e the la

In 2006, Paul Auster was awarded the Prince of Austurias Prize for Literature and inducted into the American Academy of Arts and Letters. Among his other honours are the Independent Spirit Award for the screenplay of *Smoke*. His work has been translated into more than thirty languages. He lives in Brooklyn, New York.

INVISIBLE

1967 to 2007 — three people's lives — three different perspectives . . . In New York City, in the spring of 1967, twenty-year-old Adam Walker is an aspiring poet and student at Columbia University who meets the enigmatic Frenchman Rudolf Born and his silent and seductive girlfriend, Margot. Before long, Walker finds himself caught in a perverse triangle that leads to a sudden, shocking act of violence that will alter the course of his life . . .

PAUL AUSTER

INVISIBLE

Complete and Unabridged

CHARNWOOD
Leicester

First published in Great Britain in 2009 by
Faber and Faber Limited
London

First Charnwood Edition
published 2010
by arrangement with
Faber and Faber Limited
London

British Library CIP Data

Auster, Paul, *1947 –*
    Invisible.
    1. Triangles (Interpersonal relations)- -Fiction.
    2. Friendship- -Fiction.
    3. Large type books.
    I. Title
    813.5′4–dc22

    ISBN 978–1–44480–460–7

Published by
F. A. Thorpe (Publishing)
Anstey, Leicestershire

Set by Words & Graphics Ltd.
Anstey, Leicestershire
Printed and bound in Great Britain by
T. J. International Ltd., Padstow, Cornwall

This book is printed on acid-free paper

I

I shook his hand for the first time in the spring of 1967. I was a second-year student at Columbia then, a know-nothing boy with an appetite for books and a belief (or delusion) that one day I would become good enough to call myself a poet, and because I read poetry, I had already met his namesake in Dante's hell, a dead man shuffling through the final verses of the twenty-eighth canto of the *Inferno*. Bertran de Born, the twelfth-century Provençal poet, carrying his severed head by the hair as it sways back and forth like a lantern — surely one of the most grotesque images in that book-length catalogue of hallucinations and torments. Dante was a staunch defender of de Born's writing, but he condemned him to eternal damnation for having counseled Prince Henry to rebel against his father, King Henry II, and because de Born caused division between father and son and turned them into enemies, Dante's ingenious punishment was to divide de Born from himself. Hence the decapitated body wailing in the underworld, asking the Florentine traveler if any pain could be more terrible than his.

When he introduced himself as Rudolf Born, my thoughts immediately turned to the poet. Any relation to Bertran? I asked.

Ah, he replied, that wretched creature who lost his head. Perhaps, but it doesn't seem likely, I'm afraid. No *de*. You need to be nobility for that, and the sad truth is I'm anything but noble.

I have no memory of why I was there. Someone must have asked me to go along, but who that person was has long since evaporated from my mind. I can't even recall where the party was held — uptown or downtown, in an apartment or a loft — nor my reason for accepting the invitation in the first place, since I tended to shun large gatherings at the time, put off by the din of chattering crowds, embarrassed by the shyness that would overcome me in the presence of people I didn't know. But that night, inexplicably, I said yes, and off I went with my forgotten friend to wherever it was he took me.

What I remember is this: at one point in the evening, I wound up standing alone in a corner of the room. I was smoking a cigarette and looking out at the people, dozens upon dozens of young bodies crammed into the confines of that space, listening to the mingled roar of words and laughter, wondering what on earth I was doing there, and thinking that perhaps it was time to leave. An ashtray was sitting on a radiator to my left, and as I turned to snuff out my cigarette, I saw that the butt-filled receptacle was rising toward me, cradled in the palm of a man's hand. Without my noticing them, two people had just sat down on the radiator, a man and a woman, both of them older than I was, no doubt older than anyone else in the room — he around thirty-five, she in her late twenties or early thirties.

They made an incongruous pair, I felt, Born

4

in a rumpled, somewhat soiled white linen suit with an equally rumpled white shirt under the jacket and the woman (whose name turned out to be Margot) dressed all in black. When I thanked him for the ashtray, he gave me a brief, courteous nod and said *My pleasure* with the slightest hint of a foreign accent. French or German, I couldn't tell which, since his English was almost flawless. What else did I see in those first moments? Pale skin, unkempt reddish hair (cut shorter than the hair of most men at the time), a broad, handsome face with nothing particularly distinctive about it (a generic face, somehow, a face that would become invisible in any crowd), and steady brown eyes, the probing eyes of a man who seemed to be afraid of nothing. Neither thin nor heavy, neither tall nor short, but for all that an impression of physical strength, perhaps because of the thickness of his hands. As for Margot, she sat without stirring a muscle, staring into space as if her central mission in life was to look bored. But attractive, deeply attractive to my twenty-year-old self, with her black hair, black turtleneck sweater, black miniskirt, black leather boots, and heavy black makeup around her large green eyes. Not a beauty, perhaps, but a simulacrum of beauty, as if the style and sophistication of her appearance embodied some feminine ideal of the age.

Born said that he and Margot had been on the verge of leaving, but then they spotted me standing alone in the corner, and because I looked so unhappy, they decided to come over and cheer me up — just to make sure I didn't slit my throat before the night was out. I had no idea how to interpret his remark. Was this man insulting me, I wondered, or was he actually trying to show some kindness to a lost young stranger? The words themselves had a certain playful, disarming quality, but the look in Born's eyes when he delivered them was cold and detached, and I couldn't help feeling that he was testing me, taunting me, for reasons I utterly failed to understand.

I shrugged, gave him a little smile, and said: Believe it or not, I'm having the time of my life.

That was when he stood up, shook my hand, and told me his name. After my question about Bertran de Born, he introduced me to Margot, who smiled at me in silence and then returned to her job of staring blankly into space.

Judging by your age, Born said, and judging by your knowledge of obscure poets, I would guess you're a student. A student of literature, no doubt. NYU or Columbia?

Columbia.

Columbia, he sighed. Such a dreary place.

Do you know it?

I've been teaching at the School of International Affairs since September. A visiting professor with a one-year appointment. Thankfully, it's April now, and I'll be going back to Paris in two months.

So you're French.

By circumstance, inclination, and passport. But Swiss by birth.

French Swiss or German Swiss? I'm hearing a little of both in your voice.

Born made a little clucking noise with his tongue and then looked me closely in the eye. You have a sensitive ear, he said. As a matter of fact, I *am* both — the hybrid product of a German-speaking mother and a French-speaking father. I grew up switching back and forth between the two languages.

Unsure of what to say next, I paused for a moment and then asked an innocuous question: And what are you teaching at our dismal university?

Disaster.

That's a rather broad subject, wouldn't you say?

More specifically, the disasters of French colonialism. I teach one course on the loss of Algeria and another on the loss of Indochina.

That lovely war we've inherited from you.

Never underestimate the importance of war. War is the purest, most vivid expression of the human soul.

You're beginning to sound like our headless poet.

Oh?

I take it you haven't read him.

Not a word. I only know about him from that passage in Dante.

De Born was a good poet, maybe even an excellent poet — but deeply disturbing. He wrote some charming love poems and a moving lament after the death of Prince Henry, but his real subject, the one thing he seemed to care about with any genuine passion, was war. He absolutely reveled in it.

7

I see, Born said, giving me an ironic smile. A man after my own heart.

I'm talking about the pleasure of seeing men break each other's skulls open, of watching castles crumble and burn, of seeing the dead with lances protruding from their sides. It's gory stuff, believe me, and de Born doesn't flinch. The mere thought of a battlefield fills him with happiness.

I take it you have no interest in becoming a soldier.

None. I'd rather go to jail than fight in Vietnam.

And assuming you avoid both prison and the army, what plans?

No plans. Just to push on with what I'm doing and hope it works out.

Which is?

Penmanship. The fine art of scribbling.

I thought as much. When Margot saw you across the room, she said to me: Look at that boy with the sad eyes and the brooding face — I'll bet you he's a poet. Is that what you are, a poet?

I write poems, yes. And also some book reviews for the *Spectator*.

The undergraduate rag.

Everyone has to start somewhere.

Interesting . . .

Not terribly. Half the people I know want to be writers.

Why do you say *want*? If you're already doing it, then it's not about the future. It already exists in the present.

Because it's still too early to know if I'm good enough.

Do you get paid for your articles?

Of course not. It's a college paper.

Once they start paying you for your work, then you'll know you're good enough.

Before I could answer, Born suddenly turned to Margot and announced: You were right, my angel. Your young man is a poet.

Margot lifted her eyes toward me, and with a neutral, appraising look, she spoke for the first time, pronouncing her words with a foreign accent that proved to be much thicker than her companion's — an unmistakable French accent. I'm always right, she said. You should know that by now, Rudolf.

A poet, Born continued, still addressing Margot, a sometime reviewer of books, and a student at the dreary fortress on the heights, which means he's probably our neighbor. But he has no name. At least not one that I'm aware of.

It's Walker, I said, realizing that I had neglected to introduce myself when we shook hands. Adam Walker.

Adam Walker, Born repeated, turning from Margot and looking at me as he flashed another one of his enigmatic smiles. A good, solid American name. So strong, so bland, so dependable. Adam Walker. The lonely bounty hunter in a CinemaScope Western, prowling the desert with a shotgun and six-shooter on his chestnut-brown gelding. Or else the kindhearted, straight-arrow surgeon in a daytime soap opera, tragically in love with two women at the same time.

It sounds solid, I replied, but nothing in

9

America is solid. The name was given to my grandfather when he landed at Ellis Island in nineteen hundred. Apparently, the immigration authorities found Walshinksky too difficult to handle, so they dubbed him Walker.

What a country, Born said. Illiterate officials robbing a man of his identity with a simple stroke of the pen.

Not his identity, I said. Just his name. He worked as a kosher butcher on the Lower East Side for thirty years.

There was more, much more after that, a good hour's worth of talk that bounced around aimlessly from one subject to the next. Vietnam and the growing opposition to the war. The differences between New York and Paris. The Kennedy assassination. The American embargo on trade with Cuba. Impersonal topics, yes, but Born had strong opinions about everything, often wild, unorthodox opinions, and because he couched his words in a half-mocking, slyly condescending tone, I couldn't tell if he was serious or not. At certain moments, he sounded like a hawkish right-winger; at other moments, he advanced ideas that made him sound like a bomb-throwing anarchist. Was he trying to provoke me, I asked myself, or was this normal procedure for him, the way he went about entertaining himself on a Saturday night? Meanwhile, the inscrutable Margot had risen from her perch on the radiator to bum a cigarette from me, and after that she remained standing, contributing little to the conversation, next to nothing in fact, but studying me carefully every time I spoke, her eyes fixed on me with the unblinking curiosity of a child. I confess that I enjoyed being looked at by her, even if it made me squirm a little. There was something vaguely erotic about it, I found, but I wasn't experienced enough back then to know if she was trying to send me a signal or simply looking for the sake of looking. The truth was that I had never run across people like this before, and because the two of them were so alien to me, so unfamiliar in their affect, the longer I talked to them, the more unreal they seemed to become — as if they were imaginary characters in a story that was taking place in my head.

I can't recall whether we were drinking, but if the party was anything like the others I had gone to since landing in New York, there must have been jugs of cheap red wine and an abundant stock of paper cups, which means that we were probably growing drunker and drunker as we continued to talk. I wish I could dredge up more of what we said, but 1967 was a long time ago, and no matter how hard I struggle to find the words and gestures and fugitive overtones of that initial encounter with Born, I mostly draw blanks. Nevertheless, a few vivid moments stand out in the blur. Born reaching into the inside pocket of his linen jacket, for example, and withdrawing the butt of a half-smoked cigar, which he proceeded to light with a match while informing me that it was a Montecristo, the best of all Cuban cigars — banned in America then, as they still are now — which he had managed to obtain through *a personal connection* with

11

someone who worked at the French embassy in Washington. He then went on to say a few kind words about Castro — this from the same man who just minutes earlier had defended Johnson, McNamara, and Westmoreland for their heroic work in battling the menace of communism in Vietnam. I remember feeling amused at the sight of the disheveled political scientist pulling out that half-smoked cigar and said he reminded me of the owner of a South American coffee plantation who had gone mad after spending too many years in the jungle. Born laughed at the remark, quickly adding that I wasn't far from the truth, since he had spent the bulk of his childhood in Guatemala. When I asked him to tell me more, however, he waved me off with the words *another time*.

I'll give you the whole story, he said, but in quieter surroundings. The whole story of my incredible life so far. You'll see, Mr. Walker. One day, you'll wind up writing my biography. I guarantee it.

Born's cigar, then, and my role as his future Boswell, but also an image of Margot touching my face with her right hand and whispering: Be good to yourself. That must have come toward the end, when we were about to leave or had already gone downstairs, but I have no memory of leaving and no memory of saying good-bye to them. All those things have been blotted out, erased by the work of forty years. They were two strangers I met at a noisy party one spring night in the New York of my youth, a New York that no longer exists, and that was that. I could be wrong, but I'm fairly certain that we didn't even bother to exchange phone numbers.

★ ★ ★

I assumed I would never see them again. Born had been teaching at Columbia for seven months, and since I hadn't crossed paths with him in all that time, it seemed unlikely that I would run into him now. But odds don't count when it comes to actual events, and just because a thing is unlikely to happen, that doesn't mean it won't. Two days after the party, I walked into the West End Bar following my final class of the afternoon, wondering if I might not find one of my friends there. The West End was a dingy, cavernous hole with more than a dozen booths and tables, a vast oval bar in the center of the front room, and an area near the entrance where you could buy bad cafeteria-style lunches and dinners — my hangout of choice, frequented by students, drunks, and neighborhood regulars. It happened to be a warm, sun-filled afternoon, and consequently few people were present at that hour. As I made my tour around the bar in search of a familiar face, I saw Born sitting alone in a booth at the back. He was reading a German newsmagazine (*Der Spiegel*, I think), smoking another one of his Cuban cigars, and ignoring the half-empty glass of beer that stood on the table to his left. Once again, he was wearing his white suit — or perhaps a different one, since the jacket looked cleaner and less rumpled than the one he'd been wearing Saturday night — but the white shirt was gone, replaced by something red — a deep, solid red, midway between brick and crimson.

Curiously, my first impulse was to turn around and walk out without saying hello to him. There is much to be explored in this hesitation, I believe, for it seems to suggest that I already understood that I would do well to keep my distance from Born, that allowing myself to get involved with him could possibly lead to trouble. How did I know this? I had spent little more than an hour in his company, but even in that short time I had sensed there was something off about him, something vaguely repellent. That wasn't to deny his other qualities — his charm, his intelligence, his humor — but underneath it all he had emanated a darkness and a cynicism that had thrown me off balance, had left me feeling that he wasn't a man who could be trusted. Would I have formed a different impression of him if I hadn't despised his politics? Impossible to say. My father and I disagreed on nearly every political issue of the moment, but that didn't prevent me from thinking he was fundamentally a good person — or at least not a bad person. But Born wasn't good. He was witty and eccentric and unpredictable, but to contend that war is the purest expression of the human soul automatically excludes you from the realm of goodness. And if he had spoken those words in jest, as a way of challenging yet another anti-militaristic student to fight back and denounce his position, then he was simply perverse.

Mr. Walker, he said, looking up from his magazine and gesturing for me to join him at his table. Just the man I've been looking for.

I could have invented an excuse and told him I was late for another appointment, but I didn't. That was the other half of the complex equation that represented my dealings with Born. Wary as I might have been, I was also fascinated by this peculiar, unreadable person, and the fact that he seemed genuinely glad to have stumbled into me stoked the fires of my vanity — that invisible cauldron of self-regard and ambition that simmers and burns in each one of us. Whatever reservations I had about him, whatever doubts I harbored about his dubious character, I couldn't stop myself from wanting him to like me, to think that I was something more than a plodding, run-of-the-mill American undergraduate, to see the promise I hoped I had in me but which I doubted nine out of every ten minutes of my waking life.

Once I had slid into the booth, Born looked at me across the table, disgorged a large puff of smoke from his cigar, and smiled. You made a favorable impression on Margot the other night, he said.

I was impressed by her too, I answered.

You might have noticed that she doesn't say much.

Her English isn't terribly good. It's hard to express yourself in a language that gives you trouble.

Her French is perfectly fluent, but she doesn't say much in French either.

15

Well, words aren't everything.

A strange comment from a man who fancies himself a writer.

I'm talking about Margot —

Yes, Margot. Exactly. Which brings me to my point. A woman prone to long silences, but she talked a blue streak on our way home from the party Saturday night.

Interesting, I said, not certain where the conversation was going. And what loosened her tongue?

You, my boy. She's taken a real liking to you, but you should also know that she's extremely worried.

Worried? Why on earth should she be worried? She doesn't even know me.

Perhaps not, but she's gotten it into her head that your future is at risk.

Everyone's future is at risk. Especially American males in their late teens and early twenties, as you well know. But as long as I don't flunk out of school, the draft can't touch me until after I graduate. I wouldn't want to bet on it, but it's possible the war will be over by then.

Don't bet on it, Mr. Walker. This little skirmish is going to drag on for years.

I lit up a Chesterfield and nodded. For once I agree with you, I said.

Anyway, Margot wasn't talking about Vietnam. Yes, you might land in jail — or come home in a box two or three years from now — but she wasn't thinking about the war. She believes you're too good for this world, and because of that, the world will eventually crush you.

16

I don't follow her reasoning.

She thinks you need help. Margot might not possess the quickest brain in the Western world, but she meets a boy who says he's a poet, and the first word that comes to her is *starvation*.

That's absurd. She has no idea what she's talking about.

Forgive me for contradicting you, but when I asked you at the party what your plans were, you said you didn't have any. Other than your nebulous ambition to write poetry, of course. How much do poets earn, Mr. Walker?

Most of the time nothing. If you get lucky, every now and then someone might throw you a few pennies.

Sounds like starvation to me.

I never said I planned to make my living as a writer. I'll have to find a job.

Such as?

It's difficult to say. I could work for a publishing house or a magazine. I could translate books. I could write articles and reviews. One of those things, or else several of them in combination. It's too early to know, and until I'm out in the world, there's no point in losing any sleep over it, is there?

Like it or not, you're in the world now, and the sooner you learn how to fend for yourself, the better off you'll be.

Why this sudden concern? We've only just met, and why should you care about what happens to me?

Because Margot asked me to help you, and since she rarely asks me for anything, I feel

17

honor-bound to obey her wishes.

Tell her thank you, but there's no need for you to put yourself out. I can get by on my own.

Stubborn, aren't you? Born said, resting his nearly spent cigar on the rim of the ashtray and then leaning forward until his face was just a few inches from mine. If I offered you a job, are you telling me you'd turn it down?

It depends on what the job is.

That remains to be seen. I have several ideas, but I haven't made a decision yet. Maybe you can help me.

I'm not sure I understand.

My father died ten months ago, and it appears I've inherited a considerable amount of money. Not enough to buy a château or an airline company, but enough to make a small difference in the world. I could engage you to write my biography, of course, but I think it's a little too soon for that. I'm still only thirty-six, and I find it unseemly to talk about a man's life before he gets to fifty. What, then? I've considered starting a publishing house, but I'm not sure I have the stomach for all the long-range planning that would entail. A magazine, on the other hand, strikes me as much more fun. A monthly, or perhaps a quarterly, but something fresh and daring, a publication that would stir people up and cause controversy with every issue. What do you think of that, Mr. Walker? Would working on a magazine be of any interest to you?

Of course it would. The only question is: why me? You're going back to France in a couple of months, so I assume you're talking about a

18

French magazine. My French isn't bad, but it isn't good enough for what you'd need. And besides, I go to college here in New York. I can't just pick up and move.

Who said anything about moving? Who said anything about a French magazine? If I had a good American staff to run things here, I could pop over every once in a while to check up on them, but essentially I'd stay out of it. I have no interest in directing a magazine myself. I have my own work, my own career, and I wouldn't have the time for it. My sole responsibility would be to put up the money — and then hope to turn a profit.

You're a political scientist, and I'm a literature student. If you're thinking of starting a political magazine, then count me out. We're on opposite sides of the fence, and if I tried to work for you, it would turn into a fiasco. But if you're talking about a literary magazine, then yes, I'd be very interested.

Just because I teach international relations and write about government and public policy doesn't mean I'm a philistine. I care about art as much as you do, Mr. Walker, and I wouldn't ask you to work on a magazine if it wasn't a literary magazine.

How do you know I can handle it?

I don't. But I have a hunch.

It doesn't make any sense. Here you are offering me a job and you haven't read a word I've written.

Not so. Just this morning I read four of your poems in the most recent number of the

Columbia Review and six of your articles in the student paper. The piece on Melville was particularly good, I thought, and I was moved by your little poem about the graveyard. *How many more skies above me/Until this one vanishes as well?* Impressive.

I'm glad you think so. Even more impressive is that you acted so quickly.

That's the way I am. Life is too short for dawdling.

My third-grade teacher used to tell us the same thing — with exactly those words.

A wonderful place, this America of yours. You've had an excellent education, Mr. Walker.

Born laughed at the inanity of his remark, took a sip of beer, and then leaned back to ponder the idea he had set in motion.

What I want you to do, he finally said, is draw up a plan, a prospectus. Tell me about the work that would appear in the magazine, the length of each issue, the cover art, the design, the frequency of publication, what name you'd want to give it, and so on. Leave it at my office when you're finished. I'll look it over, and if I like your ideas, we'll be in business.

★   ★   ★

Young as I might have been, I had enough understanding of the world to realize that Born could have been playing me for a dupe. How often did you wander into a bar, bump into a man you had met only once, and walk out with the chance to start a magazine — especially when the *you* in question was a twenty-year-old nothing who had yet to prove himself on any front? It was too outlandish to be believed. In all likelihood, Born had raised my hopes only in order to crush them, and I was fully expecting him to toss my prospectus into the garbage and tell me he wasn't interested. Still, on the off chance that he meant what he'd said, that he was honestly intending to keep his word, I felt I should give it a try. What did I have to lose? A day of thinking and writing at the most, and if Born wound up rejecting my proposal, then so be it.

Bracing myself against disappointment, I set to work that very night. Beyond listing half a dozen potential names for the magazine, however, I didn't make much headway. Not because I was confused, and not because I wasn't full of ideas, but for the simple reason that I had neglected to ask Born how much money he was willing to put into the project. Everything hinged on the size of his investment, and until I knew what his intentions were, how could I discuss any of the myriad points he had raised that afternoon: the quality of the paper, the length and frequency of the issues, the binding, the possible inclusion of art, and how much (if anything) he was prepared to pay the contributors? Literary magazines came in numerous shapes and guises, after all, from the mimeographed, stapled underground publications edited by young poets in the East Village to the stolid academic quarterlies to more commercial enterprises like the *Evergreen Review* to the sumptuous *objets* backed by well-heeled angels who lost thousands with every issue. I would have to talk to Born again, I realized, and so instead of drawing up a prospectus, I wrote him a letter explaining my problem. It was such a sad, pathetic document — *We have to talk about money* — that I decided to include something else in the envelope, just to convince him that I wasn't the out-and-out dullard I appeared to be. After our brief exchange about Bertran de Born on Saturday night, I thought it might amuse him to read one of the more savage works by the twelfth-century poet. I happened to own a paperback anthology of the troubadours — in English only — and my initial idea was simply to type up one of the poems from the book. When I began reading through the translation, however, it struck me as clumsy and inept, a rendering that failed to do justice to the strange and ugly power of the poem, and even though I didn't know a word of Provençal, I figured I could turn out something better working from a French translation. The next morning, I found what I was looking for in Butler Library: an edition of the complete de Born, with the original Provençal on the left and literal prose versions in French on the right. It took me several hours to complete the job (if I'm not mistaken, I missed a class because of it), and this is what I came up with:

I love the jubilance of springtime
When leaves and flowers burgeon forth,
And I exult in the mirth of bird songs

Resounding through the woods;
And I relish seeing the meadows
Adorned with tents and pavilions;
And great is my happiness
When the fields are packed
With armored knights and horses.

And I thrill at the sight of scouts
Forcing men and women to flee with their
belongings;
And gladness fills me when they are chased
By a dense throng of armed men;
And my heart soars
When I behold mighty castles under siege
As their ramparts crumble and collapse
With troops massed at the edge of the moat
And strong, solid barriers
Hemming in the target on all sides.

And I am likewise overjoyed
When a baron leads the assault,
Mounted on his horse, armed and unafraid,
Thus giving strength to his men
Through his courage and valor.
And once the battle has begun
Each of them should be prepared
To follow him readily,
For no man can be a man
Until he has delivered and received
Blow upon blow.

In the thick of combat we will see
Maces, swords, shields, and many-colored
helmets

Split and shattered,
And hordes of vassals striking in all direc-
tions
As the horses of the dead and wounded
Wander aimlessly around the field.
And once the fighting starts
Let every well-born man think only of break-
ing
Heads and arms, for better to be dead
Than alive and defeated.

I tell you that eating, drinking, and sleeping
Give me less pleasure than hearing the
shout
Of 'Charge!' from both sides, and hearing
Cries of 'Help! Help!,' and seeing
The great and the ungreat fall together
On the grass and in the ditches, and seeing
Corpses with the tips of broken, streamered
lances
Jutting from their sides.

Barons, better to pawn
Your castles, towns, and cities
Than to give up making war.

Late that afternoon, I slipped the envelope with
the letter and the poem under the door of Born's
office at the School of International Affairs. I was
expecting an immediate response, but several
days went by before he contacted me, and his
failure to call left me wondering if the magazine
project was indeed just a spur-of-the-moment
whim that had already played itself out — or,

worse, if he had been offended by the poem, thinking that I was equating him with Bertran de Born and thereby indirectly accusing him of being a warmonger. As it turned out, I needn't have worried. When the telephone rang on Friday, he apologized for his silence, explaining that he had gone to Cambridge to deliver a lecture on Wednesday and hadn't set foot in his office until twenty minutes ago.

You're perfectly right, he continued, and I'm perfectly stupid for ignoring the question of money when we spoke the other day. How can you give me a prospectus if you don't know what the budget is? You must think I'm a moron.

Hardly, I said. I'm the one who feels stupid — for not asking you. But I couldn't tell how serious you were, and I didn't want to press.

I'm serious, Mr. Walker. I admit that I have a penchant for telling jokes, but only about small, inconsequential things. I would never lead you along on a matter like this.

I'm happy to know that.

So, in answer to your question about money . . . I'm hoping we'll do well, of course, but as with every venture of this sort, there's a large element of risk, and so realistically I have to be prepared to lose every penny of my investment. What it comes down to is the following: How much can I afford to lose? How much of my inheritance can I squander away without causing problems for myself in the future? I've given it a good deal of thought since we talked on Monday, and the answer is twenty-five thousand dollars. That's my limit. The magazine will come out four times a year, and I'll put up five thousand per issue, plus another five thousand for your annual salary. If we break even at the end of the first year, I'll fund another year. If we come out in the black, I'll put the profits into the magazine, and that would keep us going for all or part of a third year. If we lose money, however, then the second year becomes problematical. Say we're ten thousand dollars in the red. I'll put up fifteen thousand, and that's it. Do you understand the principle? I have twenty-five thousand dollars to burn, but I won't spend a dollar more than that. What do you think? Is it a fair proposition or not?

Extremely fair, and extremely generous. At five thousand dollars an issue, we could put out a first-rate magazine, something to be proud of.

I could dump all the money in your lap tomorrow, of course, but that wouldn't really help you, would it? Margot is worried about your future, and if you can make this magazine work, then your future is settled. You'll have a decent job with a decent salary, and during your off-hours you can write all the poems you want, vast epic poems about the mysteries of the human heart, short lyric poems about daisies and buttercups, fiery tracts against cruelty and injustice. Unless you land in jail or get your head blown off, of course, but we won't dwell on those grim possibilities now.

I don't know how to thank you . . .

Don't thank me. Thank Margot, your guardian angel.

I hope I see her again soon.

I'm certain you will. As long as your prospectus satisfies me, you'll be seeing as much of her as you like.

I'll do my best. But if you're looking for a magazine that will cause controversy and stir people up, I doubt a literary journal is the answer. I hope you understand that.

I do, Mr. Walker. We're talking about quality . . . about fine, rarefied things. Art for the happy few.

Or, as Stendhal must have pronounced it: *ze appy foo.*

Stendhal and Maurice Chevalier. Which reminds me . . . Speaking of chevaliers, thank you for the poem.

The poem. I forgot all about it —

The poem you translated for me.

What did you think of it?

I found it revolting and brilliant. My faux ancestor was a true samurai madman, wasn't he? But at least he had the courage of his convictions. At least he knew what he stood for. How little the world has changed since eleven eighty-six, no matter how much we prefer to think otherwise. If the magazine gets off the ground, I think we should publish de Born's poem in the first issue.

★ ★ ★

I was both heartened and bewildered. In spite of my doleful predictions, Born had talked about the project as if it was already on the brink of happening, and at this point the prospectus

27

seemed to be little more than an empty formality. No matter what plan I drew up, I felt he was prepared to give it his stamp of approval. And yet, pleased as I was by the thought of taking charge of a well-funded magazine, which on top of everything else would pay me a rather excessive salary, for the life of me I still couldn't fathom what Born was up to. Was Margot really the cause of this unexpected burst of altruism, this blind faith in a boy with no experience in editing or publishing or business who just one week earlier had been absolutely unknown to him? And even if that was the case, why would the question of my future be of any concern to her? We had barely talked to each other at the party, and although she had looked me over carefully and given me a pat on the cheek, she had come across as a cipher, an utter blank. I couldn't imagine what she had said to Born that would have made him willing to risk twenty-five thousand dollars on my account. As far as I could tell, the prospect of publishing a magazine left him cold, and because he was indifferent, he was content to turn the whole matter over to me. When I thought back to our conversation at the West End on Monday, I realized that I had probably given him the idea in the first place. I had mentioned that I might look for work with a publisher or a magazine after I graduated from college, and a minute later he was telling me about his inheritance and how he was consider-ing starting up a publishing house or a magazine with his newfound money. What if I had said I wanted to manufacture toasters? Would he have answered that he was thinking about investing in a toaster factory?

It took me longer to finish the prospectus than I'd imagined it would — four or five days, I think, but that was only because I did such a thorough job. I wanted to impress Born with my diligence, and therefore I not only worked out a plan for the contents of each issue (poetry, fiction, essays, interviews, translations, as well as a section at the back for reviews of books, films, music, and art) but provided an exhaustive financial report as well: printing costs, paper costs, binding costs, matters of distribution, print runs, contributors' fees, news-stand price, subscription rates, and the pros and cons of whether to include ads. All that demanded time and research, telephone calls to printers and binders, conversations with the editors of other magazines, and a new way of thinking on my part, since I had never bothered myself with questions of commerce before. As for the name of the magazine, I wrote down several possibilities, wanting to leave the choice to Born, but my own preference was the *Stylus* — in honor of Poe, who had tried to launch a magazine with that name not long before his death.

This time, Born responded within twenty-four hours. I took that as an encouraging sign when I picked up the phone and heard his voice, but true to form he didn't come right out and say what he thought of my plan. That would have been too easy, I suppose, too pedestrian, too straightforward for a man like him, and so he toyed with me for a couple of minutes in order to

29

prolong the suspense, asking me a number of irrelevant and disjointed questions that convinced me he was stalling for time because he didn't want to hurt my feelings when he rejected my proposal.

I trust you're in good health, Mr. Walker, he said.

I think so, I replied. Unless I've contracted a disease I'm not aware of.

But no symptoms yet.

No, I'm feeling fine.

What about your stomach? No discomfort there?

Not at the moment.

Your appetite is normal, then.

Yes, perfectly normal.

I seem to recall that your grandfather was a kosher butcher. Do you still follow those ancient laws, or have you given them up?

I never followed them in the first place.

No dietary restrictions, then.

No. I eat whatever I want to.

Fish or fowl? Beef or pork? Lamb or veal?

What about them?

Which one do you prefer?

I like them all.

In other words, you aren't difficult to please.

Not when it comes to food. With other things yes, but not with food.

Then you're open to anything Margot and I choose to prepare.

I'm not sure I understand.

Tomorrow night at seven o'clock. Are you busy?

No.

Good. Then you'll come to our apartment for dinner. A celebration is in order, don't you think?

I'm not sure. What are we celebrating?

The *Stylus*, my friend. The beginning of what I hope will turn out to be a long and fruitful partnership.

You want to go ahead with it?

Do I have to repeat myself?

You're saying you liked the prospectus?

Don't be so dense, boy. Why would I want to celebrate if I hadn't liked it?

★ ★ ★

I remember dithering over what present to give them — flowers or a bottle of wine — and opting in the end for flowers. I couldn't afford a good enough bottle to make a serious impression, and as I thought the matter through, I realized how presumptuous it would have been to offer wine to a couple of French people anyway. If I made the wrong choice — which was more than likely to happen — then I would only be exposing my ignorance, and I didn't want to start off the evening by embarrassing myself. Flowers on the other hand would be a more direct way of expressing my gratitude to Margot, since flowers were always given to the woman of the house, and if Margot was a woman who liked flowers (which was by no means certain), then she would understand that I was thanking her for having pushed Born to act on my behalf. My

31

telephone conversation with him the previous afternoon had left me in a state of semishock, and even as I walked to their place on the night of the dinner, I was still feeling overwhelmed by the altogether improbable good luck that had fallen down on me. I remember putting on a jacket and tie for the occasion. It was the first time I had dressed up in months, and there I was, Mr. Important himself, walking across the Columbia campus with an enormous bouquet of flowers in my right hand, on my way to eat and talk business with *my publisher*.

He had sublet an apartment from a professor on a yearlong sabbatical, a large but decidedly stuffy, overfurnished place in a building on Morningside Drive, just off 116th Street. I believe it was on the third floor, and from the French windows that lined the eastern wall of the living room there was a view of the full, downward expanse of Morningside Park and the lights of Spanish Harlem beyond. Margot answered the door when I knocked, and although I can still see her face and the smile that darted across her lips when I presented her with the flowers, I have no memory of what she was wearing. It could have been black again, but I tend to think not, since I have a vague recollection of surprise, which would suggest there was something different about her from the first time we had met. As we were standing on the threshold together, before she even invited me into the apartment, Margot announced in a low voice that Rudolf was in a foul temper. There was a crisis of some sort back home, and he was going to have to leave for Paris tomorrow and wouldn't return until next week at the earliest. He was in the bedroom now, she added, on the telephone with Air France arranging his flight, so he probably wouldn't be out for another few minutes.

As I entered the apartment, I was immediately hit by the smell of food cooking in the kitchen — a sublimely delicious smell, I found, as tempting and aromatic as any vapor I had ever breathed. The kitchen happened to be where we headed first — to hunt down a vase for the flowers — and when I glanced at the stove, I saw the large covered pot that was the source of that extraordinary fragrance.

I have no idea what's in there, I said, gesturing to the pot, but if my nose knows anything, three people are going to be very happy tonight.

Rudolf tells me you like lamb, Margot said, so I decided to make a *navarin* — a lamb stew with potatoes and *navets*.

Turnips.

I can never remember that word. It's an ugly word, I think, and it hurts my mouth to say it.

All right, then. We'll banish it from the English language.

Margot seemed to enjoy my little remark — enough to give me another brief smile, at any rate — and then she began to busy herself with the flowers: putting them in the sink, removing the white paper wrapper, taking down a vase from the cupboard, trimming the stems with a pair of scissors, putting the flowers in the vase, and then filling the vase with water. Neither one

33

of us said a word as she went about these minimal tasks, but I watched her closely, marveling at how slowly and methodically she worked, as if putting flowers in a vase of water were a highly delicate procedure that called for one's utmost care and concentration.

Eventually, we wound up in the living room with drinks in our hands, sitting side by side on the sofa as we smoked cigarettes and looked out at the sky through the French windows. Dusk ebbed into darkness, and Born was still nowhere to be seen, but the ever-placid Margot betrayed no concern over his absence. When we'd met at the party ten or twelve days earlier, I had been rather unnerved by her long silences and oddly disconnected manner, but now that I knew what to expect, and now that I knew she liked me and thought I was *too good for this world*, I felt a bit more at ease in her company. What did we talk about in the minutes before her man finally joined us? New York (which she found to be dirty and depressing); her ambition to become a painter (she was attending a class at the School of the Arts but thought she had no talent and was too lazy to improve); how long she had known Rudolf (all her life); and what she thought of the magazine (she was crossing her fingers). When I tried to thank her for her help, however, she merely shook her head and told me not to exaggerate: she'd had nothing to do with it.

Before I could ask her what that meant, Born entered the room. Again the rumpled white pants, again the unruly shock of hair, but no

34

jacket this time, and yet another colored shirt — pale green, if I remember correctly — and the stump of an extinguished cigar clamped between the thumb and index finger of his right hand, although he seemed not to be aware that he was holding it. My new benefactor was angry, seething with irritation over whatever crisis was forcing him to travel to Paris tomorrow, and without even bothering to say hello to me, utterly ignoring his duties as host of our little celebration, he flew into a tirade that wasn't addressed to Margot or myself so much as to the furniture in the room, the walls around him, the world at large.

Stupid bunglers, he said. Sniveling incompetents. Slow-witted functionaries with mashed potatoes for brains. The whole universe is on fire, and all they do is wring their hands and watch it burn.

Unruffled, perhaps even vaguely amused, Margot said: That's why they need you, my love. Because you're the king.

Rudolf the First, Born replied, the bright boy with the big dick. All I have to do is pull it out of my pants, piss on the fire, and the problem is solved.

Exactly, Margot said, cracking the largest smile I'd yet seen from her.

I'm getting sick of it, Born muttered, as he headed for the liquor cabinet, put down his cigar, and poured himself a full tumbler of straight gin. How many years have I given them? he asked, taking a sip of his drink. You do it because you believe in certain principles, but no one else seems to give a damn. We're losing the battle, my friends. The ship is going down.

This was a different Born from the one I had come to know so far — the brittle, mocking jester who exulted in his own witticisms, the displaced dandy who blithely went about founding magazines and asking twenty-year-old students to his house for dinner. Something was raging inside him, and now that this other person had been revealed to me, I felt myself recoil from him, understanding that he was the kind of man who could erupt at any moment, that he was someone who actually *enjoyed* his own anger. He swigged down a second belt of gin and then turned his eyes in my direction, acknowledging my presence for the first time. I don't know what he saw in my face — astonishment? confusion? distress? — but whatever it was, he was sufficiently alarmed by it to switch off the thermostat and immediately lower the temperature. Don't worry, Mr. Walker, he said, doing his best to produce a smile. I'm just letting off a little steam.

He gradually willed himself out of his funk, and by the time we sat down to eat twenty minutes later, the storm seemed to have passed. Or so I thought when he complimented Margot on her superb cooking and praised the wine she had bought for the meal, but it proved to be no more than a temporary lull, and as the evening progressed, further squalls and gales came swooping down on us to spoil the festivities. I don't know if the gin and Burgundy affected Born's mood, but there was no question that he packed away a good deal of alcohol — at least twice the amount that Margot and I downed together — or if he was simply out of sorts because of the bad news he had received earlier in the day. Perhaps it was both in combination, or perhaps it was something else, but there was scarcely a moment during that dinner when I didn't feel that the house was about to catch on fire.

It began when Born raised his glass to toast the birth of our magazine. It was a gracious little speech, I thought, but when I jumped in and started mentioning some of the writers I was planning to solicit work from for the first issue, Born cut me off in mid-sentence and told me never to discuss business while eating, that it was bad for the digestion and I should learn to start acting like an adult. It was a rude and unpleasant thing to say, but I hid my injured pride by pretending to agree with him and then took another bite of Margot's stew. A moment later, Born put down his fork and said to me: You like it, Mr. Walker, don't you?

Like what? I asked.

The *navarin*. You seem to be eating it with relish.

It's probably the best meal I've had all year.

In other words, you're attracted to Margot's food.

Very much. I find it delicious.

And what about Margot herself? Are you attracted to her as well?

She's sitting right across the table from me. It seems wrong to talk about her as if she weren't here.

I'm sure she doesn't mind. Do you, Margot?

No, Margot said. Not in the least.

You see, Mr. Walker? Not in the least.

All right, then, I answered. In my opinion, Margot is a highly attractive woman.

You're avoiding the question, Born said. I didn't ask if you found her attractive, I want to know if *you* are attracted to *her*.

She's your wife, Professor Born. You can't expect me to answer that. Not here, not now.

Ah, but Margot isn't my wife. She's my special friend, as it were, but we aren't married, and we have no plans to marry in the future.

You live together. As far as I'm concerned, that's as good as being married.

Come, come. Don't be such a prude. Forget that I have any connection to Margot, all right? We're talking in the abstract here, a hypothetical case.

Fine. Hypothetically speaking, I would hypothetically be attracted to Margot, yes.

Good, Born said, rubbing his hands together and smiling. Now we're getting somewhere. But attracted to what degree? Enough to want to kiss her? Enough to want to hold her naked body in your arms? Enough to want to sleep with her?

I can't answer those questions.

You're not telling me you're a virgin, are you?

No. I just don't want to answer your questions, that's all.

Am I to understand that if Margot threw herself at you and asked you to fuck her, you wouldn't be interested? Is that what you're saying? Poor Margot. You have no idea how

38

much you've hurt her feelings.

What are you talking about?

Why don't you ask her?

Suddenly, Margot reached across the table and took hold of my hand. Don't be upset, she said. Rudolf is only trying to have some fun. You don't have to do anything you don't want to do.

Born's notion of fun had nothing to do with mine, alas, and at that stage of my life I was ill-equipped to play the sort of game he was trying to drag me into. No, I wasn't a virgin. I had slept with a number of girls by then, had fallen in and out of love several times, had suffered through a badly broken heart just two years earlier and, like most young men around the world, thought about sex almost constantly. The truth was that I would have been delighted to sleep with Margot, but I refused to allow Born to goad me into admitting it. This wasn't a hypothetical case. He actually seemed to be propositioning me on her behalf, and whatever sexual code they lived by, whatever romps and twisted dalliances they indulged in with other people, I found the whole business ugly, off-kilter, sick. Perhaps I should have spoken up and told him what I thought, but I was afraid — not of Born exactly, but of causing a rift that might lead him to change his mind about our project. I desperately wanted the magazine to work, and as long as he was willing to back it, I was prepared to put up with any amount of inconvenience and discomfort. So I did what I could to hold my ground and not lose my temper, to absorb *blow upon blow* without

39

falling from my horse, to resist him and appease him at the same time.

I'm disappointed, Born said. Until now, I took you for an adventurer, a renegade, a man who enjoys thumbing his nose at convention, but at bottom you're just another stuffed shirt, another bourgeois simpleton. How sad. You strut around with your Provençal poets and your lofty ideals, with your draft-dodger cowardice and that ridiculous necktie of yours, and you think you're something exceptional, but what I see is a pampered middle-class boy living off Daddy's money, a poseur.

Rudolf, Margot said. That's enough. Leave him alone.

I realize I'm being a bit harsh, Born said to her. But young Adam and I are partners now, and I need to know what he's made of. Can he stand up to an honest insult, or does he crumble to pieces when he's under attack?

You've had a lot to drink, I said, and from all I can gather you've had a rough day. Maybe it's time for me to be going. We can pick up the conversation when you're back from France.

Nonsense, Born replied, pounding the table with his fist. We're still working on the stew. Then there's the salad, and after the salad the cheese, and after the cheese dessert. Margot has already been hurt enough for one night, and the least we can do is sit here and finish her remarkable dinner. In the meantime, maybe you can tell us something about Westfield, New Jersey.

Westfield? I said, surprised to discover that

40

Born knew where I had grown up. How did you find out about Westfield?

It wasn't difficult, he said. As it happens, I've learned quite a bit about you in the past few days. Your father, for example, Joseph Walker, age fifty-four, better known as Bud, owns and operates the Shop-Rite supermarket on the main street in town. Your mother, Marjorie, a.k.a. Marge, is forty-six and has given birth to three children: your sister, Gwyn, in November nineteen forty-five; you in March nineteen forty-seven; and your brother, Andrew, in July nineteen fifty. A tragic story. Little Andy drowned when he was seven, and it pains me to think how unbearable that loss must have been for all of you. I had a sister who died of cancer at roughly the same age, and I know what terrible things a death like that does to a family. Your father has coped with his sorrow by working fourteen hours a day, six days a week, while your mother has turned inward, battling the scourge of depression with heavy doses of prescription pharmaceuticals and twice-weekly sessions with a psychotherapist. The miracle, to my mind, is how well you and your sister have done for yourselves in the face of such calamity. Gwyn is a beautiful and talented girl in her last year at Vassar, planning to begin graduate work in English literature right here at Columbia this fall. And you, my young intellectual friend, my budding wordsmith and translator of obscure medieval poets, turn out to have been an outstanding baseball player in high school, co-captain of the varsity team, no less. *Mens*

41

sana in corpore sano. More to the point, my sources tell me that you're a person of deep moral integrity, a pillar of moderation and sound judgment who, unlike the majority of his classmates, does not dabble in drugs. Alcohol yes, but no drugs whatsoever — not even an occasional puff of marijuana. Why is that, Mr. Walker? With all the propaganda abroad these days about the liberating powers of hallucinogens and narcotics, why haven't you succumbed to the temptation of seeking new and stimulating experiences?

Why? I said, still reeling from the impact of Born's astounding recitation about my family. I'll tell you why, but first I'd like to know how you managed to dig up so much about us in such a short time.

Is there a problem? Were there any inaccuracies in what I said?

No. It's just that I'm a little stunned, that's all. You can't be a cop or an FBI agent, but a visiting professor at the School of International Affairs could certainly be involved with an intelligence organization of some kind. Is that what you are? A spy for the CIA?

Born cracked up laughing when I said that, treating my question as if he'd just heard the funniest joke of the century. The CIA! he roared. The CIA! Why on earth would a Frenchman work for the CIA? Forgive me for laughing, but the idea is so hilarious, I'm afraid I can't stop myself.

Well, how did you do it, then?

I'm a thorough man, Mr. Walker, a man who

doesn't act until he knows everything he needs to know, and since I'm about to invest twenty-five thousand dollars in a person who qualifies as little more than a stranger to me, I felt I should learn as much about him as I could. You'd be amazed how effective an instrument the telephone can be.

Margot stood up then and began clearing plates from the table in preparation for the next course. I made a move to help her, but Born gestured for me to sit back down in my chair.

Let's return to my question, shall we? he said.

What question? I asked, no longer able to keep track of the conversation.

About why no drugs. Even the lovely Margot has a joint now and then, and to be perfectly frank with you, I have a certain fondness for weed myself. But not you. I'm curious to know why.

Because drugs scare me. Two of my friends from high school are already dead from heroin overdoses. My freshman roommate went off the rails from taking too much speed and had to drop out of college. Again and again, I've watched people climb the walls from bad LSD trips — screaming, shaking, ready to kill themselves. I don't want any part of it. Let the whole world get stoned on drugs for all I care, but I'm not interested.

And yet you drink.

Yes, I said, lifting my glass and taking another sip of wine. With immense pleasure, too, I might add. Especially with stuff as good as this to keep me company.

43

We moved on to the salad after that, followed by a plate of French cheeses and then a dessert baked by Margot that afternoon (apple tart? raspberry tart?), and for the next thirty minutes or so the drama that had flared up during the first part of the meal steadily diminished. Born was being nice to me again, and although he continued to drink glass after glass of wine, I was beginning to feel confident that we would get to the end of the dinner without another outburst or insult from my capricious, half-crocked host. Then he opened a bottle of brandy, lit up one of his Cuban cigars, and started talking about politics.

Fortunately, it wasn't as gruesome as it could have been. He was deep in his cups by the time he poured the cognac, and after an ounce or two of those burning, amber spirits, he was too far gone to engage in a coherent conversation. Yes, he called me a coward again for refusing to go to Vietnam, but mostly he talked to himself, lapsing into a long, meandering monologue on any number of disparate subjects as I sat there listening in silence and Margot washed pots and pans in the kitchen. Impossible to recapture more than a fraction of what he said, but the key points are still with me, particularly his memories of fighting in Algeria, where he spent two years with the French army interrogating *filthy Arab terrorists* and losing whatever faith he'd once had in the idea of justice. Bombastic pronouncements, wild generalizations, bitter declarations about the corruption of all governments — past, present, and future; left, right, and center — and how our so-called civilization was no more than a thin screen masking a never-ending assault of barbarism and cruelty. Human beings were animals, he said, and softminded aesthetes like myself were no better than children, diverting ourselves with hairsplitting philosophies of art and literature to avoid confronting the essential truth of the world. Power was the only constant, and the law of life was kill or be killed, either dominate or fall victim to the savagery of monsters. He talked about Stalin and the millions of lives lost during the collectivization movement in the thirties. He talked about the Nazis and the war, and then he advanced the startling theory that Hitler's admiration of the United States had inspired him to use American history as a model for his conquest of Europe. Look at the parallels, Born said, and it's not as far-fetched as you'd think: extermination of the Indians is turned into the extermination of the Jews; westward expansion to exploit natural resources is turned into eastward expansion for the same purpose; enslavement of the blacks for low-cost labor is turned into subjugation of the Slavs to produce a similar result. Long live America, Adam, he said, pouring another shot of cognac into both our glasses. Long live the darkness inside us.

As I listened to him rant on like this, I felt a growing pity for him. Horrible as his view of the world was, I couldn't help feeling sorry for a man who had descended into such pessimism, who so willfully shunned the possibility of finding any compassion, grace, or beauty in his

45

fellow human beings. Born was just thirty-six, but already he was a burnt-out soul, a shattered wreck of a person, and at his core I imagined that he must have suffered terribly, living in constant pain, lacerated by the jabbing knives of despair, disgust, and self-contempt.

Margot reentered the dining room, and when she saw the state Born was in — bloodshot eyes, slurred speech, body listing to the left as if he was about to fall off his chair — she put her hand on his back and gently told him in French that the evening was over and that he should toddle off to bed. Surprisingly, he didn't protest. Nodding his head and muttering the word *merde* several times in a flat, barely audible voice, he allowed Margot to help him to his feet, and a moment later she was guiding him out of the room toward the hall that led to the back of the apartment. Did he say good night to me? I can't remember. For several minutes, I remained in my chair, expecting Margot to return in order to show me out, but when she didn't come back after what seemed to be an inordinate length of time, I stood up and headed for the front door. That was when I saw her — emerging from a bedroom at the end of the hall. I waited as she walked toward me, and the first thing she did when we were standing next to each other was put her hand on my forearm and apologize for Rudolf's behavior.

Is he always like that when he drinks? I asked.

No, almost never, she said. But he's very upset right now and has many things on his mind.

Well, at least it wasn't dull.

You comported yourself with great discretion.

So did you. And thank you for the dinner. I'll never forget the *navarin*.

Margot gave me one of her small, fleeting smiles and said: If you want me to cook for you again, let me know. I'll be happy to give you another meal while Rudolf is in Paris.

Sounds good, I said, knowing I would never find the courage to call her but at the same time feeling touched by the invitation.

Again, another flicker of a smile, and then two perfunctory kisses, one on each cheek. Good night, Adam, she said. You will be in my thoughts.

★   ★   ★

I didn't know if I was in her thoughts or not, but now that Born was out of the country, she had entered mine, and for the next two days I could barely stop thinking about her. From the first night at the party, when Margot had trained her eyes on me and studied my face with such intensity, to the disturbing conversation Born had provoked at the dinner about the degree of my attraction to her, a sexual current had been running between us, and even if she was ten years older than I was, that didn't prevent me from imagining myself in bed with her, from wanting to go to bed with her. Was the offer to give me another dinner a veiled proposition, or was it simply a matter of generosity, a desire to help out a young student who subsisted on the wretched fare of cheap diners and warmed-over

47

cans of precooked spaghetti? I was too timid to find out. I wanted to call her, but every time I reached for the phone, I understood that it was impossible. Margot lived with Born, and even though he had insisted that marriage wasn't in their future, she was already claimed, and I didn't feel I had the right to go after her.

Then she called me. Three days after the dinner, at ten o'clock in the morning, the telephone rang in my apartment, and there she was on the other end of the line, sounding a little hurt, disappointed that I hadn't been in touch, in her own subdued way expressing more emotion than at any time since we'd met.

I'm sorry, I lied, but I was going to call you later today. You beat me to it by a couple of hours.

Funny boy, she said, seeing right through my fib. You don't have to come if you don't want to.

But I do, I answered, meaning every word of it. Very much.

Tonight?

Tonight would be perfect.

You don't have to worry about Rudolf, Adam. He's gone, and I'm free to do whatever I like. We all are. Nobody can own another person. Do you understand that?

I think so.

How do you feel about fish?

Fish in the sea or fish on a plate?

Grilled sole. With little boiled potatoes and *choux de Bruxelles* on the side. Does that appeal to you, or would you rather have something else?

No. I'm already dreaming about the sole.

48

Come at seven. And don't trouble yourself with flowers this time. I know you can't afford them.

After we hung up, I spent the next nine hours in a torment of anticipation, daydreaming through my afternoon classes, pondering the mysteries of carnal attraction, and trying to understand what it was about Margot that had worked me up to such a pitch of excitement. My first impression of her had not been particularly favorable. She had struck me as an odd and vapid creature, sympathetic at heart, perhaps, intriguing to look at, but with no electricity in her, a woman lost in some murky inner world that shut her off from true engagement with others, as if she were some silent visitor from another planet. Two days later, I had run into Born at the West End, and when he told me about her reaction to our meeting at the party, my feelings for her began to shift. Apparently she liked me and was concerned about my welfare, and when you're informed that a person likes you, your instinctive response is to like that person back. Then came the dinner. The languor and precision of her gestures as she cut the flowers and put them in the vase had stirred something in me, and the simple act of watching her move had suddenly become fascinating, hypnotic. There were depths of sensuality in her, I discovered, and the bland, uninteresting woman who seemed not to have a thought in her head turned out to be far more astute than I had imagined. She had defended me against Born at least twice during the dinner, intervening at the precise moments when things had threatened to fly out of control. Calm, always calm, barely speaking above a whisper, but each time her words had produced the desired effect. Thrown by Born's prodding insinuations, convinced that he was trying to lure me into some voyeuristic mania of his — watching me make love to Margot? — I'd assumed that she was in on it as well, and therefore I had held back and refused to play along. But now Born was on the other side of the Atlantic, and Margot still wanted to see me. It could only be for one thing. I understood now that it had always been that one thing, right from the moment she'd spotted me standing alone at the party. That was why Born had behaved so testily at the dinner — not because he wanted to instigate an evening of depraved sexual antics, but because he was angry at Margot for telling him she was attracted to me.

She cooked us dinner for five straight nights, and for five straight nights we slept together in the spare bedroom at the end of the hall. We could have used the other bedroom, which was larger and more comfortable, but neither one of us wanted to go in there. That was Born's room, the world of Born's bed, and for those five nights we made it our business to create a world of our own, sleeping in that tiny room with the single barred window and the narrow bed, which came to be known as the love bed, although love finally had nothing to do with what happened to us during those five days. We didn't fall for each other, as the saying goes, but rather we fell into

50

each other, and in the deeply intimate space we inhabited for that short, short time, our sole preoccupation was pleasure. The pleasure of eating and drinking, the pleasure of sex, the pleasure of taking part in a wordless animal dialogue that was conducted in a language of looking and touching, of biting, tasting, and stroking. That doesn't mean we didn't talk, but talk was kept to a minimum, and what talk there was tended to focus on food — *What should we eat tomorrow night?* — and the words we exchanged over dinner were wispy and banal, of no real importance. Margot never asked me questions about myself. She wasn't curious about my past, she didn't care about my opinions on literature or politics, and she had no interest in what I was studying. She simply took me for what I represented in her own mind — her choice of the moment, the physical being she desired — and every time I looked at her, I sensed that she was drinking me in, as if just having me there within arm's reach was enough to satisfy her. What did I learn about Margot during those days? Very little, almost nothing at all. She had grown up in Paris, was the youngest of three children, and knew Born because they were second cousins. They had been together for two years now, but she didn't think it would last much longer. He seemed to be growing bored with her, she said, and she was growing bored with herself. She shrugged when she said that, and when I saw the distant expression on her face, I had the terrible intuition that she already considered herself to be half dead. After that, I

51

stopped pressing her to open up to me. It was enough that we were together, and I cringed at the thought of accidentally touching on something that might cause her pain.

Margot without makeup was softer and more earthbound than the striking female object she presented to the public. Margot without clothes proved to be slight, almost meager, with small, pubescent-like breasts, slender hips, and sinewy arms and legs. A full-lipped mouth, a flat belly with a slightly protruding navel, tender hands, a nest of coarse pubic hair, firm buttocks, and extremely white skin that felt smoother than any skin I had ever touched. The particulars of a body, the irrelevant, precious details. I was tentative with her at first, not knowing what to expect, a bit awed to find myself with a woman so much more experienced than I was, a beginner in the arms of a veteran, a fumbler who had always felt shy and awkward in his nakedness, who until then had always made love in the dark, preferably under the blankets, coupling with girls who had been just as shy and awkward as he was, but Margot was so comfortable with herself, so knowledgeable in the arts of nibbling, licking, and kissing, so unreluctant to explore me with her hands and tongue, to attack, to swoon, to give herself without coyness or hesitation that it wasn't long before I let myself go. If it feels good, it's good, Margot said at one point, and that was the gift she gave me over the course of those five nights. She taught me not to be afraid of myself anymore.

I didn't want it to end. Living in that strange paradise with the strange, unfathomable Margot was one of the best, most unlikely things that had ever happened to me, but Born was due to return from Paris the next evening, and we had no choice but to cut it off. At the time, I imagined it was only a temporary ceasefire. When we said good-bye on the last morning, I told her not to worry, that sooner or later we'd figure out a way to continue, but for all my bluster and confidence Margot looked troubled, and just as I was about to leave the apartment, her eyes unexpectedly filled with tears.

I have a bad feeling, she said. I don't know why, but something tells me this is the end, that this is the last time I'll ever see you.

Don't say that, I answered. I live just a few blocks from here. You can come to my apartment anytime you want.

I'll try, Adam. I'll do my best, but don't expect too much from me. I'm not as strong as you think I am.

I don't understand.

Rudolf. Once he comes back, I think he's going to throw me out.

If he does, you can move in with me.

And live with two college boys in a dirty apartment? I'm too old for that.

My roommate isn't so bad. And the place is fairly clean, all things considered.

I hate this country. I hate everything about it except you, and you aren't enough to keep me here. If Rudolf doesn't want me anymore, I'll pack up my things and go home to Paris.

You talk as if you want it to happen, as if you're already planning to break it off yourself.

I don't know. Maybe I am.

And what about me? Haven't these days meant anything to you?

Of course they have. I've loved being with you, but we've run out of time now, and the moment you walk out of here, you'll understand that you don't need me anymore.

That's not true.

Yes, it is. You just don't know it yet.

What are you talking about?

Poor Adam. I'm not the answer. Not for you — probably not for anyone.

★ ★ ★

It was a dismal end to what had been such a momentous time for me, and I left the apartment feeling shattered, perplexed, and perhaps a little angry as well. For days afterward, I kept going over that final conversation, and the more I analyzed it, the less sense it made to me. On the one hand, Margot had teared up at the moment of my departure, confessing that she was afraid she would never see me again. That would suggest she wanted our fling to go on, but when I proposed that we begin meeting at my apartment, she had become hesitant, all but telling me it wouldn't be possible. Why not? For no reason — except that she wasn't as strong as I thought she was. I had no idea what that meant. Then she had started talking about Born, which quickly devolved into a muddle of contradictions and conflicting desires. She was worried that he was going to kick her out, but a second later that seemed to be exactly what she wanted. Even more, perhaps she was going to take the initiative and leave him herself. Nothing added up. She wanted me and didn't want me. She wanted Born and didn't want Born. Each word that came out of her mouth subverted what she had said a moment earlier, and in the end there was no way to know what she felt. Perhaps she didn't know herself. That struck me as the most plausible explanation — Margot in distress, Margot pulled apart by equal and opposite forces — but after spending those five nights with her, I couldn't help feeling hurt and abandoned. I tried to keep my spirits up — hoping she would call, hoping she would change her mind and come rushing back to me — but deep down I knew it was finished, that her fear of never seeing me again was in fact a prophecy, and that she was gone from my life for good.

Meanwhile, Born was back in New York, but a full week had gone by and I still hadn't heard from him. The longer his silence went on, the more I realized how much I was dreading his call. Had Margot told him what she and I had been up to during his absence? Were the two of them still together, or was she already back in France? After three or four days, I found myself hoping that he had forgotten about me and that I would never have to see him again. There would be no magazine, of course, but I hardly cared about that now. I had betrayed him by sleeping with his girlfriend, and even if he had more or less encouraged me to do it, I wasn't proud of what I had done — especially after Margot had told me that I didn't need her anymore, which meant, I now understood, that she didn't need me anymore. I had created a mess for myself, and coward that I probably was, I would have preferred to hide under my bed than have to face either one of them.

But Born hadn't forgotten me. Just when I was beginning to think the story was over, he called early one evening and asked me to drop by his apartment for a chat. That was the word he used — *chat* — and I was amazed by how chipper he sounded on the phone, positively bursting with energy and good cheer.

Sorry for the delay, he said. A thousand pardons, Walker, but I've been busy, busy, juggling this and that, a thousand things, for which I beg a thousand pardons, but time is a-wasting, and the moment has come to sit down and talk business. I owe you a check for the first issue, and after we've had our little chat, I'll take you out for dinner somewhere. It's been a while, and I believe we have some catching up to do.

I didn't want to go, but I went. Not without trepidation, not without a flutter of panic twitching in my stomach, but in the end I felt I had no choice. By some miracle, the magazine appeared to be alive, and if he wanted to talk to me about it, if he was in fact ready to start writing checks to support the cause, I didn't see how I could turn down his invitation. *I believe we have some catching up to do.* Like it or not, I was about to find out if Born knew what had been going on behind his back — and, if he did know, exactly what he had done about it.

He was dressed in white again: the full suit, the shirt open at the collar, but clean and unrumpled this time, the perfect hidalgo. Freshly shaven, his hair combed, looking nattier and more pulled together than I had ever seen him. A warm smile when he opened the door, a firm shake of the hand as I entered the apartment, a friendly pat on the shoulder as he led me toward the liquor cabinet and asked me what I wanted to drink, but no Margot, no sign of her anywhere, and while that didn't necessarily mean anything, I was beginning to suspect the worst. We sat down near the French windows overlooking the park, I on the sofa, he in a large chair opposite, facing each other across the coffee table, Born grinning with contentment, so pleased with himself, so terribly happy as he told me that his trip to Paris had been a resounding success and the knotty problem that had been bedeviling his colleagues was now untangled at last. Then, after a few desultory questions about my studies and the books I had been reading lately, he leaned back in his chair and said, apropos of nothing: I want to thank you, Walker. You've done me an important service.

Thank me? For what?

For showing me the light of truth. I feel greatly in your debt.

I still don't know what you're talking about.

Margot.

What about her?

She betrayed me.

How? I asked, trying to play dumb but feeling ridiculous, crumpling up with shame as Born continued to smile at me.

She slept with you.

She told you that?

Whatever her faults might be, Margot never lies. If I'm not mistaken, you spent five straight nights with her — right here in this apartment.

I'm sorry, I said, looking down at the floor, too embarrassed to meet Born's gaze.

Don't be sorry. I fairly pushed you into it, didn't I? If I had been in your shoes, I probably would have done the same thing. It was obvious that Margot wanted to sleep with you. Why would a healthy young man turn down an opportunity like that?

If you wanted her to do it, then why do you feel betrayed?

Ah, but I didn't want her to do it. I was only pretending.

And why would you pretend?

To test her loyalty, that's why. And the tramp fell for the bait. Don't worry, Walker. I'm well rid of her, and I have you to thank for getting her out the door.

Where is she now?

Paris, I presume.

Did you push her out, or did she leave because she wanted to?

That's difficult to say. Probably a little of both. Let's call it a separation by mutual consent.

Poor Margot . . .

A wonderful cook, a wonderful fuck, but at

bottom just another mindless slut. Don't feel sorry for her, Walker. She isn't worth it.

Harsh words for someone who shared your life for two years.

Perhaps. As you've already noticed, my mouth tends to run away from me at times. But facts are facts, and the fact is I'm not getting any younger. It's time for me to think about marriage, and no sane man would consider marrying a girl like Margot.

Do you have someone in mind, or is that just a statement of future intentions?

I'm engaged. As of two weeks ago. Yet one more thing I accomplished on my trip to Paris. That's why I'm in such a good mood tonight.

Congratulations. And when is the happy day?

It's still not clear. There are complicated issues involved, and the wedding can't take place until next spring at the earliest.

A pity to wait so long.

It can't be helped. Technically, she's still married to someone else, and we have to wait for the law to do its work. Not that it isn't worth it. I've known this woman since I was your age, and she's an exemplary person, the partner I've longed for all my life.

If you care about her so much, why have you been with Margot for the past two years?

Because I didn't know I was in love with her until I saw her again in Paris.

Exit Margot, enter wife. Your bed won't be empty for long, will it?

You underestimate me, young man. Much as I'd like to move in with her now, I'm going to hold off until we're married. It's a question of principle.

Chivalry in action.

That's it. Chivalry in action.

Like our old friend from Périgord, the ever-gentle, peace-loving Bertran.

The mention of the poet's name seemed to stop Born dead in his tracks. *Merde!* he said, thwacking his knee with the palm of his left hand, I almost forgot. I owe you money, don't I? Sit tight while I look for my checks. I won't be a minute.

With those words Born bounced out of his chair and began rushing toward the other end of the apartment. I stood up to stretch my legs, and by the time I reached the dining room table, which was no more than ten or twelve feet from the sofa, he had already returned. Brusquely pulling out a chair, he sat down, opened his checkbook, and started to write — using a speckled green fountain pen, I remember, with a thick nib and blue-black ink.

I'm giving you six thousand, two hundred and fifty dollars, he said. Five thousand to pay for the first issue, plus twelve fifty to cover a fourth of your annual salary. Take your time, Adam. If you can put the contents together by . . . let's see . . . by the end of August or the beginning of September, that will be soon enough. I'll be long gone by then, of course, but we can stay in contact through the post, and if something urgent comes up, you can call me and reverse the charges.

It was the largest check I had ever seen, and

when he tore it out of the book and handed it to me, I looked down at the sum and felt dizzy with apprehension. Are you sure you want to go ahead with it? I asked. This is an awful lot of money, you know.

Of course I want to go ahead with it. We made a deal, and now it's up to you to assemble the best first issue you possibly can.

But Margot's out of the picture now. You're under no obligation to her anymore.

What are you talking about?

It was Margot's idea, remember? You gave me this job because of her.

Nonsense. It was my idea from the start. The only thing Margot ever wanted was to crawl into bed with you. She couldn't have cared less about jobs or magazines or the precarious state of your future. If I told you she was the one who put me up to it, that was only because I didn't want to embarrass you.

Why in the world would you do this for me?

To be perfectly honest, I don't know. But I see something in you, Walker, something I like, and for some inexplicable reason I find myself willing to take a gamble on you. I'm betting that you'll make a success of it. Prove me right.

★ ★ ★

It was a warm spring evening, a soft and beautiful evening with a cloudless sky overhead, the smell of flowers in the air, and no wind at all, not even the faintest hint of a breeze. Born was planning to take me to a Cuban restaurant on

61

Broadway and 109th Street (the Ideal, a favorite spot of his), but as we walked westward across the Columbia campus, he proposed that we continue on past Broadway and head for Riverside Drive, where we could stop to look at the Hudson for a few moments, and then make our way downtown along the edge of the park. It was that kind of a night, he said, and since we weren't in any rush, why not prolong the journey a bit and take advantage of the good weather? So we took our little stroll in the pleasant spring air, talking about the magazine, about the woman Born was planning to marry, about the trees and shrubs in Riverside Park, about the geological composition of the New Jersey Palisades across the river, and I remember that I felt happy, awash in a sense of well-being, and whatever misgivings I might have had about Born were beginning to melt away, or at least had been put in abeyance for now. He hadn't blamed me for allowing myself to be seduced by Margot. He had just given me a check for an enormous amount of money. He wasn't haranguing me with his warped political ideas. For once, he seemed to be relaxed and undefensive, and perhaps he really had fallen in love, perhaps his life was turning in a new and better direction, and for that one night, in any case, I was willing to give him every benefit of the doubt.

We crossed over to the eastern sidewalk of Riverside Drive and began walking downtown. Several streetlamps had burned out, and as we approached the corner of West 112th, we found ourselves entering a block-long stretch of murk and darkness. Night had fallen in earnest by then, and it was difficult to see anything more than a yard or two in front of us. I lit up a cigarette, and through the glow of the match burning near my mouth, I glimpsed the shadowy outline of a figure emerging from a blackened doorway. A second later, Born grabbed my arm and told me to stop. Just that one word: *Stop*. I let the match fall from my hand and tossed the cigarette into the gutter. The figure was coming toward us, unmistakably walking in our direction, and after a few more steps I saw that it was a black kid dressed in dark clothes. He was rather short, probably no more than sixteen or seventeen, but after another three or four steps, I finally understood why Born had grabbed my arm, finally saw what he had already seen. The kid was holding a gun in his left hand. The gun was pointed at us, and just like that, with a single tick of the clock, the entire universe had changed. The kid wasn't a person anymore. He was that gun and nothing else, the nightmare gun that lived in every New Yorker's imagination, the heartless, inhuman gun that was destined to find you alone one night on a darkened street and send you to an early grave. Fork it over. Empty your pockets. Shut up. A moment earlier, I had been on top of the world, and now, suddenly, I was more afraid than I had ever been in my life.

The kid stopped about two feet in front of us, pointed the gun at my chest, and said: Don't move.

He was close enough now for me to see his

face, and as far as I could tell he looked scared, not at all confident about what he was doing. How could I have known this? Perhaps it was something in his eyes, or perhaps I had detected a slight tremor in his lower lip — I can't be sure. Fear made me blind, and whatever sense I had of him must have come to me through my pores, a subliminal osmosis, so to speak, knowledge without consciousness, but I was almost certain that he was a beginner, a novice thug out on his first or second job.

Born was standing to my left, and after a moment I heard him say: What do you want from us? There was a small quiver in his voice, but at least he had managed to speak, which was more than I was capable of doing just then.

Your money, the kid said. Your money and your watch. Both of you. Wallets first. And be quick about it. I ain't got all night.

I reached into my pocket for my billfold, but Born unexpectedly chose to make a stand. A stupid move, I thought, an act of defiance that could wind up getting us both killed, but there wasn't a thing I could do about it.

And what if I don't want to give you my money? he asked.

Then I'll shoot you, mister, the kid said. I'll shoot you and take your wallet anyway.

Born let out a long, histrionic sigh. You're going to regret this, little man, he said. Why don't you just run along now and leave us alone?

Why don't you just shut your fucking mouth and give me your wallet? the kid answered, thrusting the gun into the air a couple of times for emphasis.

As you wish, Born replied. But don't say I didn't warn you.

I was still looking at the kid, which meant that I had only a vague, peripheral view of Born, but at the last second I turned my head slightly to the left and saw him reach into the inside breast pocket of his jacket. I assumed he was going for his billfold, but when his hand emerged from the pocket it was bunched up into a fist, as if he was hiding something, concealing some object in his closed palm. I couldn't begin to guess what that thing might have been. An instant later, I heard a click, and the blade of a knife jumped out of its sheath. With a hard, upward thrust, Born immediately stabbed the kid with the switch-blade — straight in the stomach, a dead-center hit. The boy grunted as the steel tore through his flesh, grabbed his stomach with his right hand, and slowly sank to the ground.

Shit, man, he said. It ain't even loaded.

The gun fell out of his hand and clattered onto the sidewalk. I could barely absorb what I was seeing. Too many things had happened in too short a time, and none of them seemed quite real anymore. Born swept up the gun and dropped it into the side pocket of his jacket. The kid was moaning now, clutching his stomach with both hands and writhing around on the pavement. It was too dark to make out much of anything, but after a few moments I thought I saw blood oozing onto the ground.

We have to get him to a hospital, I finally said.

There's a phone booth up on Broadway. You wait with him here and I'll run to make the call.

Don't be an idiot, Born said, grabbing hold of my jacket and giving me a good hard shake. No hospitals. The boy is going to die, and we can't have anything to do with it.

He won't die if an ambulance gets here within ten or fifteen minutes.

And if he lives, then what? Do you want to spend the next three years of your life in court?

I don't care. Walk away from it if you like. Go home and drink another bottle of gin, but I'm running off to Broadway right now to call for an ambulance.

Fine. Have it your own way. We'll pretend to be good little Boy Scouts, and I'll sit here with this piece of garbage and wait for you to come back. Is that what you want? How stupid do you think I am, Walker?

I didn't bother to answer him. Instead, I turned on my heels and started running up 112th Street toward Broadway. I was gone for ten minutes, fifteen minutes at the most, but when I returned to the spot where I'd left Born and the wounded boy, they had both disappeared. Except for a patch of congealing blood on the sidewalk, there was no sign that either one of them had ever been there.

★ ★ ★

I went home. There was no point in waiting for the ambulance now, so I climbed back up the hill toward Broadway and headed downtown. My

66

mind was blank, incapable of producing a single coherent thought, but as I unlocked the door of the apartment, I realized that I was sobbing, had in fact been sobbing for the past several minutes. Luckily, my roommate was out, which spared me the trouble of having to talk to him in that state. I went on crying in my room, and when the tears finally stopped, I tore up Born's check and put the pieces in an envelope, which I mailed to him early the next morning. There was no accompanying letter. I was confident that the gesture spoke for itself and that he would understand I was finished with him and wanted nothing more to do with his filthy magazine.

That afternoon, the late edition of the *New York Post* reported that the body of eighteen-year-old Cedric Williams had been discovered in Riverside Park with over a dozen knife wounds gouged into his chest and stomach. There was no doubt in my mind that Born was responsible. The moment I'd left him to call for the ambulance, he had picked up the bleeding Williams and carried him into the park to finish off the job he had started on the sidewalk. Considering the amount of traffic that moves along Riverside Drive, I found it incredible that no one had spotted Born crossing the street with the kid in his arms, but according to the paper, the investigators working on the case had yet to establish any leads.

Knowing what I did, I clearly had an obligation to call the local precinct house and tell them about Born and the knife and the attempt by Williams to hold us up. I chanced upon the article while drinking a cup of coffee in the Lions Den, the snack bar on the ground floor of the undergraduate student center, and rather than use a public phone, I decided to walk to my apartment on 107th Street and make the call from there. I still hadn't told anyone about what had happened. I had tried to reach my sister in Poughkeepsie — the one person I was prepared to unburden myself to — but she hadn't been in. Once I arrived at my apartment building, I collected my mail in the lobby before taking the elevator upstairs. There was only one letter for me: a stampless, hand-delivered envelope with my name written across the front in block letters, folded up in thirds and then shoved through a narrow slot in the mailbox. I opened it in the elevator on my way up to the ninth floor. *Not a word, Walker. Remember: I still have the knife, and I'm not afraid to use it.*

There was no signature at the bottom, but that hardly seemed necessary. It was a vicious threat, and now that I had seen Born in action, now that I had witnessed the brutality he was capable of, I felt certain he wouldn't hesitate to carry it out. He would come after me if I tried to turn him in. If I did nothing, he would leave me alone. I still had every intention of calling the police, but the day passed, and then more days passed, and I couldn't bring myself to do it. Fear reduced me to silence, but the fact was that only silence could protect me from having to cross paths with him again, and that was all that mattered to me now: to keep Born out of my life forever.

This failure to act is far and away the most

reprehensible thing I have ever done, the low point in my career as a human being. Not only did it allow a killer to walk free, but it also had the insidious effect of forcing me to confront my own moral weakness, to recognize that I had never been the person I had thought I was, that I was less good, less strong, less brave than I had imagined myself to be. Horrid, implacable truths. My cowardice sickened me, and yet how not to be afraid of that knife? Born had stuck it into Williams's belly without the slightest compunction or regret, and even if the first stab could have been justified as an act of self-defense, what about the twelve others he had delivered in the park, the cold-blooded decision to kill? After torturing myself for close to a week, I finally found the courage to call my sister again, and when I heard myself spewing out the whole sordid business to Gwyn over the course of our two-hour conversation, I realized that I didn't have a choice. I had to step forward. If I didn't talk to the police, I would lose all respect for myself, and the shame of it would go on haunting me for the rest of my life.

I'm fairly certain they believed my story. I gave them Born's note, for one thing, and although it lacked a signature, the knife was mentioned, the threat was explicit, and if there was any doubt concerning the author's identity, a handwriting expert could easily confirm that it had been composed by Born. There was also the bloodstain on the sidewalk near the corner of Riverside Drive and West 112th Street. And then there was my emergency call for the ambulance, which tallied with their records, and the additional fact that I was able to tell them that no one had been present at the scene when the ambulance arrived. At first, they were reluctant to believe that a professor at Columbia University's School of International Affairs could commit such a nasty street crime, let alone that such a person would walk around with a switchblade in his pocket, but in the end they assured me they would look into it. I left the police station convinced that the matter would soon be closed. It was the end of May, which meant there were still two or three weeks to go before the semester ended, and because I had put off reporting to the police for six long days following the discovery of Williams's corpse, I figured that Born must have thought his threatening note had done its job. But I was wrong, miserably and tragically wrong. As promised, the police did go to question him, but they quickly learned from an administrator at the School of International Affairs that Professor Born had returned to Paris earlier in the week. His mother had died quite suddenly, they were told, and with so little time remaining in the semester, his final classes were going to be taught by a substitute. In other words, Professor Born would not be coming back.

He had been frightened of me, after all. In spite of the note, he had assumed I would ignore his threat and go to the police anyway. Yes, I did go — but not soon enough, not soon enough by half, and because I gave him that extra time, he had pounced at the opportunity and run, fleeing the country and escaping the jurisdiction of New York's laws. I knew for a fact that the story about his mother's death was a sham. During our first conversation at the party in April, he had told me that both his parents were dead, and unless his mother had been resurrected in the interim, I was hard-pressed to see how she could have died twice. When the detective called to tell me what had happened, I felt crushed, humiliated, numb. Born had defeated me. He had shown me something about myself that filled me with revulsion, and for the first time in my life I understood what it was to hate someone. I could never forgive him — and I could never forgive myself.

Back in the dark ages of our youth, Walker and I had been friends. We entered Columbia together in 1965, two eighteen-year-old freshmen from New Jersey, and over the next four years we moved in the same circles, read the same books, shared the same ambitions. Then our class graduated, and I lost contact with him. In the early seventies, I ran into someone who told me Adam was living in London (or maybe it was Rome, he wasn't sure), and that was the last time I heard anyone mention his name. For the next thirty-something years, he rarely entered my thoughts, but whenever he did, I would find myself wondering how he had managed to disappear so thoroughly. Of all the young misfits from our little gang at college, Walker was the one who had struck me as the most promising, and I figured it was inevitable that sooner or later I would begin reading about the books he had written or come across something he had published in a magazine — poems or novels, short stories or reviews, perhaps a translation of one of his beloved French poets — but that moment never came, and I could only conclude that the boy who had been destined for a life in the literary world had gone on to concern himself with other matters.

A little less than a year ago (spring 2007), a UPS package was delivered to my house in

Brooklyn. It contained the manuscript of Walker's story about Rudolf Born (Part I of this book), along with a cover letter from Adam that read as follows:

Dear Jim,

Forgive the intrusion after such a long silence. If memory serves, it's been thirty-eight years since we last talked, but I recently came across an announcement that you'll be doing an event in San Francisco next month (I live in Oakland), and I was wondering if you might have some free time to spend with me — perhaps dinner at my house, for example — since I'm in urgent need of help, and I believe you're the only person I know (or knew) who can give it to me. I say this not to alarm you but because of the enormous admiration I have for the books you have written — which have made me so proud of you, so proud to have once counted myself among your friends.

By way of anticipation, I enclose a still-not-finished draft of the first chapter of a book I am trying to write. I want to go on with it but seem to have hit a wall of struggle and uncertainty — *fear* might be the word I'm looking for — and I'm hoping that a talk with you might give me the courage to climb over it or tear it down. I should add (in case you're in doubt) that it is not a work of fiction.

At the risk of sounding melodramatic, I should also add that I am not well, am in

76

fact slowly dying of leukemia, and will be lucky to hang on for another year. Just so you know what you're getting yourself into, in case you choose to get into it. I look a fright these days (no hair! thin as a twig!), but vanity has no place in my world anymore, and I have done my best to come to terms with the thing that has happened to me, even as I fight on with the treatments. A couple of centuries ago, sixty used to be considered old, and since none of us thought we would live past thirty, reaching the double of that isn't half bad, is it?

I could go on, but I don't want to take up any more of your time. Sending you this manuscript was not an easy decision (you must be inundated by countless letters from cranks and would-be novelists), but I'll be glad to fill you in on my comings and goings of the past four decades if you decide to accept my invitation — which I fervently hope you will. As for the ms., save it for the plane trip to California if you're too busy between now and then. It's short enough to be consumed in less than an hour.

Hoping for a response.

Yours in solidarity,

Adam Walker

It hadn't been a close friendship — no shared confidences, no long one-on-one talks, no letters exchanged — but there was no question that I admired Walker, and I had no doubt that he looked on me as an equal, since he never failed

77

to show me anything but respect and goodwill. He was a bit timid, I remember, a trait that seemed odd in a person of such keen intelligence who also happened to be one of the best-looking boys on campus — *handsome as a movie star*, as a girlfriend of mine once put it. But better to be shy than arrogant, I suppose, better to blend in delicately than to intimidate everyone with your insufferable human perfection. He was something of a loner, then, but amiable and droll whenever he emerged from his cocoon, with a sharp, offbeat sense of humor, and what I especially liked about him was the broad range of his interests, his ability to talk about Cavalcanti, say, or John Donne, and then, with the same acumen and knowledge, turn around and tell you something about baseball that had never occurred to you before. Concerning his inner life, however, I knew nothing. Beyond the fact that he had an older sister (a remarkable beauty, by the way, leading one to suspect that the entire Walker clan had been blessed with the genes of angels), I knew nothing about his family or background, and certainly nothing about the death of his little brother. Now Walker himself was dying, a month past his sixtieth birthday he was beginning to say his farewells, and after reading his hesitant, touching letter, I couldn't help thinking that this was the start, that the bright young men of yore were at last turning old, and before long our whole generation would be gone. Rather than follow Adam's advice and ignore his manuscript until I was on the plane to California, I sat down and read it immediately.

How to describe my response? Fascination, amusement, a growing sense of dread, and then horror. If I hadn't been told it was a true story, I probably would have plunged in and taken those sixty-plus pages for the beginning of a novel (writers do, after all, sometimes inject characters who bear their own names into works of fiction), and then I might have found the ending implausible — or perhaps too abrupt, which would have made it unsatisfying — but because I approached it as a piece of autobiography from the start, Walker's confession left me shaken and filled with sorrow. Poor Adam. He was so hard on himself, so contemptuous of his weakness in relation to Born, so disgusted with his petty aspirations and youthful strivings, so sick over his failure to recognize that he was dealing with a monster, but who can blame a twenty-year-old boy for losing his bearings in the blur of sophistication and depravity that surrounds a person like Born? *He had shown me something about myself that filled me with revulsion.* But what had Walker done wrong? He had called for an ambulance on the night of the stabbing, and then, after a momentary lapse of courage, he had gone and talked to the police. Under the circumstances, no one could have done more than that. Whatever revulsion Walker felt about himself could not have been caused by how he behaved at the end. It was the beginning that distressed him, the simple fact that he had allowed himself to be seduced, and he had gone on torturing himself about it for the rest of his life — to such an extent that now, even as his life was ending, he felt driven to march back into the past and tell the story of his shame. According to his letter, this was only the first chapter. I wondered what could possibly come next.

★ ★ ★

I wrote back to Walker that evening, assuring him that I had received his package, expressing concern and sympathy over the state of his health, telling him that in spite of everything I was happy to have heard from him after so many years, was moved by his kind words about the books I had published, and so on. Yes, I promised, I would adjust my schedule to make sure I could go to his house for dinner and would gladly discuss the problems he was having with the second chapter of his memoir. I don't have a copy of my letter, but I remember that I wrote it in a spirit of encouragement and support, calling the chapter he had sent me both *excellent* and *disturbing*, or words to that effect, and telling him I felt the project was well worth seeing through to the end. I needn't have said anything more, but curiosity got the better of me, and I concluded with what might have been an impertinence. Forgive me for asking, I wrote, but I'm not sure I can wait until next month to find out what happened to you after we last saw each other. If you're feeling up to it, I would welcome another letter before I head for your neck of the woods. Not a blow-by-blow account, of course, but the gist, whatever you care to tell me.

Not wanting to entrust my letter to the vagaries of the U.S. Postal Service, I shipped it by express mail the following morning. Two days later, I received Walker's express mail response.

Gratified, thankful, looking forward to next month.

In answer to your question, I'm more than happy to oblige you, although I'm afraid you'll find my story rather dull. June 1969. We shook hands, I remember, vowed to stay in touch, and then walked off in opposite directions, never to meet again. I went back to my parents' house in New Jersey, planning to visit for a couple of days, got drunk with my sister that night, tripped, fell down the stairs, and broke my leg. Bad luck, it would seem, but in the end it was the best thing that could have happened to me. Ten days later, *Greetings!*, and an invitation from the federal government to show up for my army physical. I hobbled into the draft board on crutches, was given a I-Y deferment because of the broken leg, and by the time the break mended, the Selective Service had instituted the lottery. I wound up drawing a high number, an obscenely high number (346), and all of a sudden, literally in a single flash, the confrontation I had been dreading for so long was permanently erased from my future.

Beyond that early gift from the gods, I mostly bumped along, struggling to keep my balance, lurching fitfully between bouts of optimism and blinding stretches of despair. Unaccountable, perplexing, perplexed. In the fall of 1969 I moved to London — not because England attracted me, but because I couldn't stand living in America anymore. The poison of Vietnam, the tears of Vietnam, the blood of Vietnam. We were all out of our minds back then, weren't we? All driven to madness by a war we detested and couldn't stop. So I left our fair country, found myself a shithole flat in Hammersmith, and spent the next four years toiling in the sewers of Grub Street — cranking out countless freelance book reviews and accepting any translation that came my way, French books mostly, one or two in Italian, regurgitating into English everything from a dull academic history of the Middle East to an anthropological study of voodoo to crime fiction. Meanwhile, I continued writing my crabbed, gnostic poems. In 1972, a book was published by an obscure small press based in Manchester, an edition of three or four hundred copies, one review in an equally obscure little magazine, sales in the neighborhood of fifty — echoing those hilarious lines from *Krapp's Last Tape* (which I remember you were so fond of): 'Seventeen copies sold, of which eleven at trade price to free circulating libraries beyond the seas. Getting known.' Getting known indeed.

I pushed on with it for another year, and then, after a bitter, anguished debate with myself, I concluded that I wasn't making sufficient progress and stopped. It's not that I thought my work was bad. There were occasional sparks, a few poems that seemed to have something fresh and urgent about them, lines I felt genuinely proud of, but by and large the results were mediocre, and the prospect of living out my life as a mediocrity frightened me into quitting.

The London years. The somber revelations of dashed hopes, loveless sex in the beds of prostitutes, one serious liaison with an English girl named Dorothy that crashed to a sudden halt when she found out I was Jewish. But, believe it or not, in spite of how grim all this must sound to you, I think I was growing stronger, finally beginning to grow up and take charge of my life. I finished my last poem in June 1973, ceremoniously burned it in the kitchen sink, and went back to America. I had sworn not to return until the last U.S. soldier had left Vietnam, but I had a new plan now, and I didn't have time for such highminded claptrap anymore. I was going to throw myself into the trenches and fight it out with my bare fists. Good-bye, literature. Welcome to the thing-in-itself, the sensorium of the real.

Berkeley, California. Three years of law school. The idea was to do some good, to work with the poor, the downtrodden, to involve myself with the spat-upon and the invisible and see if I couldn't defend them against the cruelties and indifference of American society. More highminded claptrap? Some might think so, but it never felt that way to me. From poetry to justice, then. Poetic justice, if you will. For the sad fact remains: there is far more poetry in the world than justice.

Now that my illness has forced me to stop working, I've had ample time to ponder my motives for choosing the life I did. In a very concrete way, I think it started that night in 1967 when I saw Born stab Cedric Williams in the belly — and then, after I had run off to call for an ambulance, carry him into the park and murder him. For no reason, no reason whatsoever, and then, even worse, for him to have gotten away with it, to have skipped the country and never to have been judged for his crime. It would be impossible to overstate how terribly this grieved me, has continued to grieve me. Justice betrayed. The anger and frustration have not diminished, and if that is how I feel, if this sense of justice is what burns most brightly in me, then I'm certain I chose the correct path for myself.

Twenty-seven years of legal aid work, community activism in the black neighborhoods of Oakland and Berkeley, rent strikes, class action suits against various corporations, police brutality cases, the list goes on.

In the long run, I don't think I've accomplished much. A number of satisfying victories, yes, but this country is no less cruel now than it was then, perhaps more cruel than ever, and yet to have done nothing would have been impossible for me. I would have felt that I was living in a fraudulent relation with myself.

Am I starting to sound like a self-righteous prig? I hope not.

Income was meager, of course. The kind of work I did does not a rich man make. But there were family resources that fell into my lap — my lap and my sister's lap — following the deaths of our parents (mother in 1974, father in 1976). We sold the house and our father's supermarket for a considerable sum, and because Gwyn is a clever and practical woman, she invested the money well, which meant that I always had enough to live on (modestly, but comfortably) without worrying too much about what my work brought in. Playing the system in order to beat the system. A fine little twist of hypocrisy, I suppose, but everyone has to put food on the table, everyone needs a roof over his head. Alas, medical bills have made a severe dent in my savings these past two years, but I think I'll have enough to carry me through to the end — assuming I don't last too long, which doesn't appear likely.

As for matters of the heart, I staggered along in my clumsy, retarded way for a good many years, too many years, crawling in and out of various beds, falling in and out of love with various women, but never felt any temptation to settle down and marry until I was thirty-six, when I met the one person who ever really counted for me, a social worker by the name of Sandra Williams — yes, the same last name that belonged to the murdered boy, a slave name, a common slave name borne by hundreds of thousands if not millions of African-Americans — and although an interracial marriage can pose numerous social problems for the couple (from both camps), I never considered it to be an impediment, for the truth was that I loved Sandra, loved her from the first day to the last. A wise woman, a brave woman, a spirited and beautiful woman, just six months younger than I was, already married and divorced when we met, with a twelve-year-old girl, Rebecca, my stepdaughter, herself now married and the mother of two, and the nineteen years I spent with Sandra turned me into someone better than I had been, better than I would have been alone or with anyone else, and now that she is dead (of cervical cancer, five years ago), not a day goes by when I don't long for her. My only regret is that we never managed to have children together, but making a family is beyond the power of a man who turns out to have been born sterile.

What more to say? I am well cared for by my housekeeper (who will cook dinner for us on the night of your visit), I see Rebecca and her family often, I talk to my sister on the telephone nearly every day, I have many friends. When health permits, I continue to devour books (poems, history, novels, among them yours — the instant they are published), still take an active interest in baseball (an incurable disease), and fitfully indulge in the escapism of watching films (thanks to a DVD player, loyal friend to the solitaries and shut-ins of this world). But mostly I think about the past, the old days, that long-ago year (1967) when so much happened to me, happened in me and around me, the unexpected turns and discoveries of that year, the madness of that year, which pushed me toward the life I wound up living, for both good and bad. Nothing like a fatal illness to sharpen one's thoughts, to make one want to tote up the accounts, to produce a final reckoning. The plan is to write the book in three parts, three chapters. Not a long book, not a complicated book, but it has to be done right, and to be stuck in the second part has become a source of terrible discombobulation. Rest assured, I am not expecting you to solve the problem for me. But I have a suspicion, perhaps a groundless suspicion, that a talk with you would give me the kick in the pants I need. Beyond that — and before that — that is, above and beyond my minuscule travails, there will be the tremendous pleasure of seeing you again . . .

I had been hoping for a word from him, but it never occurred to me that he would write more than a couple of paragraphs, that he would be willing to put in the time and effort to share such a full account of himself with me — I, who was hardly more than a stranger to him at that point. *Many friends* or not, he must have been lonely, I thought, he must have been more than a little desperate, and while I still couldn't grasp why I was the person he had chosen to be his confessor, he had latched on to me in such a way as to make it all but unthinkable not to do everything I could for him. How swiftly the weather changes. A dying friend had reentered my life after an absence of close to forty years, and suddenly I felt an obligation not to let him down. But what kind of help could I give him? He was having trouble with his book, and for some inexplicable reason he had deluded himself into thinking I had the power to say the magic words that would get him started again. Did he expect me to hand him a prescription for a pill that cured struggling authors of their writer's block? Was that all he wanted from me? It seemed so paltry, so painfully beside the point. Walker was an intelligent man, and if his book needed to be written, he would find a way to do it.

That was more or less what I told him in my next letter. Not straight off, since there were other subjects to be addressed first (my sadness over his wife's death, my surprise over his choice of profession, my admiration for the work he had done and the battles he had fought), but once those matters had been dispensed with, I said quite bluntly and simply that I believed he would figure it out on his own. Fear is a good thing, I continued, repeating the word he had used in his first letter, fear is what drives us to take risks and extend ourselves beyond our normal limits, and any writer who feels he is standing on safe ground is unlikely to produce anything of value. As for the wall he had mentioned, I said that everyone hits those walls, and more often than not the condition of being stuck arises from a flaw in the writer's thinking — i.e., he doesn't fully understand what he is trying to say or, more subtly, he has taken a wrong approach to his subject. By way of example, I told him about the problems I had encountered while working on an early book of mine — also a memoir (of sorts), which had been divided into two parts. Part One was written in the first person, and when I began Part Two (which was more directly about myself than the previous part), I continued writing in the first person, grew more and more dissatisfied with the results, and eventually stopped. The pause lasted several months (difficult months, anguished months), and then one night the solution came to me. My approach had been wrong, I realized. By writing about myself in the first person, I had smothered myself and made myself invisible, had made it impossible for me to find the thing I was looking for. I needed to separate myself from myself, to step back and carve out some space between myself and my subject (which was myself), and therefore I returned to the beginning of Part Two and began

89

writing it in the third person. *I* became *He*, and the distance created by that small shift allowed me to finish the book. Perhaps he (Walker) was suffering from the same problem, I suggested. Perhaps he was too close to his subject. Perhaps the material was too wrenching and personal for him to write about it with the proper objectivity in the first person. What did he think? Was there a chance that a new approach might get him up and running again?

When I sent the letter, my trip to California was still six weeks off. Walker and I had already set the date and time of our dinner, he had furnished me with directions to his house, and I wasn't anticipating another letter from him before my departure. A month went by, perhaps a little longer than that, and then, when I was least expecting it, he contacted me again. Not by mail this time, but by telephone. Years had passed since our last conversation, but I recognized his voice at once — and yet (how to express this?) it wasn't quite the same voice I remembered, or else it was the same but with something added to it or subtracted from it, the same voice in a slightly different register: Walker at one remove from himself and the world, incapacitated, ill, speaking softly, slowly, with a barely perceptible flutter embedded in each word that escaped from his mouth, as if he were summoning all his strength to push the air up through his windpipe and into the phone.

Hi there, Jim, he said. I hope I'm not interrupting your dinner.

Not at all, I replied. We won't be eating for

90

another twenty or thirty minutes.

Good. It must be cocktail hour, then. Assuming you still drink.

I still drink. Which is exactly what we're doing now. My wife and I just opened a bottle of wine, and we're gradually swilling ourselves into a stupor as a chicken roasts in the oven.

The pleasures of domestic life.

And what about you? How are things on your end?

Couldn't be better. A minor setback last month, but all is well again, and I've been working my head off. I wanted you to know that.

Working on the book?

Working on the book.

Which means you're unstuck.

That's why I called. To thank you for your last letter.

A new approach, then?

Yes, and it helped enormously.

This is good news.

I hope so. Rather brutal stuff, I'm afraid. Ugly things I haven't had the heart or the will to look at in years, but I'm past it now and furiously mapping out the third chapter.

You mean the second chapter is finished?

A draft. I came to the end about ten days ago.

Why didn't you send it to me?

I don't know. Too nervous, I guess. Too unsure of myself.

Don't be ridiculous.

I was thinking it might be better to wait until the whole thing was done before showing it to you.

No, no, send me the second part now. We can talk about it when I see you in Oakland next week.

After you read it, you might not want to come.

What are you talking about?

It's disgusting, Jim. Every time I think about it, it makes me want to puke.

Send it anyway. No matter what my reaction is, I promise I won't back out of the dinner. I want to see you again.

And I want to see you.

Good. Then it's settled. The twenty-fifth at seven o'clock.

You've been very kind to me.

I haven't done anything.

More than you know, good sir, more than you know.

Try to take care of yourself, all right?

I'll do my best.

See you on the twenty-fifth, then.

Yes, the twenty-fifth. At the stroke of seven.

★ ★ ★

It was only after we hung up that I realized how unsettling this conversation had been for me. For one thing, I felt certain that Walker was lying about the state of his health — which was not good, not good at all, and no doubt growing worse by the minute — and while it was perfectly understandable that he should want to hide the truth from me, to deflect any impulse on my part to pity him by toughing it out with a stoic's false cheerfulness (*Couldn't be better!*), I

92

nevertheless felt (and this is something of a paradox) a tone of *self*-pity running through his words, as if from the beginning to the end of our talk he had been fighting back tears, willing himself not to lose his grip and start weeping into the phone. His physical condition was already a cause for grave concern, but now I was just as worried about the condition of his mind. At certain points during our conversation, he had sounded like a man on the brink of a mental breakdown, a man holding himself together with nothing more than a few frayed pieces of string and wire. Was it possible that writing the new chapter of his book had depleted him to such an extent? Or was that only one element among several, among many? Walker was dying, after all, and perhaps the mere fact of his impending death, the corrosive horror of that impending death, had become too much for him to face anymore. And yet, the trembling, tearful catch in his voice could just as easily have been caused by an adverse reaction to a medicine he was taking, a side effect of some drug that was helping to keep him alive. I didn't know. I didn't know anything, but after the lucid, forthright depiction of himself in the first part of his book, along with the two articulate and courageous letters he had sent me, I found myself a bit thrown by how different he sounded in person. I wondered what it would be like to spend an evening in his company, enclosed in the private world of his dwindling, devastated self, and for the first time since accepting his invitation I was beginning to dread our encounter.

Two days after the phone call, the second part of his book arrived at my house in a FedEx envelope. A brief cover letter informed me that he had at last come up with a title, *1967*, and that each chapter would be headed by the name of a season. The first part was *Spring*, the part I had just been sent was *Summer*, and the part he was working on now was *Fall*. I had already heard him describe the new pages to me over the phone, and with the words *brutal, ugly,* and *disgusting* still fresh in my mind, I braced myself for something unbearable, a story that would be even more harsh and troubling than *Spring*.

SUMMER

Spring turns into summer. For you it is the summer after the spring of Rudolf Born, but for the rest of the world it is the summer of the Six-Day War, the summer of race riots in more than one hundred American cities, the Summer of Love. You are twenty years old and have just finished your second year of college. When war breaks out in the Middle East, you think about joining the Israeli army and becoming a soldier, even though you are an avowed pacifist and have never shown any interest in Zionism, but before you can come to a decision and make any plans, the war suddenly ends, and you remain in New York.

Nevertheless, you feel a strong urge to quit the country, to be anywhere but where you are now, and therefore you have already gone to the dean of students and told him that you want to sign up for the Junior Year Abroad Program (after a lengthy consultation with your father, who has grudgingly given his approval). You have chosen Paris. You are not going there simply because you are fond of Paris, which you visited for the first time two summers ago, but because you are keen to perfect your French, which is adequate now but could be better. You are aware that Born is in Paris, or at least you assume he is, but you weigh the odds in your mind and figure your chances of running into him are slight. And if such an event should occur, you feel prepared to handle it in a manner appropriate to the circumstances. How difficult would it be to turn your head and walk on past him? That is what you tell yourself, in any case, but in your innermost heart of hearts you play out scenes in which you do not turn your head, in which you confront him in the middle of the street and strangle him to death with your bare hands.

You live in a two-bedroom apartment in a building on West 107th Street between Broadway and Amsterdam Avenue. Your roommate has just graduated and is leaving the city, and because you need someone else to share the place with you, you have already invited your sister to occupy the other bedroom — for, as luck would have it, her years at Vassar have come to an end, and she is about to begin graduate work in the English Department at Columbia. You and your sister have always been close — best friends, co-conspirators, obsessed guardians of your dead brother's memory, fellow students of literature, confidants — and you are pleased with the arrangement. It is only for the summer, of course, since you will be winging off to Paris in September, but for part of June and all of July and August you will be together, dwelling under the same roof for the first time in years. After you are gone, your sister will take over the lease and find another person to live in the room you have vacated.

Your family is well-off, but not exceedingly well-off, not rich by the standards of the rich, and although your father is generous enough to provide you with an allowance to cover basic expenses, more money is needed for the books and records you want to buy, the films you want to see, the cigarettes you want to smoke, and so you begin looking for a summer job. Your sister has already found one for herself. She is just sixteen months older than you are, but her interactions with the world have always been more sensible and prudent than yours, and within days of learning that she would be studying at Columbia and sharing an apartment with you on West 107th Street, she set about looking for a job compatible with her interests and talents. Consequently, everything has been arranged in advance, and immediately after she arrives in New York, she begins working as an editorial assistant for a large commercial publisher in midtown. You, on the other hand, in your scattershot, haphazard way, put off the search until the last minute, and because you resist the idea of spending forty hours a week in an office with a tie around your neck, you jump at the first opportunity that presents itself. A friend has left town for the summer, and you apply to fill his spot as a page at Butler Library on the Columbia campus. The salary is less than half of what your sister earns, but you console yourself with the thought that you can walk to and from your job, which will exempt you from the ordeal of having to cram yourself twice daily into a subway car filled with hordes of sweating commuters.

You are given a test before they hire you. A senior librarian hands you a stack of cards, perhaps eighty cards, perhaps a hundred cards, each one bearing the title of a book, the name of the author of that book, the year of the publication of that book, and a Dewey decimal number that indicates where that book must be shelved. The librarian is a tall, grim-faced woman of around sixty, a certain Miss Greer, and already she seems suspicious of you, determined not to give an inch. Because she has just met you and cannot possibly know who you are, you imagine that she is suspicious of all young people — as a matter of principle — and therefore what she sees when she looks at you is not you as yourself but you as yet one more guerrilla fighter in the war against authority, an unruly insurrectionist who has no business barging into the sanctum of her library and asking for work. Such are the times you live in, the times you both live in. She instructs you to put the cards in order, and you can sense how deeply she wants you to fail, how happy it will make her to reject your application, and because

97

you want the job just as much as she doesn't want you to have it, you make sure that you don't fail. Fifteen minutes later, you hand her the cards. She sits down and begins looking through them, one by one, one after the other, all the way through to the end, and as you watch the skeptical expression on her face melt into a kind of bafflement, you know that you have done well. The stony face cracks a little smile. She says: No one ever gets it perfect. This is the first time I've seen it happen in thirty years.

You work from ten in the morning until four in the afternoon, Monday through Friday. You make it a habit to arrive promptly, entering the broad and pretentious faux-classical building designed by James Gamble Rogers with your lunch in a brown paper bag. Pomp and stuffiness aside, the building never fails to impress you with its bulk and grandeur, but the crowning touch of idiocy, you feel, the greatest embarrassment of all, are the names of the illustrious dead chiseled into the façade — Herodotus, Homer, Plato, along with numerous others — and every morning you imagine how different the library would look if it were adorned with other sets of names: the names of jazz musicians, for example (Fats Waller, Charlie Parker, Benny Goodman), or movie goddesses from the 1940s (Ingrid Bergman, Hedy Lamarr, Gene Tierney), or obscure, barely remembered baseball players (Gus Zernial, Wayne Terwilliger, Clyde Kluttz), or, quite simply, the names of your friends. And so the day begins. You go in through the front door, the heavy front door with its polished brass

98

fittings, walk up the marble staircase, glance at the portrait of Eisenhower (former university president, then the president who reigned over your childhood), and enter a small room to the right of the front desk, where you say good morning to Mr. Goines, your supervisor, a small man with owl glasses and a protruding belly, who doles out your chores for the day. Essentially, there are only two tasks to perform. Either you are putting books back on shelves or sending newly requested books to the main desk via dumbwaiter from one of the floors above. Each job has its advantages and disadvantages, and each can be carried out by anyone possessing the mental skills of a fruit fly.

When putting books onto the shelves, you must confirm and then reconfirm that the Dewey decimal number of the book you are shelving is one notch above the book to its left and one notch below the book to its right. The books are loaded onto a wooden cart equipped with four wheels, roughly fifty to a hundred books for each shelving session, and as you guide your little vehicle through the labyrinthine stacks, you are alone, always and everlastingly alone, since the stacks are off-limits to everyone but library personnel, and the only other person you will ever see is one of your fellow pages, manning the desk in front of the dumbwaiter. Each of the several floors is identical to all the others: an immense windowless space filled with row upon row of towering gray metal shelves, all of them stuffed to capacity with books, thousands of books, tens of thousands of books, hundreds of thousands of books, a million books, and at times even you, who love books as much as anyone on this earth, become stupefied, anxious, even nauseated when you consider how many billions of words, how many trillions of words those books contain. You are shut off from the world for hours every day, inhabiting what you come to think of as an airless bubble, even if there must be air because you are breathing, but it is dead air, air that has not stirred in centuries, and in that suffocating environment you often feel drowsy, drugged to the point of semiconsciousness, and have to fight off the urge to lie down on the floor and go to sleep.

Still, your shelving missions sometimes lead to unexpected discoveries, and the cloud of boredom that envelops you is momentarily lifted. Chancing upon a 1670 edition of *Paradise Lost*, for example. It is not the original printing from 1667, but very nearly so, a copy that came off the presses during Milton's lifetime, a book the poet conceivably could have held in his hands, and you marvel that this precious tome is not locked away in some temperature-controlled vault for rare books but is sitting out in the open in the musty stacks. Why is this discovery so important to you, why do your hands tremble as you open the book and begin scanning its pages? Because you have spent the past several months immersed in John Milton, studying Milton more closely than any poet you have ever read. During the tormented spring of Rudolf Born, you were one of several undergraduates enrolled in Edward Tayler's class, the renowned Milton course taught by the finest professor you had all year, attending both lectures and seminars, carefully plowing your way through *Areopagitica, Paradise Lost, Paradise Regained, Samson Agonistes*, and a host of shorter works, and now that you have come to love Milton and rank him above all other poets of his time, you feel an instant surge of happiness when you stumble across this book, this three-hundred-year-old book, while making your lugubrious rounds as a shelver in the stacks of Butler Library.

Unfortunately, such moments of happiness do not come often. It is not that you are particularly unhappy with your job at the library, but as time goes by and the hours you spend there accumulate, it becomes increasingly difficult for you to keep your mind on what you are supposed to be doing, mindless as those tasks might be. A sense of unreality invades you each time you set foot in the silent stacks, a feeling that you are not truly there, that you are trapped in a body that has ceased to belong to you. And so it happens that one afternoon, just two weeks after you earned your job with the only perfect test score in the annals of pagedom, as you find yourself on yet another shelving foray, working in an aisle of medieval German history, you are half startled out of your wits when someone taps you on the shoulder from behind. You instinctively wheel around to confront the person who touched you — no doubt someone who has slipped unnoticed into this restricted area to attack and/or rob the first victim he can find — and there, much to your relief, is Mr. Goines, looking at you with a sad expression on his face. Without saying a word, he lifts his right hand into the air, crooks his forefinger at you, and with an impatient, wiggling gesture beckons you to follow him. The little man waddles down the aisle, turns right when he comes to the corridor, walks past one row of shelves, then a second, and makes another right turn into an aisle of medieval French history. You and your cart were in this aisle just twenty minutes earlier, shelving several books on life in tenth-century Normandy, and sure enough, Mr. Goines goes straight to the spot where you were working. He points to the shelf and says, Look at this, and so you bend down and look. At first, you fail to notice anything out of the ordinary, but then Mr. Goines pulls two books off the shelf, two books separated by a distance of about twelve inches, with three or four books standing between them. Your supervisor shoves the two books close to your face, making it clear that he wants you to read the Dewey decimal numbers affixed to the spines, and it is only then that you become aware of your error. You have reversed the placement of the books, putting the first where the second should be and the second where the first should be. Please, Mr. Goines says, in a rather supercilious voice, don't ever do it again. If a book is put in the wrong place, it can be lost for twenty years or more, maybe forever.

It is a small matter, perhaps, but you feel humiliated by your negligence. Not that the two books in question could have been lost (they were on the same shelf, after all, just inches away from each other), but you understand the point Mr. Goines is trying to make, and although you bristle at the condescending tone he adopts with you, you apologize and promise to be more vigilant in the future. You think: Twenty years! Forever! You are astounded by the idea. Put something in the wrong place, and even though it is still there — quite possibly smack under your nose — it can vanish for the rest of time.

You return to your cart and continue shelving books of medieval German history. Until now, you have not known you are being spied upon. It puts a sickening taste in your mouth, and you tell yourself to be careful, to keep on your toes, to take nothing for granted ever again, not even in the benign, soporific precincts of a university library.

Shelving expeditions eat up approximately half your day. The other half is spent sitting behind a small desk on one of the upper floors, waiting for a pneumatic tube to come flying up through the intestines of the building with a withdrawal slip commanding you to retrieve this or that book for the student or professor who has just asked for it below. The pneumatic tube makes a distinctive, clattering noise as it speeds upward toward its destination, and you can hear it from the moment it begins its ascent. The stacks are distributed among several floors, and since you are just one of several pages sitting at desks on those several floors, you don't know if the pneumatic tube with the withdrawal slip rolled up inside it is headed for you or one of your colleagues. You don't find out until the last

103

second, but if it is indeed meant for you, the metallic cylinder comes bursting out of an opening in the wall behind you and lands in the box with a propulsive thud, which instantly triggers a mechanism that turns on the forty or fifty red lightbulbs that line the ceiling from one end of the floor to the other. These lights are essential, for it often happens that you are away from your desk when the tube arrives, in the process of searching for another book, and when you see the lights go on you are alerted to the fact that a new order has just come in. If you are not away from your desk, you pull the withdrawal slip out of the tube, go off to find the book or books that are wanted, return to your desk, tuck the withdrawal slips into the books (making sure that the top portion is sticking out by a couple of inches), load the books into the dumbwaiter in the wall behind your desk, and push the button for the second floor. To top off the operation, you return the empty tube by squeezing it into a little hole in the wall. You hear a pleasant *whoosh* as the cylinder is sucked into the vacuum, and more often than not you will go on standing there for a moment, following the sound of the clattering missile as it plunges through the pipe on its way downstairs. Then you return to your desk. You settle into your chair. You sit and wait for the next order.

On the surface, there is nothing to it. What could be simpler or less challenging than loading books into a dumbwaiter and pushing a button? After the drudgery of shelving, you would think your stints behind the desk would come as a welcome respite. As long as there are no books to retrieve (and there are many days when the pneumatic tube is sent to you just three or four times in as many hours), you can do whatever you want. You can read or write, for example, you can stroll around the floor and poke into arcane volumes, you can draw pictures, you can sneak an occasional nap. At one time or another, you manage to do all those things, or make an attempt to do them, but the atmosphere in the stacks is so oppressive, you find it difficult to focus your attention for any length of time on the book you are reading or the poem you are trying to write. You feel as if you are trapped inside an incubator, and little by little you come to understand that the library is good for one thing and one thing only: indulging in sexual fantasies. You don't know why it happens to you, but the more time you spend in that unbreathable air, the more your head fills with images of naked women, beautiful naked women, and the only thing you can think about (if *thought* is the appropriate word in this context) is fucking beautiful naked women. Not in some sensuously decked-out boudoir, not in some tranquil Arcadian meadow, but right here on the library floor, rolling around in sweaty abandon as the dust of a million books hovers in the air around you. You fuck Hedy Lamarr. You fuck Ingrid Bergman. You fuck Gene Tierney. You couple with blondes and brunettes, with black women and Chinese women, with all the women you have ever lusted after, one by one, two by two,

105

three by three. The hours inch along, and as you sit at your desk on the fourth floor of Butler Library, you feel your cock grow hard. It is always hard now, always hard with the hardest of hard-ons, and there are times when the pressure becomes so great that you leave your desk, dash down the corridor to the men's room, and wank into the toilet. You are disgusted with yourself. You are appalled by how quickly you give in to your desires. As you zip up you swear it will never happen again, which is exactly what you said to yourself twenty-four hours ago. Shame stalks you as you return to your desk, and you sit down wondering if there isn't something seriously wrong with you. You decide that you have never been more lonely, that you are the loneliest person in the world. You think you might be headed for a crack-up.

★ ★ ★

Your sister says to you: What do you think, Adam? Should we go home for the weekend or stay here and sweat it out in New York?

Let's stay, you answer, as you contemplate the bus ride to New Jersey and the long hours you would have to spend talking to your parents. If it gets too hot in the apartment, you say, we can always go to the movies. There are some good things playing at the New Yorker and the Thalia on Saturday and Sunday, and the air-conditioning will cool us off.

It is early July, and you and your sister have been living together for two weeks now. Since all

106

your friends have vanished for the summer, Gwyn is the only person you have seen — not counting the people you work with at the library, but they don't count for much. You have no girlfriend at the moment (Margot was the last woman you slept with), and your sister has recently parted ways with the young professor she was involved with for the past year and a half. Therefore, you have only each other for company, but there is nothing wrong with that as far as you are concerned, and all in all you are more than satisfied with the way things have worked out since she moved in with you. You are entirely at ease in her company, you can talk more openly with her than anyone else you know, and your relations are remarkably free of conflict. Every now and then, she becomes annoyed with you for neglecting to wash the dishes or leaving a mess in the bathroom, but each time you fall down on the domestic front you promise to mend your lackadaisical habits, and little by little you have been improving.

It is a happy arrangement, then, just as you imagined it would be when you proposed the idea in the first place, and now that you are slowly going to pieces at your job in the Castle of Yawns, you understand that living in the apartment with your sister is no doubt helping you keep your sanity, that more than anyone else she has the power to lighten the despair you carry around inside you. On the other hand, the fact that you are together again has produced some curious effects, consequences you did not foresee when the two of you discussed the possibility of joining forces back in the spring. Now you ask yourself how you could have been so blind. You and Gwyn are brother and sister, you belong to the same family, and therefore it is only natural, during the course of the long conversations you have with each other, that family matters should sometimes be mentioned — remarks about your parents, references to the past, memories of small details from the life you shared as children — and because these subjects have been unearthed so often during the weeks you have spent together, you find yourself thinking about them even when you are alone. You don't want to think about them, but you do. You have spent the past two years consciously trying to avoid your parents, doing everything you can to keep them at arm's length, and you have gone back to Westfield only when you were certain that Gwyn was going to be there as well. You still love your parents, but you don't particularly like them anymore. You came to this conclusion after your sister went off to college, leaving you alone with them for your last two years of high school, and when you finally went off to college yourself, you felt as if you had broken out of prison. It's not that you pride yourself for feeling the way you do — in fact, you are revolted by it, appalled by your coldness and lack of compassion — and you constantly berate yourself for accepting money from your father, who supports you and pays your tuition, but you need to be in college in order to stay away from him and your mother, and since you have no money of your own, and since your father earns too much for you to qualify for a scholarship, what choice do you have but to wallow in the ignominy of your two-faced position? So you run, and as you run you know you are running for your life, and unless you maintain the distance between you and your parents, you will begin to wither and die, just as surely as your brother Andy died when he drowned in Echo Lake on August 10, 1957, that small lake in New Jersey with its eerily appropriate name, for Echo too withered and died, and after her beloved Narcissus drowned, there was nothing left of her but a heap of bones and the wailing of her disembodied, inextinguishable voice.

You don't want to think about these things. You don't want to think about your parents and the eight years you spent walled up in a house of grief. You were ten at the time of Andy's death, and both you and Gwyn had been shipped off to a summer camp in New York State, which meant that neither one of you was present when the accident occurred. Your mother was alone with the seven-year-old Andy, planning to spend a week in the little lakeside bungalow your father bought in 1949 when you and your sister were no more than tots, the site of family summers, the site of smoky barbecues and mosquito-ridden sunsets, and the irony was that they were in the process of selling the place, this was to be the last summer at Echo Lake, just an hour's drive from home but no longer the calm retreat it had been now that all the new houses were going up, and so, with her two oldest kids away, your mother succumbed to a burst of nostalgia and decided to haul Andy out to the lake, even though your father was too busy to go with them. Andy wasn't much of a swimmer at that point, was still struggling to get the hang of it, but he had a daredevil streak in him, and he incited mischief with such hell-bent exuberance that everyone thought he was destined to earn an advanced degree in Practical Jokes. On the third day of the visit, sometime around six in the morning, with your mother still asleep in her room, Andy got it into his head to go for an unchaperoned swim. Before leaving, the seven-year-old adventurer sat down to write this short, semi-literate message — *Deere Mom Ime in the lake Lov Andy* — then tiptoed out of the bungalow, jumped into the water, and drowned. *Ime in the lake*.

You don't want to think about it. You have run away now, and you don't have the heart to return to that house of screams and silences, to listen to your mother howling in the bedroom upstairs, to reopen the medicine cabinet and count the bottles of tranquilizers and antidepressants, to think about the doctors and the breakdowns and the suicide attempt and the long stay in the hospital when you were twelve. You don't want to remember your father's eyes and how for years they seemed to look right through you, nor his robotic daily drill of waking at six sharp every morning and not returning from work until nine at night, or his refusal to mention the name of his dead son to you or your sister. You rarely saw him anymore, and with your mother all but incapable of tending the house and preparing

110

meals, the ritual of the family dinner came to an end. The chores of cleaning and cooking were handled by a succession of so-called maids, principally worn-out black women in their fifties and sixties, and because on most nights your mother preferred to eat alone in her room, it was usually just you and your sister, sitting face to face at the pink Formica table in the kitchen. Where your father ate his dinner was a mystery to you. You imagined that he went to restaurants, or perhaps the same restaurant every night, but he never said a word about it.

It is painful for you to think about these things, but now that your sister is with you again, you can't help yourself, the memories come rushing in on you against your will, and when you sit down to work on the long poem you started in June, you often find yourself stopping in mid-phrase, staring out the window, and reminiscing about your childhood.

You realize now that you began running away from them much earlier than you suspected. If not for Andy's death, you probably would have remained a compliant, dutiful son until the hour you left home, but once the household began to fall apart — with your mother withdrawing into a state of permanent guilt-racked mourning and your father scarcely present anymore — you had to look elsewhere for some kind of sustainable existence. In the circumscribed world of childhood, elsewhere meant school and the ball fields you played on with your friends. You wanted to excel at everything, and because you were lucky enough to have been endowed with reasonable intelligence and a strong body, your grades were always near the top of your class and you stood out in any number of sports. You never sat down and thought any of this through (you were too young for that), but these successes helped to nullify some of the grimness that surrounded you at home, and the more you succeeded, the more you asserted your independence from your mother and father. They wished you well, of course, they were not actively against you, but a moment arrived (you could have been eleven) when you began to crave the admiration of your friends as much as you craved your parents' love.

Hours after your mother was carted off to the mental hospital, you swore an oath on your brother's memory to be a good person for the rest of your life. You were alone in the bathroom, you remember, alone in the bathroom fighting back tears, and by good you meant honest, kind, and generous, you meant never making fun of anyone, never feeling superior to anyone, and never picking a fight with anyone. You were twelve years old. When you were thirteen, you stopped believing in God. When you were fourteen, you spent the first of three consecutive summers working in your father's supermarket (bagging, shelving, manning the register, signing in deliveries, removing trash — thus perfecting the skills that would lead to your exalted position as a page at the Columbia library). When you were fifteen, you fell in love with a girl named Patty French. Later that year, you told your sister that you were going to become a poet. When you

112

were sixteen, Gwyn left home and you went into internal exile.

Without Gwyn, you never would have made it that far. Much as you wanted to forge a life for yourself beyond the grasp of your family, home was where you lived, and without Gwyn to protect you in that home, you would have been smothered, annihilated, driven to the edge of madness. Early memories non-existent, but you first see her as a five-year-old as the two of you sit naked in the bathtub, your mother washing Gwyn's hair, the shampoo foaming up in frothy white spikes and bizarre undulations as your sister throws back her head, laughing, and you look on in rapt wonder. Already, you loved her more than anyone else in the world, and until you were six or seven you assumed that you would always live with her, that you would end up as man and wife. Needless to add that you sometimes squabbled and played nasty tricks on each other, but not habitually, not half as often as most siblings do. You looked so much alike, with your dark hair and gray-green eyes, with your elongated bodies and smallish mouths, so alike that you could have passed for male and female versions of the same person, and then in jumped the fair-skinned Andy with his blond curls and short, chubby frame, and right from the start you both found him a comical personage, a clever midget in soggy diapers who had joined the family for the sole purpose of entertaining you. For the first year of his life, you treated him like a toy or pet dog, but then he began to talk, and you reluctantly decided that he must be human. A real person, then, but contrary to you and your sister, who tended to be restrained and well mannered, your little brother was a dervish of fluctuating moods, alternately boisterous and sulky, prone to sudden, uncontrollable crying fits and long spurts of jungle-crazy laughter. It couldn't have been easy for him — trying to crack into the inner circle, trying to keep up with his big sister and brother — but the gap narrowed as he grew older, the frustrations gradually diminished, and near the end the crybaby was developing into a good kid — more than a little daft at times (*Ime in the lake*) but nevertheless a good kid.

Just before Andy was born, your parents moved you and your sister into adjoining bedrooms on the third floor. It was a separate realm up there under the eaves, a small principality cut off from the rest of the house, and after the cataclysm of Echo Lake in August 1957, it became your refuge, the only spot in that fortress of sorrow where you and your sister could escape your grieving parents. You grieved too, of course, but you grieved in the way children do, more selfishly, perhaps more solemnly, and for many months you and your sister tortured yourselves by recounting all the less-than-kind things you had ever done to Andy — the taunts, the cutting remarks, the teasing insults, the slaps and shoves, the too hard punches — as if compelled by some shadowy sense of guilt to do penance, to grovel in your wickedness by endlessly rehearsing the slew of misdemeanors you had committed over the years. These recitations always took place at night, in the dark after you had gone to bed, the two of you talking through the open door between your rooms, or else one of you in the other's bed, lying side by side on your backs, looking up at the invisible ceiling. You felt like orphans then, with the ghosts of your parents haunting the floor below, and sleeping together became a natural reflex, an abiding comfort, a remedy to ward off the shakes and tears that came so often in the months after Andy's death.

Intimacies of this sort were the unquestioned ground of your relations with your sister. It went all the way back to the beginning, to the very edge of conscious memory, and you cannot recall a single moment when you felt shy or afraid in her presence. You took baths with her when you were small children, you eagerly explored each other's bodies in games of 'doctor,' and on stormy afternoons when you were confined to the house, Gwyn's preferred activity was jumping on the bed together stark naked. Not just for the pleasure of the jumping, as she put it, but because she liked to see your penis flopping up and down, and diminutive as that organ must have been at that point in your life, you readily obliged her, since it always made her laugh, and nothing made you happier than to see your sister laugh. How old were you then? Four years old? Five years old? Eventually, children begin to recoil from the rowdy, Caliban nudism of toddlerhood, and by the time they reach the age of six or seven the barriers of modesty have already gone up. For some reason, this failed to happen with you and Gwyn. No more splashing in the tub, perhaps, no more doctor games, no more jumping on the bed, but still, an altogether un-American casualness as far as your bodies were concerned. The door of the bathroom you shared was often left open, and how many times did you walk past that door and catch sight of Gwyn peeing into the toilet, how many times did she glimpse you stepping from the shower without a stitch of clothing on? It felt perfectly natural to see each other naked, and now, in the summer of 1967, as you put down your pen and look out the window to think about your childhood, you ponder this lack of inhibition and conclude that it must have been because you felt your body belonged to her, that each of you belonged to the other, and therefore it would have been unimaginable to act differently. It's true that as time went on you both became somewhat more reserved, but even when your bodies began to change, you did not completely withdraw from each other. You remember the day Gwyn walked into your room, sat down on the bed, and lifted her blouse to show you the first, tiny swell of her nipples, the earliest sign of her incipient, growing breasts. You remember showing her your first pubic hair and one of your first adolescent erections, and you also remember standing next to her in the bathroom and looking at the blood run down her legs when she had her first period. Neither one of you thought twice about going to the other when these miracles occurred. Life-altering events demanded a witness, and what better

116

person to serve that role than one of you?

Then came the night of the grand experiment. Your parents were going away for the weekend, and they had decided that you and your sister were old enough to take care of yourselves without supervision. Gwyn was fifteen and you were fourteen. She was nearly a woman, and you were just emerging from boyhood, but both of you were trapped in the throes of early teenage desperation, thinking about sex from morning to night, masturbating incessantly, out of your minds with desire, your bodies burning with lustful fantasies, longing to be touched by someone, to be kissed by someone, ravenous and unfulfilled, aroused and alone, damned. The week before your parents' departure, the two of you had openly discussed the dilemma, the great contradiction of being old enough to want it but too young to get it. The world had played a trick on you by forcing you to live in the mid-twentieth century, citizens of an advanced industrial nation no less, whereas if you had been born into a primitive tribe somewhere in the Amazon or the South Seas, you would no longer still be virgins. That was when you hatched your plan — immediately following that conversation — but you waited until your parents were gone before you put it into action.

You were going to do it once, just once. It was supposed to be an experiment, not a new way of life, and no matter how much you enjoyed it, you would have to stop after that one night, because if you went on with it after that, things could get out of hand, the two of you could easily get

117

carried away, and then there would be the problem of having to account for bloody sheets, not to mention the grotesque possibility, the unthinkable possibility, which neither of you dared to talk about out loud. Anything and everything, you decided, but no penetration, the whole gamut of opportunities and positions, as much as you both wanted for as long as you both wanted it, but it would be a night of sex without intercourse. Since neither one of you had engaged in sex with anyone before, that prospect was exciting enough, and you spent the days leading up to your parents' departure in a delirium of anticipation — frightened to death, shocked by the boldness of the plan, crazed.

It was the first chance you ever had to tell Gwyn how much you loved her, to tell her how beautiful you thought she was, to push your tongue inside her mouth and kiss her in the way you had dreamed of doing for months. You were trembling when you took off your clothes, trembling from head to toe when you crawled into the bed and felt her arms tighten around you. It was dark in the room, but you could dimly make out the gleam in your sister's eyes, the contours of her face, the outline of her body, and when you crawled under the covers and felt the nakedness of that body, the bare skin of your fifteen-year-old sister pressing against the bare skin of your own body, you shuddered, feeling almost breathless from the onrush of sensations coursing through you. You lay in each other's arms for several moments, legs entwined, cheeks touching, too awed to do anything but cling to each other and hope you wouldn't burst apart from sheer terror. Eventually, Gwyn began to run her hands along your back, and then she brought her mouth toward your face and kissed you, kissed you hard, with an aggression you had not been expecting, and as her tongue shot into your mouth, you understood that there was no better thing in the world than to be kissed in the way she was kissing you, that this was without argument the single most important justification for being alive. You went on kissing for a long spell, the two of you purring and pawing at each other as your tongues flailed and saliva slid down from your lips. At last, you screwed up your courage and placed your palms on her breasts, her small, still not fully grown breasts, and for the first time in your life you said to yourself: I am touching a girl's naked breasts. After you had run your hands over them for a while, you began to kiss the places you had touched, to flick your tongue around the nipples, to suck the nipples, and you were surprised when they grew firmer and more erect, as firm and erect as your penis had been since the moment you climbed on top of your naked sister. It was too much for you to handle, this initiation into the glories of female anatomy pushed you beyond your limits, and without any prompting from Gwyn you suddenly had your first ejaculation of the night, a ferocious spasm that wound up all over her stomach. Mercifully, whatever embarrassment you felt was short-lived, for even as the juices were pouring out of you, Gwyn had begun to laugh, and by way of toasting your accomplishment, she merrily rubbed her hand across her belly.

It went on for hours. You were both so young and inexperienced, both so charged up and indefatigable, both so crazy in your hunger for each other, and because you had promised that this would be the only time, neither one of you wanted it to end. So you kept at it. With the strength and stamina of your fourteen years, you quickly rebounded from your accidental discharge, and as your sister gently put her hand around your rejuvenated penis (sublime transport, inexpressible joy), you forged on with your anatomy lesson by roaming your hands and mouth over other areas of her body. You discovered the delicious, down-soft regions of nape and inner thigh, the indelible satisfactions of back hollow and buttocks, the almost unbearable delight of the licked ear. Tactile bliss, but also the smell of the perfume Gwyn had put on for the occasion, the ever more sweaty slickness of your two bodies, and the little symphony of sounds you both made throughout the night, singly and together: the moans and whimpers, the sighs and yelps, and then, when Gwyn came for the first time (rubbing her clitoris with the middle finger of her left hand), the sound of air surging in and out of her nostrils, the accelerating speed of those breaths, the triumphant gasp at the end. The first time, followed by two other times, perhaps even a third. In your own case, beyond the early solo bungle, there was the hand of your sister wrapped around your penis, the hand moving up and down as you lay on your back in a fog of mounting excitation, and then there was her mouth, also moving up and down, her mouth around your once-again hard penis, and the profound intimacy you both felt when you came into that mouth — the fluid of one body passing into another, the intermingling of one person with another, conjoined spirits. Then your sister fell back onto the bed, opened her legs, and told you to touch her. Not there, she said, here, and she took your hand and guided you to the place where she wanted you to be, the place where you had never been, and you, who had known nothing before that night, slowly began your education as a human being.

★   ★   ★

Six years later, you are sitting in the kitchen of the apartment you share with your sister on West 107th Street. It is early July 1967, and you have just told her that you would prefer to stay in New York for the weekend, that you have no interest in trekking out to your parents' house on the bus. Gwyn is sitting across the table from you, dressed in blue shorts and a white T-shirt, her long dark hair pinned up on her head because of the heat, and you notice that her arms are tanned, that in spite of the office job that keeps her indoors for much of the day, she has been out in the sun often enough for her skin to have acquired a lovely ginger-brown cast, which somehow reminds you of the color of pancakes. It is six-thirty on a Thursday evening, and you are both home from work, drinking beer directly

121

from the can and smoking unfiltered Chesterfields. In an hour or so, you will be going out to dinner at an inexpensive Chinese restaurant — more for the air-conditioning than the food — but for now you are content to sit and do nothing, to recompose yourself after another tedious day at the library, which you have begun referring to as the Castle of Yawns. After your comment about not wanting to go to New Jersey, you have no doubt that Gwyn will start talking about your parents. You are prepared for that, and talk you will if you must, but you nevertheless hope the conversation will not last too long. The nine millionth chapter in the saga of Marge and Bud. When did you and your sister start calling your parents by their first names? You can't remember precisely, but more or less around the time Gwyn left home for college. They are still Mom and Dad when you are with them, but Marge and Bud when you and your sister are alone. A slight affectation, perhaps, but it helps to separate them from you in your mind, to create an illusion of distance, and that is what you need, you tell yourself, that is what you need more than anything else.

I don't get it, your sister says to you. You never want to go there anymore.

I wish I did, you answer, shrugging defensively, but every time I set foot in that house, I feel I'm being sucked back into the past.

Is that so terrible? You're not going to tell me all your memories are bad. That would be ridiculous. Ridiculous and untrue.

No, no, not all bad. Good and bad together.

But the strange thing is, whenever I'm there, it's the bad ones I think about. When I'm not there, I mostly think about the good.

Why don't I feel that way?

I don't know. Maybe because you're not a boy.

What difference does that make?

Andy was a boy. There were two of us once, and now there's only me — sole survivor of the shipwreck.

So? Better one than none, for God's sake.

It's their eyes, Gwyn, the expression on their faces when they look at me. One minute, I feel as if I'm being reproached. Why you? they seem to be asking me. Why did you get to live when your brother didn't? And the next minute, their eyes are drowning me with tenderness, a worried, nauseating, overprotective love. It makes me want to jump out of my shoes.

You're exaggerating. There's no reproach, Adam. They're so proud of you, you should hear them carry on when you're not there. Endless hymns to the wonder boy they created, the crown prince of the Walker dynasty.

Now you're the one who's exaggerating.

Not really. If I didn't like you so much, I'd feel jealous.

I don't know how you can stand it. Watching them together, I mean. Every time I look at them, I ask myself why they're still married.

Because they want to be married, that's why.

It makes no sense. They can't even talk to each other anymore.

They've been through fire together, and they don't have to talk now if they don't feel like it. As

123

long as they want to stay together, it's none of our business how they manage their lives.

She used to be so beautiful.

She's still beautiful.

She's too sad to be beautiful. No one that sad can still be beautiful.

You stop for a moment to absorb what you have just said. Then, turning your eyes away from your sister, unable to look at her as you formulate the next sentence, you add:

I feel so sorry for her, Gwyn. I can't tell you how many times I've wanted to call the house and tell her that everything is okay, that she can stop hating herself now, that she's punished herself long enough.

You should do it.

I don't want to insult her. Pity is such an awful, useless emotion — you have to bottle it up and keep it to yourself. The moment you try to express it, it only makes things worse.

Your sister smiles at you, somewhat inappropriately, you feel, but when you study her face and see the grave and pensive look in her eyes, you understand that she has been hoping you would say something like this, that she is relieved to hear that you are not quite as walled off and coldhearted as you make yourself out to be, that there is some compassion in you, after all. She says: Okay, little brother. You'll sweat it out in New York if you like. But, just for your information, a trip back home every now and then can lead to some rather interesting discoveries.

Such as?

Such as the box I found under my bed the last time I was there.

What was in it?

Quite a few things, actually. One of them happened to be the play we wrote together in high school.

I shudder to think . . .

King Ubu the Second.

Did you take a look at it?

I couldn't resist.

And?

Not too hot, I'm afraid. But there were some funny lines, and two of the scenes almost made me laugh. When Ubu arrests his wife for burping at the table, and the bit when Ubu declares war on America so he can give it back to the Indians.

Adolescent drivel. But we had a good time, didn't we? I can remember rolling around on the floor and laughing so hard that my stomach hurt.

We took turns writing sentences, I think. Or was it whole speeches?

Speeches. But don't make me swear to it in court. I could be wrong.

We were crazy back then, weren't we? Both of us — each one as crazy as the other. And no one ever guessed. They all thought we were successful, well-adjusted kids. People looked up to us, we were envied, and deep down we were both nuts.

Again you look into your sister's eyes, and you can sense that she wants to talk about the grand experiment, a subject neither one of you has mentioned in years. Is it worth going into now,

125

you wonder, or should you deflect the conversation onto something else? Before you can decide what to do, she says:

I mean, what we did that night was absolutely insane.

Do you think so?

Don't you?

Not really. My dick was sore for a week afterward, but I still look back on it as the best night of my life.

Gwyn smiles, disarmed by your insouciant attitude toward what most people would consider to be a crime against nature, a mortal sin. She says: You don't feel guilty?

No. I felt blameless then, and I feel blameless now. I always assumed you felt the same way.

I want to feel guilty. I tell myself I should feel guilty, but the truth is that I don't. That's why I think we were insane. Because we walked away from it without any scars.

You can't feel guilty unless you think you've done something wrong. What we did that night wasn't wrong. We didn't hurt anyone, did we? We didn't force each other to do anything we didn't want to do. We didn't even go all the way. What we did was a little youthful experimenting, that's all. And I'm glad we did it. To be honest, my only regret is that we didn't do it again.

Ah. So you were thinking the same thing I was.

Why didn't you tell me?

I was too scared, I guess. Too scared that if we kept on doing it, we might find ourselves in real trouble.

So you found yourself a boyfriend instead. Dave Cryer, the king of the animals.

And you fell for Patty French.

Water under the bridge, comrade.

Yes, it's all water under the bridge now, isn't it?

★ ★ ★

You and your sister talk about the past, then, and your parents' silent marriage, and your dead brother, and the childish farce you wrote in tandem one spring vacation years ago, but these matters take up no more than a small fraction of the time you spend together. Another fraction is consumed in brief conversations concerning household maintenance (shopping, cleaning, cooking, paying the rent and utility bills), but the bulk of the words you exchange that summer are about the present and the future, the war in Vietnam, books and writers, poets, musicians, and filmmakers, as well as the stories you bring home from your respective jobs. You and your sister have always talked, the two of you have been engaged in a complex, ongoing dialogue since your earliest childhood, and this willingness to share your thoughts and ideas is probably what best defines your friendship. It turns out that you agree about most things, but by no means all things, and you enjoy duking it out over your differences. Your spats about the relative merits of various writers and artists have a somewhat comical aspect to them, however, since it rarely happens that either of you

127

manages to persuade the other to change his or her opinion. Case in point: you both consider Emily Dickinson to be the supreme American poet of the nineteenth century, but whereas you have a soft spot for Whitman, Gwyn dismisses him as bombastic and crude, a false prophet. You read one of the shorter lyrics out loud to her (*The Dalliance of the Eagles*), but she remains unconvinced, telling you she's sorry, but a poem about eagles fucking in midair leaves her cold. Case in point: she admires *Middlemarch* above all other novels, and when you confess to her that you never made it past page 50, she urges you to give it another try, which you do, and once again you give up before reaching page 50. Case in point: your positions on the war and American politics are nearly identical, but with the draft staring you in the face the instant you leave college, you are far more vociferous and hotheaded than she is, and whenever you launch into one of your apoplectic rants against the Johnson administration, Gwyn smiles at you, sticks her fingers in her ears, and waits for you to stop.

You both love Tolstoy and Dostoyevsky, Hawthorne and Melville, Flaubert and Stendhal, but at that stage of your life you cannot stomach Henry James, while Gwyn argues that he is the giant of giants, the colossus who makes all other novelists look like pygmies. You are in complete harmony about the greatness of Kafka and Beckett, but when you tell her that Céline belongs in their company, she laughs at you and calls him a fascist maniac. Wallace Stevens yes, but next in line for you is William Carlos Williams, not T. S. Eliot, whose work Gwyn can recite from memory. You defend Keaton, she defends Chaplin, and while you both howl at the sight of the Marx Brothers, your much-adored W. C. Fields cannot coax a single smile from her. Truffaut at his best touches you both, but Gwyn finds Godard pretentious and you don't, and while she lauds Bergman and Antonioni as twin masters of the universe, you reluctantly tell her that you are bored by their films. No conflicts about classical music, with J. S. Bach at the top of the list, but you are becoming increasingly interested in jazz, while Gwyn still clings to the frenzy of rock and roll, which has stopped saying much of anything to you. She likes to dance, and you don't. She laughs more than you do and smokes less. She is a freer, happier person than you are, and whenever you are with her, the world seems brighter and more welcoming, a place where your sullen, introverted self can almost begin to feel at home.

The conversation continues throughout the summer. You talk about books and films and the war, you talk about your jobs and your plans for the future, you talk about the past and the present, and you also talk about Born. Gwyn knows you are suffering. She understands that the experience still weighs heavily on you, and again and again she patiently listens to you tell the story, again and again the same story, the obsessive story that has wormed itself into your soul and become an integral part of your being. She tries to reassure you that you acted well, that there was nothing else you could have done, and while you agree that you could not have prevented Cedric Williams's murder, you know that your cowardly hesitation before going to the police allowed Born to escape unpunished, and you cannot forgive yourself for that. Now it is Friday, the first evening of the early July weekend you have chosen to spend in New York, and as you and your sister sit at the kitchen table, drinking your postwork beers and smoking your cigarettes, the conversation once again turns to Born.

I've been mulling it over, Gwyn says, and I'm pretty sure the whole thing started because Born was sexually attracted to you. It wasn't just Margot. It was the two of them together.

Startled by your sister's theory, you pause for a moment to consider whether it makes any sense, painfully reviewing your tangled relations with Born from this altered perspective, but in the end you say no, you don't agree.

Think about it, Gwyn persists.

I am thinking about it, you answer. If it were true, then he would have made a pass at me. But he didn't. He never tried to touch me.

It doesn't matter. Chances are, he wasn't even aware of it himself. But a man doesn't fork over thousands of dollars to a twenty-year-old stranger because he's worried about his future. He does it out of a homoerotic attraction. Born fell in love with you, Adam. Whether he knew it himself is irrelevant.

I'm still not convinced, but now that you mention it, I wish he *had* made a pass at me. I would have punched him in the face and told him to fuck off, and then we never would have taken that walk down Riverside Drive, and the Williams kid never would have been killed.

Has anyone ever tried something like that with you?

Like what?

Another man. Has another man ever made a move on you?

I've gotten some curious stares, but no one's ever said anything to me.

So you've never done it.

Done what?

Have sex with another guy.

God no.

Not even when you were little?

What are you talking about? Little boys don't have sex. They can't have sex — for the simple reason that they're little boys.

I don't mean little little. I'm talking about just after puberty. Thirteen, fourteen years old. I thought all boys that age liked to jerk each other off.

Not me.

What about the famous circle jerk? You must have taken part in one of those.

How old was I the last year I went to summer camp?

I can't remember.

Thirteen . . . It must have been thirteen, because I started working at the Shop-Rite when I was fourteen. Anyway, the last year I went to camp, some of the boys in my cabin did that. Six or seven of them, but I was too shy to join in.

Too shy or too put off?

A little of both, I guess. I've always found the male body somewhat repellent.

Not your own, I hope.

I mean other men's bodies. I have no desire to touch them, no desire to see them naked. To tell you the truth, I've often wondered why women are drawn to men. If I were a woman, I'd probably be a lesbian.

Gwyn smiles at the absurdity of your remark. That's because you're a man, she says.

And what about you? Have you ever been attracted to another girl?

Of course. Girls are always getting crushes on each other. It comes with the territory.

I mean sexually attracted. Have you ever felt the urge to sleep with a girl?

I just spent four years at an all-girls college, remember? Things are bound to happen in a claustrophobic atmosphere like that.

Really?

Yes, really.

You never told me.

You never asked.

Did I have to? What about the No-Secrets Pact of nineteen sixty-one?

It's not a secret. It's too unimportant to qualify as a secret. For the record — just so you don't get the wrong impression — it happened exactly twice. The first time, I was stoned on pot. The second time, I was drunk.

And?

Sex is sex, Adam, and all sex is good, as long as both people want it. Bodies like to be touched

132

and kissed, and if you close your eyes, it hardly matters who's touching and kissing you.

As a statement of principle, I couldn't agree with you more. I just want to know if you enjoyed it, and if you did enjoy it, why you haven't done it more often.

Yes, I enjoyed it. But not enormously, not as much as I enjoy having sex with men. Contrary to your view on the subject, I adore men's bodies, and I have a particular fondness for the thing they have that women's bodies don't. Being with a girl is pleasant enough, but it doesn't have the power of a good, old-fashioned two-sex tumble.

Less bang for your buck.

Exactly. Minor league.

Bush league, as it were.

Stifling a laugh, Gwyn flings her cigarette pack at you and shouts in pretend anger: You're impossible!

★ ★ ★

That is precisely what you are: impossible. The moment the word flies out of your sister's mouth, you regret your lewd and feeble joke, and for the rest of the evening and long into the following day, the word sticks to you like a curse, like some pitiless condemnation of who and what you are. Yes, you are impossible. You and your life are impossible, and you wonder how on earth you managed to find your way into this cul-de-sac of despair and self-loathing. Is Born alone responsible for what has happened to you?

133

Can a single momentary lapse of courage have damaged your belief in yourself so badly that you no longer have faith in your future? Just months ago you were going to set the world on fire with your brilliance, and now you think of yourself as stupid and inept, a moronic masturbation machine trapped in the dead air of an odious job, a nobody. If not for Gwyn, you might think about checking yourself into a hospital. She is the only person you can talk to, the only person who makes you feel alive. And yet, happy as you are to be with her again, you know that you mustn't overburden her with your troubles, that you can't expect her to transform herself into the divine surgeon who will cut open your chest and mend your ailing heart. You must help yourself. If something inside you is broken, you must put it back together with your own two hands.

*   *   *

After twenty-four hours of bleak introspection, the agony slowly subsides. The turnaround begins on Saturday, the second evening of the early July weekend you have chosen to spend in Manhattan. After dinner, you and your sister ride the 104 bus down Broadway to the New Yorker theater and walk into the coolness of that dark space to watch Carl Dreyer's 1955 film, *Ordet* (The Word). Normally, you would not be interested in a film about Christianity and matters of religious faith, but Dreyer's direction is so exact and piercing that you are quickly swept up into the story, which begins to remind you of a piece of music, as if the film were a visual translation of a two-part invention by Bach. The aesthetics of Lutheranism, you whisper into Gwyn's ear at one point, but since she has not been privy to your thoughts, she has no idea what you are talking about and returns your comment with a bewildered frown.

There is little need to rehash the intricacies of the story. Compelling as those twists and turns might be, they amount to just one story among an infinity of stories, one film among a multitude of films, and if not for the end, *Ordet* would not have affected you more than any other good film you have seen over the years. It is the end that counts, for the end does something to you that is wholly unexpected, and it crashes into you with all the force of an axe felling an oak.

The farm woman who has died in childbirth is stretched out in an open coffin as her weeping husband sits beside her. The mad brother who thinks he is the second coming of Christ walks into the room holding the hand of the couple's young daughter. As the small group of mourning relatives and friends looks on, wondering what blasphemy or sacrilege is about to be committed at this solemn moment, the would-be incarnation of Jesus of Nazareth addresses the dead woman in a calm and quiet voice. Rise up, he commands her, lift yourself out of your coffin and return to the world of the living. Seconds later, the woman's hands begin to move. You think it must be a hallucination, that the point of view has shifted from objective reality to the mind of the addled brother. But no. The woman

135

opens her eyes, and just seconds after that she sits up, fully restored to life.

There is a large crowd in the theater, and half the audience bursts out laughing when they see this miraculous resurrection. You don't begrudge them their skepticism, but for you it is a transcendent moment, and you sit there clutching your sister's arm as tears roll down your cheeks. What cannot happen has happened, and you are stunned by what you have witnessed.

Something changes in you after that. You don't know what it is, but the tears you shed when you saw the woman come back to life seem to have washed out some of the poison that has been building up inside you. The days pass. At various moments, you think your small breakdown in the balcony of the New Yorker theater might be connected to your brother, Andy, or, if not to Andy, then to Cedric Williams, or perhaps to both of them together. At other moments, you are convinced that by some strange, sympathetic overlapping of subject and object, you felt you were watching yourself rise from the dead. Over the next two weeks, your step gradually becomes less heavy. You still feel doomed, but you sense that when the day comes for you to be led to the scaffold, you might have it in you to crack a parting joke or exchange pleasantries with your hooded executioner.

★ ★ ★

Every year since your brother's death, you and your sister have celebrated his birthday. Just the

136

two of you, with no parents, relatives, or other guests allowed. For the first three years, when you were both still young enough to spend your summers at sleepaway camp, you would hold the party in the open air, the two of you tiptoeing out of your cabins in the middle of the night and running across the darkened ball fields up to the meadow on the northern edge of the campgrounds and then bolting into the woods with flashlights illuminating your path through the trees and underbrush — each one of you holding a cupcake or cookie, which you had stolen from the mess hall after dinner that evening. For three consecutive summers after your camp days ended, you both worked in your father's supermarket, and therefore you were at home on the twenty-sixth of July and could celebrate the birth of your brother in Gwyn's bedroom on the third floor of the house. The next two years were the most difficult, since you both traveled during those summers and were far apart on the appointed day, but you managed to perform truncated versions of the ritual over the telephone. Last year, you took a bus to Boston, where Gwyn was shacked up with her then boyfriend, and the two of you went out to a restaurant to lift a glass in honor of the departed Andy. Now another July twenty-sixth is upon you, and for the first summer in a long while you are together again, about to throw your little fête in the kitchen of the apartment you share on West 107th Street.

It is not a party in the traditional sense of the word. Over the years, you and your sister have developed a number of strict protocols regarding the event, and with slight variations, depending on how old you have been, each July twenty-sixth is a reenactment of all the previous July twenty-sixths of the past ten years. In essence, the birthday dinner is a conversation divided into three parts. Food is served and eaten, and once the three-part talk is finished, a small chocolate cake appears, ornamented by a single candle burning in the center. You do not sing the song. You mouth the words in unison, speaking softly, barely raising your voices above a whisper, but you do not sing them. Nor do you blow the candle out. You let it burn down to a stub, and then you listen to it sizzle as the flame is extinguished in the ooze of the chocolate frosting. After a slice of cake, you open a bottle of scotch. Alcohol is a new element, not introduced until 1963 (the last of the supermarket summers, when you were sixteen and Gwyn was seventeen), but for the next two years you were apart and drinkless, and last year you were in a public place, which meant you had to watch your consumption. This year, alone in your New York apartment, you both aim to get good and drunk.

Gwyn has put on lipstick and makeup for the dinner, and she comes to the table wearing gold hoop earrings and a pale green summer shift, which makes the green of her gray-green eyes appear even more vivid. You are in a white oxford shirt with short sleeves and a button-down collar, and around your neck is the only tie you own, the same tie Born ridiculed you for

138

wearing last spring. Gwyn laughs when she sees you in that getup and says you look like a Mormon — one of those earnest young men who go around the world knocking on doors and giving out pamphlets, a proselytizer on a holy mission. Nonsense, you tell her. You don't have a crew cut, and your hair isn't blond, and therefore you could never be confused with a Mormon. Still and all, Gwyn says, you look mighty, mighty strange. If not a Mormon, she continues, then perhaps a fledgling accountant. Or a math student. Or a wannabe astronaut. No, no, you shoot back at her — a civil rights worker in the South. All right, she says, you win, and an instant later you remove both the tie and the shirt, leave the kitchen, and change into something else. When you return, Gwyn smiles but says nothing further about your clothes.

As usual, the weather is hot, and because you don't want to increase the temperature in the kitchen, you have refrained from using the oven and prepared a light summer meal that consists of chilled soup, a platter of cold cuts (ham, salami, roast beef), and a lettuce-and-tomato salad. There is also a loaf of Italian bread, along with a bottle of chilled Chianti encased in a straw covering (the cheap wine of choice among students of the period). After taking your first sips of the cold watercress soup, you begin the three-part conversation. That is the core of the experience for you, the single most important reason for staging this annual event. All the rest — the meal, the cake, the candle, the words of the happy birthday song, the booze — are mere trappings.

Step One: You talk about Andy in the past tense, dredging up everything you can recall about him while he was still alive. Invariably, this is the longest portion of the ritual. You remember your memories of past years, but additional ones always seem to spring forth from your unconscious as well. You try to keep the tone light and cheerful. This is not an exercise in morbidity, it is a celebration, and laughter is permitted at all times. You repeat some of his early mispronunciations of words: hangaburger for hamburger, human bean for human being, chuthers for each other — as in *They kissed their chuthers* — and the perfectly logical but demented *Mommy's Ami*, following a reference by your mother to the city of Miami. You talk about his bug collection, his Superman cape, and his bout with the chicken pox. You remember teaching him how to ride a bicycle. You remember his aversion to peas. You remember his first day of school (tears and torment), his skinned elbows, his hiccuping fits. Just seven years on this earth, but every year you and Gwyn come to the same conclusion: the list is inexhaustible. And yet, every year, you can't help feeling that a little more of him has vanished, that in spite of your best efforts, less and less of him is coming back to you, that you are powerless to stop him from fading away.

Step Two: You talk about him in the present tense. You imagine what kind of person he would have become if he were still alive today. For ten

140

years now, he has been living this shadow existence inside you, a phantom being who has grown up in another dimension, invisible yet breathing, breathing and thinking, thinking and feeling, and you have followed him since the age of eight, for more years after death than he ever managed to live, and now that he is seventeen, the gap between you has become ever smaller, ever less significant, and it shocks you, it shocks you and your sister simultaneously, to realize that at seventeen he is probably no longer a virgin, that he has smoked pot and gotten drunk, that he shaves and masturbates, drives a car, reads difficult books, is thinking about what college to go to, and is on the brink of becoming your equal. Gwyn starts to cry, saying that she can't stand it anymore, that she wants to stop, but you tell her to hang on for a few more minutes, that the two of you never have to do this again, that this will be the last birthday party for the rest of your lives, but for Andy's sake you have to see this one through to the end.

Step Three: You talk about the future, about what will happen to Andy between now and his next birthday. This has always been the easiest part, the most enjoyable part, and in past years you and Gwyn have sailed through the game of predictions with immense enthusiasm and brio. But not this year. Before you can begin the third and last part of the conversation, your over-wrought sister clamps her hand over her mouth, gets up from her chair, and rushes out of the kitchen.

You find her in the living room, sobbing on the

sofa. You sit down next to her, put your arm around her shoulders, and talk to her in a soothing voice. Calm down, you say. It's all right, Gwyn. I'm sorry . . . sorry I pushed you so hard. It's my fault.

You feel the thinness of her quaking shoulders, the delicate bones beneath her skin, her heaving rib cage pressing against your own ribs, her hip against your hip, her leg against your leg. In all the years you have known her, you doubt you have ever seen her so miserable, so crushed by sadness.

It's no good, she finally says, her eyes cast downward, addressing her words to the floor. I've lost contact with him. He's gone now, and we'll never find him again. In two weeks, it will have been ten years. That's half your life, Adam. Next year, it will be half of mine. That's too long. The space keeps growing. The time keeps growing, and every minute he drifts farther and farther away from us. Good-bye, Andy. Send us a postcard someday, all right?

You don't say anything. You sit there with your arm around your sister and let her go on crying, knowing that it would be useless to intervene, that you must allow the explosion to run its course. How long does it last? You haven't the faintest idea, but a moment eventually comes when you notice that the tears have stopped. With your left hand, the free hand that is not around her shoulders, you take hold of her chin and turn her face toward you. Her eyes are red and swollen. Rivulets of mascara have run down her cheeks. Mucus is dribbling from her nose.

You withdraw your left hand, put it into the back pocket of your pants, and pull out a handkerchief. You begin dabbing her face with the cloth. Little by little, you wipe away the tears, the snot, and the black mascara, and throughout the long, meticulous procedure, your sister doesn't move. Looking at you intently, her eyes washed clean of any discernible emotion, she sits in absolute stillness as you repair the damage left by the storm. When the job is finished, you stand up and say to her: Time for a drink, Miss Walker. I'll go get the scotch.

You march off to the kitchen. A minute later, when you return to the living room with a bottle of Cutty Sark, two glasses, and a pitcher of ice cubes, she is exactly where she was when you left her — sitting on the sofa, her head leaning against the backrest, eyes shut, breathing normally again, purged. You put down the drinking equipment on one of the three wooden milk crates that stand side by side in front of the sofa, the battered, upside-down boxes that you and your former roommate dragged off the street one day and which now serve as your excuse for a coffee table. Gwyn opens her eyes and gives you a wan, exhausted smile, as if asking you to forgive her for her outburst, but there is nothing to forgive, nothing to talk about, nothing you could ever hold against her, and as you set about pouring the drinks and putting ice into the glasses, you feel relieved that the business with Andy is over, relieved that there will be no more birthday celebrations for your absent brother, relieved that you and your sister have at last put this childish thing behind you.

You hand Gwyn her drink and then sit down beside her on the sofa. For several minutes, neither one of you says a word. Sipping your scotches and staring ahead at the wall in front of you, you both know what is going to happen tonight, you feel it as a certainty in your blood, but you also know that you have to be patient and give the alcohol time to do its work. When you lean forward to prepare the second round of drinks, Gwyn starts talking to you about her broken romance with Timothy Krale, the thirty-year-old assistant professor who entered her life more than eighteen months ago and left it this past April, at roughly the same moment you were shaking Born's hand for the first time. The teacher of her class on modernist poetry, of all things, the man risked his job by going after her, and she fell hard for him, especially in the beginning, during the first wild months of furtive assignations and weekend jaunts to distant motel rooms in forgotten towns across upstate New York. You yourself met him a number of times, and you understood what Gwyn saw in him, you concurred that Krale was an attractive and intelligent fellow, but you also sensed that there was something desiccated about the man, a detachment from others that made it difficult for you to warm up to him. It didn't surprise you when Gwyn turned down his proposal of marriage and put a stop to the affair. She told him that she felt too young, that she wasn't ready to commit herself over the long term, but that wasn't the real reason, she explains to you now,

144

she left him because he wasn't a kind enough lover. Yes, yes, she says, she knows he loved her, loved her as much as he was capable of loving anyone, but she found him selfish in bed, inattentive, too driven by his own needs, and she couldn't imagine herself tolerating such a man for the rest of her life. She turns to you now, and with a look of utmost seriousness and conviction in her eyes, she sets forth her definition of love, wanting to know if you share her opinion or not. Real love, she says, is when you get as much pleasure from giving pleasure as you do from receiving it. What do you think, Adam? Am I right or wrong? You tell her she is right. You tell her it is one of the most perceptive things she has ever said.

When does it start? When does the idea revolving in both your minds manifest itself as action in the physical world? Midway through the third drink, when Gwyn hunches forward and puts her glass down on the makeshift table. You have promised yourself that you will not make the first move, that you will hold back from touching her until she touches you, for only then will you know beyond all doubt that she wants what you want and that you have not misread her desires. You are a little drunk, of course, but not egregiously so, not so far gone that you have lost your wits, and you fully understand the import of what you are about to do. You and your sister are no longer the floundering, ignorant puppies you were on the night of the grand experiment, and what you are proposing now is a monumental transgression, a dark and iniquitous thing according to the laws of man and God. But you don't care. That is the simple truth of the matter: you are not ashamed of what you feel. You love your sister. You love her more than any person you have known or will ever know on the face of this wretched earth, and because you will be leaving the country in approximately one month, not to return for an entire year, this is your only chance, the only chance for both of you, since it is all but inevitable that a new Timothy Krale will walk into Gwyn's life while you are gone. No, you have not forgotten the vow you took when you were twelve years old, the promise you made to yourself to live your life as an ethical human being. You want to be a good person, and every day you struggle to follow the oath you swore on your dead brother's memory, but as you sit on the sofa watching your sister put her glass down on the table, you tell yourself that love is not a moral issue, desire is not a moral issue, and as long as you cause no harm to each other or anyone else, you will not be breaking your vow.

A moment later, you put down your glass as well. The two of you lean back on the sofa, and Gwyn takes hold of your hand, intertwining her fingers with yours. She asks: Are you afraid? You tell her no, you're not afraid, you're extremely happy. Me too, she says, and then she kisses you on the cheek, very gently, no more than the faintest nuzzle, the merest brush of her mouth against your skin. You understand that everything must go slowly, must build by the smallest of increments, that for a long while it will be a

146

halting, tentative dance of yes and no, and you prefer it that way, for if either one of you should have second thoughts, there will be time to back down and call it off. More often than not, what stirs the imagination is best kept in the imagination, and Gwyn is aware of that, she is wise enough to know that the distance between thought and deed can be enormous, a gulf as large as the world itself. So you test the waters cautiously, baby step by baby step, grazing your mouths against each other's necks, grazing your lips against each other's lips, but for many minutes you do not open your mouths, and although you have wrapped your arms around each other in a tight embrace, your hands do not move. A good half hour goes by, and neither one of you shows any inclination to stop. That is when your sister opens her mouth. That is when you open your mouth, and together you fall headfirst into the night.

★ ★ ★

There are no rules anymore. The grand experiment was a one-time-only event, but now that you are both past twenty, the strictures of your adolescent frolic no longer hold, and you go on having sex with each other every day for the next thirty-four days, right up to the day you leave for Paris. Your sister is on the pill, there are spermicidal creams and jellies in her bureau drawer, condoms are available to you, and you both know that you are protected, that the unmentionable will never come to pass, and therefore you can do anything and everything to each other without fear of destroying your lives. You don't discuss it. Beyond the brief exchange on the night of your brother's birthday (*Are you afraid? No, I'm not afraid*) you never say a word about what is happening, refuse to explore the ramifications of your month-long affair, your month-long marriage, for that is finally what it is, you are a young married couple now, a pair of newlyweds trapped in the throes of constant, overpowering lust — sex beasts, lovers, best friends: the last two people left in the universe.

Outwardly, your lives go on as before. Five days a week, the alarm clock wakes you early in the morning, and after a minimal breakfast of orange juice, coffee, and buttered toast, you both rush out of the apartment and head for your jobs, Gwyn to her office on the twelfth floor of a glass tower in the heart of Manhattan and you to your dreary clerk's post in the Palace of Null. You would prefer to have her within your sight at all times, would be perfectly content if she were never apart from you for a single minute, but if these unavoidable separations cause you a measure of pain, they also increase your longing for her, and perhaps that isn't a bad thing, you decide, for you spend your days in the thrall of breathless anticipation, agitated and alert, counting the hours until you can see her and hold her again. Intense. That is the word you use to describe yourself now. You are intense. Your feelings are intense. Your life has become increasingly intense.

At work, you no longer sit behind your desk

fantasizing about Ingrid Bergman and Hedy Lamarr. From time to time, an erection still threatens to burst through your pants, but you don't need to touch it anymore, and you have stopped running to the men's room at the end of the corridor. This is the library, after all, and thoughts about naked women are an inextricable part of working in the library, but the only naked body you think about now belongs to your sister, the real body of the real woman you share your nights with, and not some figment who exists only in your brain. There is no question that Gwyn is just as beautiful as Hedy Lamarr, perhaps even more beautiful — undoubtedly more beautiful. This is an objective fact, and you have spent the past seven years watching men stop dead in their tracks to stare at her as she walks past them on the street, have witnessed how many quick, astonished turns of the head, how many surreptitious glances on the subway, in restaurants, in theaters — hundreds and hundreds of men, and every one of them with the same leering, misty, dumbfounded look in his eyes. Yes, it is the face that launched a thousand hopes, the face that spawned a thousand dirty dreams, and as you wait at your desk for the next pneumatic tube to come rattling up from the second floor, you see that face in your head, you're looking into Gwyn's large, animated, gray-green eyes, and as those eyes look into yours, you watch her undo the back of her white summer dress and let it slide down the length of her tall, slender body.

You sit in baths together. That is the new

149

postwork routine, and rather than spend that hour in the kitchen as you did before your brother's birthday party, you now hoist your beers and puff on your cigarettes while soaking in a lukewarm bath. Not only does it provide respite from the heaviness of the dogday heat, but it gives you yet another chance to look at each other's naked bodies, which you never seem to tire of doing. Again and again, you tell your sister how much you love to look at her, that you adore every centimeter of her vibrant, luminous skin, and that beyond the overtly feminine places all men think about, you worship her elbows and knees, her wrists and ankles, the backs of her hands and her long, thin fingers (you could never be attracted to a woman with short thumbs, you tell her one day — an absurd but utterly sincere pronouncement), and that you are both mystified and enchanted by how a body as delicate as hers can also be as strong as it is, that she is both a swan and a tiger, a mythological being. She is fascinated by the hair that has grown on your chest (a recent development of the past twelve months) and has an unflagging interest in the mutabilities of your penis: from the limp, dangling member depicted in biology textbooks to the full-bore phallic titan at the summit of arousal to the shrunken, exhausted little man in postcoital retreat. She calls your dick a variety show. She says it has multiple personalities. She claims she wants to adopt it.

Now that you are living on such intimate terms with her, Gwyn has emerged as a slightly different person from the one you have known all your life. She is both funnier and more salacious than you imagined, more vulgar and idiosyncratic, more passionate, more playful, and you are startled to learn how deeply she exults in filthy language and the bizarre slang of sex. Gwyn has rarely sworn in your presence. She is a literate, well-educated girl who speaks in full, grammatical sentences, but except for the night of the grand experiment long ago, you have known nothing about her sexuality, and therefore you could not have guessed that she would grow up into a woman who likes to talk about sex as well as have it. Common twentieth-century words do not interest her. She shuns the term *making love*, for example, in favor of older, more hilarious locutions, such as rumpty-rumpty, quaffing, and bonker bang. A good orgasm is referred to as a bone-shaker. Her ass is a rumdadum. Her crotch is a slittie, a quim, a quim-box, a quimsby. Her breasts are boobs and tits, boobies and titties, her twin girls. At one time or another, your penis is a bong, a blade, a slurp, a shaft, a drill, a quencher, a queller, a lancelot, a lightning rod, Charles Dickens, Dick Driver, and Adam Junior. The words excite and amuse her, and once you recover from your initial shock, you are excited and amused as well. In the grip of approaching orgasm, however, she tends to revert to the contemporary standbys, falling back on the simplest, crudest words in the English lexicon to express her feelings. Cunt, pussy, fuck. Fuck me, Adam. Again and again. Fuck me, Adam. For an entire month you are the captive of that word, the willing prisoner of

151

that word, the embodiment of that word. You dwell in the land of flesh, and your cup runneth over. Surely goodness and mercy shall follow you all the days of your life.

Still, you and your sister never talk about what you are doing. You don't even have a conversation to discuss why you don't talk about it. You are living in the confines of a shared secret, and the walls of that space are built by silence, an insane silence that can be broken only at the risk of bringing those walls down upon your heads. So you sit in your lukewarm bath, you slather each other with soap, you make love on the floor before dinner, you make love in Gwyn's bed after dinner, you sleep like stones, and early in the morning the alarm clock rousts you back to consciousness. On the weekends, you take long rambles through Central Park, resisting the temptation to hold hands, to kiss in public. You go to the movies. You go to plays. The poem you started in June has not advanced by a single line since the night of Andy's birthday, but you don't care, you have other things to absorb your attention now, and time is passing quickly, there are fewer and fewer days before your departure, and you want to spend every moment you can with her, to live out the mad thing you have done together to the very end of the time that is left.

★   ★   ★

The last day comes. For seventy-two hours, you have been living in a state of constant turmoil, of

152

ever-mounting dread. You don't want to go. You want to cancel the trip and stay in New York with your sister, but at the same time you understand that this is out of the question, that the month you have lived with her in unholy matrimony was made possible only by the fact that it was for one month, that there was a limit to how long your incestuous rampage could go on, and because you can't bear to face the truth that it is over now, you feel broken and bereft, benumbed by sorrow.

To make matters worse, you have to spend your last day in New York with your parents. Bud and Marge drive their big car into the city to treat you and your sister to a farewell family lunch at an expensive midtown restaurant — and then on to the airport for last kisses, last hugs, last good-byes. Your nervous, overmedicated mother says little during the meal, but your father is in uncommonly good spirits that day. He keeps addressing you as *son* rather than by your name, and while you know that your father intends no harm, you find this verbal tic annoying, since it seems to deprive you of your personhood and transform you into an object, a thing. Not Adam but Son, as in my son, my creation, my heir. Bud says he envies you for the adventure that awaits you in Paris, meaning Paris as the capital of loose women and late-night naughtiness (ha ha, wink wink), and though he himself never had such an opportunity, could never even afford to go to college, much less spend a year studying in a foreign country, he is clearly proud of himself for having done well enough in the money department to be backing his offspring's trip to Europe, symbol of the good life, the rich life, an emblem of middle-class American success, of which he is one of Westfield, New Jersey's shining examples. You cringe and endure, struggling not to lose your patience, wishing you could be alone with Gwyn. As usual, your sister is calm and composed, alert to the tensions underlying the occasion but stubbornly pretending not to notice them. On the way to the airport, you sit together in the backseat of the car. She takes hold of your hand and squeezes it hard, not loosening her grip throughout the entire forty-minute ride, but that is the only hint she gives of what she is feeling on this horrible day, this day of days, and somehow it is not enough, this hand squeezing your hand is not enough, and from this day forward you know that nothing will ever be enough again.

At the departure gate, your mother puts her arms around you and begins to cry. She can't stand the thought of not seeing you for a whole year, she says, she will miss you, she will worry about you day and night, and please remember to eat enough, send letters, call if you feel homesick, I will always be there for you. You hug her tightly, thinking, My poor mother, my poor wretched mother, and tell her that everything will be fine, but you are by no means certain of that, and your words lack conviction, you can hear your voice trembling as you speak. Over your mother's shoulder, you see your father observing you with that distant, shut-down look

154

in his eyes, and you know he doesn't have the first idea what to make of you, that you have always been a mystery to your father, a person beyond understanding, but now, for once in your life, you find yourself in accord with him, for the truth of the matter is that you, too, have no idea what to make of yourself, and yes, even to yourself, you are a person beyond understanding.

A last look at Gwyn. There are tears in your sister's eyes, but you can't tell if they are meant for you or your mother, if they are an expression of private anguish or sympathy for the overwrought woman who has been weeping in her son's arms. Now that the end has come, you want Gwyn to suffer as much as you are suffering. Pain is the only thing that holds you together now, and unless her pain is as great as yours, there will be nothing left of the small, perfect universe you have lived in for the past month. It is impossible to know what she is thinking, and because your parents are standing less than three feet from you, you cannot ask. You take her in your arms and whisper: I don't want to go. You say it again: I don't want to go. And then you step back from her, put your head down, and go.

One week after I read the text of *Summer*, I was in Oakland, California, ringing the doorbell of Walker's house. I hadn't written or called to tell him what I thought of the second part of his book, nor had he written or called to ask. I felt it would be better to hold back from giving any comments until I saw him in person, and with our scheduled dinner looming up on the immediate horizon, my chance would come soon enough. I couldn't explain why it was so important to me, but I wanted him to be looking into my eyes when I told him that I was not disgusted by what he had written, that I did not find it brutal or ugly (to quote his words back to him), and that my wife, who had now read the first and second parts of the book, felt the same as I did. That was the little speech I rehearsed in my head as the taxi took me across the bridge from San Francisco to Oakland, but I never managed to say what I wanted to say. It turned out that Walker had died just twenty-four hours after he'd sent me the manuscript, and by the time I reached the front door of his house, his ashes had been in the ground for three days.

Rebecca was the one who told me these things, the same Rebecca Adam had talked about in the second letter I received from him, his thirty-five-year-old stepdaughter, a tall, broad-shouldered woman with light brown skin, penetrating eyes, and an attractive if not conventionally pretty face, who referred to her mother's white husband not as her stepfather but as her father. I was glad to hear her use that word, glad to know that Walker had been capable of inspiring that degree of love and loyalty in a child who had not been born to him. That one word seemed to tell me everything about the sort of life he had built for himself in this small house in Oakland with Sandra Williams and her daughter, who eventually became his daughter, and who, even after her mother's death, had stayed by him until the end.

Rebecca broke the news to me just seconds after she opened the door and let me into the house. I shouldn't have been surprised, but I was. In spite of the weakness and fear I had detected in his voice when we talked on the phone, in spite of my certainty that he was coming to the end, I hadn't thought it would happen just yet, I had assumed there was still some time left — enough time for us to have our dinner, at any rate, perhaps even enough time for him to finish his book. When Rebecca spoke the words *My father passed six days ago*, I felt so rattled, so unwilling to accept the finality of her statement that a sudden wave of dizziness rushed through my head, and I had to ask her if I could sit down. She walked me over to a chair in the living room, then went into the kitchen to fetch a glass of water. When she returned, she apologized for her stupidity, even though no apologies were necessary, and even though she was anything but stupid.

I didn't find out that you and my father were planning to have dinner tonight until less than an hour ago, she said. Ever since the funeral, I've been coming to the house and sorting through his things, and it didn't enter my fat little head until six o'clock this evening to open his date book and see if there were any appointments I had to cancel. When I saw the thing for seven o'clock, I immediately called your house in Brooklyn. Your wife gave me the number of your hotel in San Francisco, but when I called them, they said you weren't in your room. I figured you were already on your way here, so I called my husband, told him to feed the kids, and stuck around here waiting for you to show up. You might not be aware of it, but you rang the bell exactly on the dot of seven.

That was the deal, I said. I promised to be here at the stroke of seven. I thought your father would be amused by my punctuality.

I'm sure he would have been, she replied, with a touch of sadness in her voice.

Before I could say anything, she changed the subject and again apologized for something that needed no apology. I was planning to call you within the next few days, she said. Your name is on the list, and I'm sorry I didn't get around to it sooner. Dad had a lot of friends, a ton of friends. So many people to contact, and then there was the funeral to arrange, and a million other things to take care of, and I suppose you could say I've been a bit swamped. Not that I'm complaining. It's better to keep yourself busy at a time like this than to sit around and mope, don't you think?

161

But I'm really sorry I didn't get in touch with you earlier. Dad was so happy when you wrote back to him last month. He's been talking about you ever since I can remember, I feel as if I've known you all my life. His friend from college, the one who went on to make a name for himself out in the big world. It's an honor to meet you at last. Not the best of circumstances, I know, but I'm glad you're here.

Me too, I said, feeling somewhat calmed by the patter of her resonant, soothing voice. Your father was writing something, I continued. Did you know about that?

He mentioned it to me. A book called *1967*.

Have you read it?

No.

Not a word?

Not a single letter. A couple of months ago, he told me that if he died before he finished it, he wanted me to delete the text from his computer. Just wipe it out and forget it, he said, it's of no importance.

So you erased it?

Of course I did. It's a sin to disobey a person's dying wish.

Good, I thought to myself. Good that this woman won't have to set eyes on Walker's manuscript. Good that she won't have to learn about her father's secret, which surely would have hurt her deeply, confused her, devastated her. I could take it in my stride, but that was only because I didn't belong to Walker's family. But imagine his child having to read those fifty pages. Unthinkable.

162

We were sitting face to face in the living room, each one of us planted in a soft, tattered armchair. Minimal furnishings, a couple of framed posters on the wall (Braque, Miró), another wall lined with books from top to bottom, a cotton throw rug in the center of the room, and a warm California dusk hovering outside the windows, yellowish and dim: the comfortable but modest life Walker had referred to in his letter. I drank down the last of the water Rebecca had given me and put the glass on the round short-legged table that stood between us. Then I said: What about Adam's sister? I used to know her a little bit back in the sixties, and I've often wondered what happened to her.

Aunt Gwyn. She lives back east, so I never got to know her very well. But I've always liked her. A generous, funny woman, and she and my mom hit it off, they were solid together. She came out for the funeral, of course, stayed right here in the house, and went home just this morning. My dad's death really shook her up. We all knew he was sick, we all knew he wasn't going to last long, but she wasn't around at the end, she didn't see how he was slipping away from us, and so she wasn't expecting it to happen so soon. She cried her heart out at the funeral, I mean really broke down and sobbed, and all I could do was hold her and try not to break down myself. My little Adam, she kept saying. My poor little Adam.

Poor little Gwyn.

Poor little everyone, Rebecca said, as her own eyes suddenly began to glisten. A few seconds later, a single tear fell from her left eye and slid down her cheek, but she didn't bother to wipe it away.

Is she married?

To an architect named Philip Tedesco.

I've heard of him.

Yes, he's very well known. They've been married for a long time and have two grown-up daughters. One of them is exactly my age.

The last time I saw Gwyn, she was a graduate student in English literature. Did she ever get her PhD?

I'm not sure. What I do know is that she works in publishing. She's director of a university press in the Boston area. A big one, a prominent one, but for the life of me I can't remember the name of it just now. Dammit. Maybe it will come to me later.

Don't worry about it. It's not important.

Without thinking, I reached into my pocket and pulled out a tin of Schimmelpennincks, the tiny Dutch cigars I have smoked since my early twenties. I was about to open the lid, saw Rebecca looking at me, and hesitated. Before I could ask her if it was all right to smoke in the house, she sprang out of her chair and said: I'll get you an ashtray. Matter-of-fact, sympathetic, one of the last Americans who had not joined the ranks of the Tobacco Police. Then she added: I think there's one in my father's study — at which point she smacked the heel of her hand against her forehead and muttered angrily: Good God, I don't know what's wrong with me today.

Is there a problem? I asked, bewildered by

how upset she had become.

I have something for you, she said. It's sitting on my father's desk, and I forgot all about it until this minute. I was going to mail it to you, but then, when I looked in the date book and saw you were coming here tonight, I told myself I could give it to you in person. But I swear, if I hadn't mentioned my father's study, I would have let you walk out of this house empty-handed. I think I must be going senile.

So I accompanied her into the study, a midsize room on the ground floor with a wooden desk, another wall packed with books, filing cabinets, a laptop computer, and a telephone — not so much a lawyer's miniature home office as a place to think, a vestige of Walker's early life as a poet. A nine-by-twelve manila envelope had been placed on top of the shut computer. Rebecca picked it up and handed it to me. My name was written out across the front in block letters, and just below my name, in much smaller cursive, I read: Notes for *Fall*.

Dad gave this to me two days before he died, Rebecca said. It must have been around six o'clock, because I remember coming here straight from my job at the hospital to check in on him. He said he'd talked to you on the phone about two hours earlier, and that if and when, in the event of, I don't want to say the word anymore, in the event of his you-know-what, I was to get this to you as quickly as possible. He looked so drained . . . so worn out when he said that to me, I could see he'd taken a bad turn, that his strength was beginning to leave him.

165

Those were his last two requests. To delete the *1967* file from his computer and give you the envelope. Here it is. I have no idea what Notes for *Fall* means. Do you?

No, I lied. Not the foggiest notion.

★ ★ ★

Back in my hotel room later that night, I opened the envelope and pulled out a short, handwritten letter from Walker and thirty-one single-spaced pages of notes that he had typed up on his computer and then printed out for me. The letter read as follows:

Five minutes after our telephone conversation. Deepest thanks for the encouragement. First thing tomorrow morning, I will have my housekeeper send you the second chapter by express mail. If you find it repugnant, which I fear you will, please accept my apologies. As for the pages in this envelope, you will see that they are the outline for the third part. Written in great haste — telegraphic style — but working quickly helped bring back memories, a deluge of memories, and now that the outline is finished, I don't know if I have it in me to work it up into a proper piece of prose. I feel exhausted, frightened, perhaps a little deranged. I will put the printed-out ms. into an envelope and give it to my daughter, who will send it to you in case I don't hold on long enough to have our

166

famous, much talked about dinner. So weak, so little left, time running out. I will be robbed of my old age. I try not to feel bitter about it, but sometimes I can't help myself. Life is shit, I know, but the only thing I want is more life, more years on this godforsaken earth. As for the enclosed pages, do with them what you will. You are a pal, the best of men, and I trust your judgment in all things. Wish me luck on my journey. With love, Adam.

Reading that letter filled me with an immense, uncontainable sadness. Just hours before, Rebecca had jolted me with the news that Walker was dead, and now he was talking to me again, a dead man was talking to me, and I felt that as long as I held the letter in my hand, as long as the words of that letter were still before my eyes, it would be as if he had been resurrected, as if he had been momentarily brought back to life in the words he had written to me. A strange response, perhaps, no doubt an embarrassingly doltish response, but I was too distraught to censor the emotions that were running through me, and so I read the letter six or seven more times, ten times, twelve times, enough times to have learned every word of it by heart before I found the courage to put it away.

I went to the minibar, poured two little bottles of scotch into a tall glass, and then returned to the bed, where I sat down with the résumé of the third and final part of Walker's book.

Telegraphic. No complete sentences. From

167

beginning to end, written like this. Goes to the store. Falls asleep. Lights a cigarette. In the third person this time. Third person, present tense, and therefore I decided to follow his lead and render his account in exactly that way — third person, present tense. *As for the enclosed pages, do with them what you will.* He had given me his permission, and I don't feel that turning his encrypted, Morse-code jottings into full sentences constitutes a betrayal of any kind. Despite my editorial involvement with the text, in the deepest, truest sense of what it means to tell a story, every word of *Fall* was written by Walker himself.

FALL

Walker arrives in Paris a month before his classes are scheduled to begin. He has already rejected the idea of living in a student dormitory and therefore must arrange for his own housing. On the first morning after crossing the Atlantic, he returns to the hotel he stayed in for several weeks during his first visit to Paris two years before. He plans to use it as a base while he searches for better lodgings elsewhere, but the half-drunk manager with the two-day stubble of beard remembers him from his earlier visit, and when Walker mentions that he will be staying for an entire year, the man offers him a monthly rate that averages out to less than two dollars a night. Nothing is expensive in the Paris of 1967, but even by the standards of that time this is an exceedingly low rent, almost an act of charity, and Walker impulsively decides to accept the man's offer. They shake hands on it, and then the man ushers him into the back room for a glass of wine. It is ten o'clock in the morning. As Walker puts the glass to his mouth and takes his first sip of the acrid *vin ordinaire*, he says to himself: Good-bye, America. For better or worse, you are in Paris now. You must not allow yourself to fall apart.

The Hôtel du Sud is a decrepit, crumbling establishment on the rue Mazarine in the sixth arrondissement, not far from the Odéon metro station on the Boulevard Saint-Germain. In America, a building in such a state of disrepair would be condemned for demolition, but this is not America, and the broken-down eyesore Walker now inhabits is nevertheless a historic structure, erected in the seventeenth century, he thinks, perhaps even earlier, which means that in spite of its filthiness and dilapidation, in spite of the creaking, worn-out steps of the cramped circular staircase, his new digs are not entirely without charm. Granted, his room is a disaster area of brittle, peeling wallpaper and cracked wooden floor planks, the bed is an ancient spring contraption with a caved-in mattress and rock-hard pillows, the small desk wobbles, the desk chair is the least comfortable chair in all of Europe, and one door of the armoire is missing, but setting aside these disadvantages, the room is fairly spacious, light pours through the two sets of double windows, and no noise can be heard from the street. When the manager opens the door and lets him in for the first time, Walker instantly feels that this will be a good place for writing poems. In the long run, that is the only thing that counts. This is the kind of room poets are supposed to work in, the kind of room that threatens to break your spirit and forces you into constant battle with yourself, and as Walker deposits his suitcase and typewriter by the foot of the bed, he vows to spend no less than four hours a day on his writing, to bear down on his work with more diligence and concentration than ever before. It doesn't matter that there is no telephone, that the toilet is a communal toilet at the end of the hall, that there is nowhere to shower or bathe, that everything around him is old. Walker is young, and this is the room where he means to reinvent himself.

There is university business to be taken care of, the tedium of consulting with the director of the Junior Year Abroad Program, selecting courses, filling out forms, attending an obligatory luncheon to meet the other students who will be in Paris for the year. There are just six of them (three Barnard girls and three Columbia boys), and while they all seem earnest and friendly, more than willing to accept him as a member of the gang, Walker makes up his mind to have as little to do with them as possible. He has no inclination to become part of a group, and he certainly doesn't want to waste his time speaking English. The whole point in coming to Paris is to perfect his French. In order to do that, the shy and reticent Walker will have to embolden himself to make contact with the natives.

On an impulse, he decides to call Margot's parents. He remembers that the Jouffroys live on the rue de l'Université in the seventh arrondissement, not terribly far from his hotel, and he hopes they will be able to tell him where he can find her. Why he should want to see Margot again is a difficult question to answer, but for now Walker doesn't even bother to ask it. He has been in Paris for six days, and the truth is that he is beginning to feel somewhat lonely. Rather than renege on his plan not to fraternize with his fellow students, he has steadfastly stuck to himself, spending every morning in his room, parked at his wobbly desk writing and rewriting his newest poems, and then, after hunger drives him down into the street to search for food (most often at the student cafeteria around the corner on the rue Mazet, where he can buy a tasteless but filling lunch for one or two francs), he has consumed the rest of the daylight hours by walking aimlessly around the city, browsing in bookstores, reading on park benches, alive to the world around him but not yet immersed in it, still feeling his way, not unhappy, no, but wilting a little from the constant solitude. Except for Born, Margot is the one person in all of Paris with whom he has shared anything in the past. If she and Born are together again, then he must and will avoid her, but if it turns out that they are well and truly separated, that the breakup has indeed continued for these past three-plus months, then what possible harm can come from

171

seeing her for an innocent cup of coffee? He doubts she will have any interest in renewing physical relations with him, but if she does, he would welcome the chance to sleep with her again. After all, it was the reckless, unbridled Margot who unleashed the erotic maelstrom in him that led to the furies of late summer. He is certain of the connection. Without Margot's influence, without Margot's body to instruct him in the intricate workings of his own heart, the story with Gwyn never would have been possible. Margot the fearless, Margot the silent, Margot the cipher. Yes, he very much wants to see her again, even if it is only for an innocent cup of coffee.

He walks to the café on the corner, buys a telephone *jeton* from the barman, and then goes downstairs to look up the Jouffroys' number in the directory. He is heartened when the phone is answered on the first ring — then shocked when the person on the other end proves to be Margot herself.

Walker insists on conducting the conversation in French. Back in the spring, they spoke to each other in French a number of times, but mostly they communicated in English, and even if Margot is a person of few words, Walker knows she can express herself more comfortably in her own language. Now that he is in Paris, he aims to give Margot's Frenchness back to her, wondering if she might not show herself to be a somewhat different person in her own country and her own tongue. The real Margot, as it were, at home in the city where she was born, and not

172

some disaffected, hostile visitor stuck in an America she could barely tolerate.

They run through the common litany of questions and answers. What in the world is he doing in Paris? How are things? Was it pure luck that she picked up the phone or has she moved in with her parents? What is she doing now? Does she have time to join him for a cup of coffee? She hesitates for a moment and then surprises him by answering: Why not? They arrange to meet at La Palette in an hour.

It is four o'clock in the afternoon, and Walker arrives first, ten minutes in advance. He orders a cup of coffee and then sits there for half an hour, growing more and more convinced that she has stood him up, but just when he is about to leave, Margot wanders in. Moving in that slow, distracted way of hers, the flicker of a smile parting her lips, kissing him warmly on both cheeks, she settles into the chair across from him. She doesn't apologize for her lateness. Margot is not a person who would do that kind of thing, and he doesn't expect it from her, he would never dream of asking her to play by anyone's rules but her own.

En français, alors? she says.

Yes, he answers, speaking to her in French. That's why I'm here. To practice my French. Since you're the only French person I know, I was hoping I could practice with you.

Ah, so that's it. You want to use me to further your education.

In a manner of speaking, yes. But speaking is only part of it. That is, we don't have to talk

173

every minute if you don't want to.

Margot smiles, then changes the subject by asking him for a cigarette. As he lights the Gauloise for her, Walker looks at Margot and suddenly understands that he will never be able to separate her in his mind from Born. It is a grotesque realization, and it utterly smashes the playful, seductive tone he was trying to initiate. He was foolish to call her, he tells himself, foolish to think he could talk her into bed again by acting as if the horrors of the spring had never happened. Even if Margot is no longer a part of Born's life, she is tied to Born in Walker's memory, and to look at her is no different from looking at Born himself. Unable to stop himself, he begins telling her about the stroll down Riverside Drive on that May evening after she left New York. He describes the stabbing to her. He tells her point-blank that Born is without question the murderer of Cedric Williams.

He watches Margot's face carefully as he recounts the gruesome particulars of that night and the days that followed, and for once she looks like a normal human being to him, an undead fellow creature with a conscience and a capacity to feel pain, and in spite of his fondness for Margot, he discovers that he enjoys punching her like this, hurting her like this, destroying her faith in a man she lived with for two years, a man she supposedly loved. Margot is crying now. He wonders if he is doing this to her because of the way she treated him in New York. Is this his revenge for having been dumped without warning at the beginning of their affair? No, he

174

doesn't think so. He is talking to her because he understands that he can no longer look at her without seeing Born, and therefore this is the last time he will ever see her, and he wants her to know the truth before they go their separate ways. When he finishes telling the story, she stands up from the table and rushes off in the direction of the toilets.

He can't be certain if she will be coming back. She has taken her purse with her to the women's room, and since the weather outdoors is warm and mild, she was not wearing a coat or jacket when she entered the café, which means that no coat or jacket is slung over the back of her chair. Walker decides to give her a quarter of an hour, and if she hasn't returned to the table by then, he will get up and leave. Meanwhile, he asks the waiter for another drink. No, not coffee this time, he says. Make it a beer.

Margot is gone for just under ten minutes. When she sits down in her chair again, Walker notices the puffiness around her lids, the glassy sheen in her eyes, but her makeup is intact, and her cheeks are no longer smudged with mascara. He thinks: Gwyn's mascara on the night of Andy's birthday; Margot's mascara on a September afternoon in Paris; the weeping mascara of death.

Forgive me, she says to him in a subdued voice. These things you've told me . . . I don't . . . I don't know what to think anymore.

But you believe me, don't you?

Yes, I believe you. No one would ever make up something like that.

I'm sorry. I didn't want to upset you, but I thought you should know what happened — just in case you ever felt tempted to go back to him.

The strange thing is, I'm not surprised . . .

Did Born ever hit you?

Just once. A slap across the face. A hard, angry slap across the face.

Just once?

Just once. But there's violence in him. Under all the charm and witty jokes, there's real anger, real violence. I hate to admit it now, but I think it excited me. Never knowing if I could trust him or not, never knowing what he was going to do next. He only hit me that one time, but he got into a couple of fights while we were together, fights with other men. You've seen his temper. You know what he's like when he's drunk. I think it goes back to his days in the army, the war, the awful things he did during the war. Torturing prisoners. He once confessed to me that he tortured prisoners in Algeria. He denied it the next day, but I didn't believe him, even though I pretended to. The first story was the truth, I know it.

What about the knife he carries in his pocket? Didn't that ever scare you?

I take people as they are, Adam. I don't ask a lot of questions. If he wanted to carry a knife, I figured that was his business. He said it was a dangerous world and a man had to protect himself. After what happened to you that night in New York, you can't really argue with him, can you?

My sister has a theory. I don't know if it's a

good theory, but she thinks Born started talking to me at the party because he felt a sexual attraction. A homoerotic attraction, as she put it. What do you think? Is she on to something or not?

It's possible. Anything is possible.

Did he ever talk to you about being attracted to men?

No. But that's neither here nor there. I can't tell you what he did before I started living with him. I can't even account for all the things he did while we were together. Who knows what a person's secret desires are? Unless the person acts on them or talks about them, you don't have a clue. The only thing I can talk about is what I saw with my own eyes — and what I saw was this. Very early in our relationship, Rudolf and I had a threesome with another man. It was my idea. Rudolf went along with it to please me, to prove that he was willing to do anything I asked him to do. The other man was an old friend of mine, someone I'd slept with before, an extremely good-looking guy. If Rudolf was attracted to this person, he would have kissed him, wouldn't he? He would have gone for his cock and sucked him off. But he didn't do those things. He liked watching me with François, I could see he was very hot when he saw François's cock go into me, but he didn't touch him in a sexual way. Does that prove anything? I don't know. All I can tell you is that when we saw you at the party in New York, I told Rudolf you were one of the most beautiful boys I had ever seen. He agreed with me. He said you looked like a tormented Adonis, Lord Byron on the verge of a nervous break-down. Does that mean he was attracted to you? Maybe yes, maybe no. You're a special case, Adam, and what makes you special is that you have no idea of the effect you have on other people. It seems perfectly plausible to me that a straight man could get a crush on you. Maybe that's what happened to Rudolf. But I can't know for certain, because even if he did fall for you, he never said a word about it.

He's getting married. Did you know that? At least he said he was the last time I saw him.

Yes, I know. I know all about it. That was my exit visa out of the affair. Good-bye to the double-crossing slut Margot, hello to the angelic Hélène Juin.

You sound bitter . . .

No, not bitter. Confused. I know her, you see, I've known her for a long time, and it just doesn't make any sense to me. Hélène must be five or six years older than Rudolf, she has an eighteen-year-old daughter, and all I can say about her is that she's very dull, very ordinary, very proper. A nice person, of course, a nice, hardworking bourgeois person with a tragic story, but I don't understand what he sees in her. Crazy Rudolf will be bored out of his mind.

He said he loved her.

He probably does. But that doesn't mean he should marry her.

Tragic story. Something to do with her first husband, right? I didn't quite understand what he was talking about.

Juin is a close friend of Rudolf's. Six or seven years ago, he was in a bad car accident. Crushed to pieces, fractured skull, all sorts of internal injuries, but somehow he managed to survive. Or nearly survive. He's been in a coma ever since, more or less brain-dead, on life support in a hospital. For years, Hélène refused to give up hope, but his condition never improved, it never will improve, and finally her friends and family persuaded her to file for a divorce. When it goes through next spring, she'll be free to marry again. Good for her, but the last person I thought she'd go for was Rudolf. I've sat through at least a dozen dinners with the two of them, and I never sensed any strong feeling on either side. Friendship, yes, but no . . . no . . . what's the word I'm looking for?

Sparks.

That's it. No sparks.

You still miss him, don't you?

Not anymore. Not after what you've told me today.

But you did.

I did. I didn't want to, but I did.

The man is a maniac, you know.

True. But what law says you can't love a maniac?

They both fall silent after that, at a loss for more words, more thoughts. Margot looks at her watch, and Walker imagines she is about to tell him she's late for another appointment, that she has to run. Instead, she asks him if he has plans for dinner tonight, and if he doesn't, would he care to go to a restaurant with her? She knows a

179

good place on the rue des Grands Augustins and will gladly treat him if he is low on money. Walker wants to tell her that it won't be possible, that he doesn't think he can see her anymore, that he believes they should put a stop to their friendship, but he can't bring himself to say the words. He is too lonely to refuse her offer, too weak-minded to turn his back on the only person he knows in Paris. Yes, he says, he would love to have dinner with her, but it's still early, not even six o'clock, and what will they do in the meantime? Anything you want, Margot says, meaning, quite literally, anything he wants, and because the thing he wants most is to crawl into bed with her, he suggests they walk over to his hotel on the rue Mazarine so he can show her his ridiculously ugly hellhole of a room. Since thoughts of sex are never far from Margot's mind, she quickly understands Walker's intentions, then goes on to demonstrate that understanding by giving him a little smile.

I wasn't very nice to you in New York, was I? she says.

You were extremely nice to me. At least for a while. But then, no, not very nice.

I'm sorry I hurt you. It was a bad time for me. I didn't know what I was doing, and then, all of a sudden, the only thing I wanted was to get out of New York. Try not to hold it against me.

I don't. I admit that I felt angry for a few weeks, but it didn't last longer than that. I stopped blaming you a long time ago.

We can be friends now, can't we?

I hope so.

Nothing too intense, mind you. Not every minute, not every day. I'm not ready for that. I'm not sure I'll ever be ready for that again. But we can take care of each other a little bit. It might be good for both of us.

As they make their way to the hotel, Walker senses that the woman beside him is no longer the same Margot he met in New York last spring. He was right to think she would be somewhat different in her own language, in her own city, in the wake of her split-up with Born, and after the conversation in the café, he can only conclude that she is more forthright, more articulate, more vulnerable than he previously imagined. Still, even as he anticipates their imminent arrival at the hotel — the mounting of the circular stairs, the key entering the lock of his door, the shedding of their clothes, the sight of Margot's small, naked body, the feel of her body against his — he wonders if he hasn't committed a colossal mistake.

At first, things do not go well. Margot says nothing about his room, because she is either too polite or too indifferent to bother mentioning it, but Walker can't help seeing it through her eyes, and he is overcome with embarrassment, appalled at himself for having dragged her up to such a tawdry, dismal place. It puts him in a foul mood, and when the two of them sit down on the bed and begin to kiss, he feels absent, alarmingly disengaged. Margot pulls back and asks if anything is wrong. Don't get weird on me, Adam, she says. This is supposed to be fun, remember?

181

He can't tell her that he is thinking about Gwyn, that the moment their mouths touched he was seized by a memory of the last time his mouth touched the mouth of his sister, and as he struggles to kiss Margot now, the only thought in his mind is that he will never be able to hold his sister in this way again.

I don't know what's wrong with me, he says. I feel so sad . . . so bloody fucking sad.

Maybe I should go, Margot says, gently patting his back. Sex isn't compulsory, after all. We can try again another day.

No, don't leave. I don't want you to leave. Just give me a little time. I'll be all right, I promise.

Margot gives him the time, and eventually he begins to emerge from his melancholic funk, not fully perhaps, but enough to feel aroused when she slides out of her dress and he puts his arms around her bare skin, enough to make love to her, enough to make love to her twice, and in the pause between couplings, as they drink from the bottle of red wine he carried up to his room earlier that day, Margot further arouses him with graphic stories about her sexual encounters with other women, her passion for touching and kissing large breasts (because hers are so small), for licking and fondling women's crotches, for thrusting her tongue deep into women's assholes, and while Walker can't tell if these are true stories or simply a ploy to get him hard again for their second go at it, he enjoys listening to this dirty talk, just as he enjoyed listening to Gwyn's dirty talk in the apartment on West 107th Street. He wonders if words aren't an essential element of sex, if talking isn't finally a more subtle form of touching, and if the images dancing in our heads aren't just as important as the bodies we hold in our arms. Margot tells him that sex is the one thing in life that counts for her, that if she couldn't have sex she would probably kill herself to escape the boredom and monotony of being trapped inside her own skin. Walker doesn't say anything, but as he comes into her for the second time, he realizes that he shares her opinion. He is mad for sex. Even in the grip of the most crushing despair, he is mad for sex. Sex is the lord and the redeemer, the only salvation on earth.

They never make it to the restaurant. After finishing off the bottle of wine, they both fall asleep and forget about dinner. Early the next morning, just before dawn, Walker opens his eyes and discovers that he is alone in bed. A piece of paper is lying on the pillow next to him, a note from Margot: *Sorry. The bed was too uncomfortable. Call me next week.*

He asks himself if he will have the courage to call. Then, more to the point, he asks himself if he will have the courage not to call, if he can resist seeing her again.

★ ★ ★

Two days later, he is sitting at an outdoor café on the place Saint-André des Arts, nursing a glass of beer and writing in a small notebook. It is six o'clock in the evening, the end of another workday, and now that Walker has begun to

183

settle into the rhythms of Paris, he understands that this is probably the city's most inspiriting hour, the transition from work to home, the streets thronged with men and women rushing back to their families, to their friends, to their solitary lives, and he enjoys being outside among them, encircled by the vast collective exhale filling the air. He has just written a brief letter to his parents and a longer letter to Gwyn, and now he is trying to write something cogent about the work of George Oppen, a contemporary American poet whom he greatly admires. He copies out these lines from Oppen's most recent book, *This In Which*:

Impossible to doubt the world: it can be
    seen
And because it is irrevocable

It cannot be understood, and I believe that
    fact is lethal.

He is about to jot down some comments on this passage, but before he can proceed a shadow falls across the page of the notebook. He glances up, and there, standing directly in front of him, is Rudolf Born. Before Walker can say or do anything, the future husband of Hélène Juin sits down in the empty chair beside him. Walker's pulse begins to race. He is breathless, speechless. It wasn't supposed to happen this way, he tells himself. If and when they crossed paths, he was the one who was going to spot Born, not the other way around. He was going to be walking

184

down a crowded street, in a position to avert his eyes and escape unnoticed. That was how he always saw it in his head, and now here he is out in the open, defenseless, sitting on his dumb, sorry ass, unable to pretend Born isn't there, trapped.

The white suit is gone, replaced by a cream-colored jacket, and a silk foulard is hanging around his neck, a blue-and-green patterned affair no doubt worn to bounce off the light blue of his shirt — still and ever the rumpled dandy, Walker thinks, wearing the same sardonic smile as of old.

Well, well, Born says, with false good humor, pronouncing the words in such a way as to emphasize their falseness. We meet again, Walker. What a pleasant surprise.

Walker knows that he is going to have to talk to him, but for the time being he can't get any words out of his mouth.

I was hoping I'd run into you, Born continues. Paris is such a small city, it was bound to happen sooner or later.

Who told you I was here? Walker finally asks. Margot?

Margot? I haven't talked to Margot in months. I didn't even know she was in town.

Who was it, then?

You forget that I taught at Columbia. I have Columbia connections, and the head of your program just happens to be a friend of mine. I had dinner with him the other night, and he was the one who told me. He said you were living in some fleabag on the rue Mazarine. Why didn't

185

you go to Reid Hall? The rooms might not be as big there, but at least they aren't crawling with bugs.

Walker has no desire to discuss his living arrangements with Born, no interest in wasting his breath on small talk. Ignoring the question, he says: I haven't forgotten, you know. I still think about it all the time.

Think about what?

What you did to that boy.

I didn't do anything to him.

Please . . .

One thrust, that was all. You were there. You saw what happened. He was going to shoot us. If I hadn't attacked first, we both would have been killed.

But the gun wasn't loaded.

We didn't know that, did we? He said he was going to shoot, and when someone points a gun at me and says he's going to shoot, I take him at his word.

What about the park? Over twelve more stab wounds after the first one. Why on earth did you do that?

I didn't. I know you don't believe me, but I had nothing to do with that. Yes, I carried him into the park after you left, but by the time I got there he was already dead. Why would I go on stabbing someone after he was dead? All I wanted was to get out of there as quickly as I could.

Then who did it?

I have no idea. A sick person. A goblin of the night. New York is a sinister place, after all. It could have been anyone.

I talked to the police, you know. In spite of your not so subtle warning.

I figured you would. That's why I left in such a hurry.

If you were innocent, why not stay and fight it out in court?

For what? They would have acquitted me in the end, and I couldn't afford to lose all the time it would have taken to defend myself. The kid deserved to die. The kid died. That's all there is to it.

No remorse, then.

No remorse. None whatsoever. I don't even blame you for turning against me and going to the police. You did what you thought was right. Mistakenly, of course, but that's your problem, not mine. I saved your life, Adam. Remember that. If the gun had been loaded, you'd still be thanking me for what I did. The fact that it wasn't loaded doesn't really change anything, does it? As long as we thought it was loaded, it was loaded.

Walker is willing to concede the point, but there is still the question of the park, the question of how and when the boy died, and he has no doubt that Born's version of events is untrue — for the simple reason that it could not have happened so quickly. A single stab wound to the stomach can lead to death, but inevitably it is a slow and protracted death, which means that Williams must have been alive when Born reached the park, and therefore the additional wounds that ended up killing the boy were inflicted by Born himself. Nothing else makes sense. Why would another person go to the trouble of stabbing a dead teenager more than a dozen times? If Williams was still breathing when Born left the park, it might be possible to build an argument for a second attacker — far-fetched but possible — but only if the object was to steal the boy's money, and the police told Walker back in the spring that no robbery had taken place. The kid's wallet was found in his pocket, and sixteen untouched dollars were inside the wallet, which eliminates theft as a motive for the crime. *Why would I go on stabbing someone after he was dead?* Because he wasn't dead, and you kept on plunging your knife into him until you made sure he was, and then, even after you finished the job, you continued stabbing him because you were engulfed by rage, because you were out of your mind and enjoyed what you were doing.

I don't want to talk about it anymore, Walker says, reaching into his pocket and pulling out some coins to pay for his beer. I have to go.

Suit yourself, Born replies. I was hoping we could bury the hatchet and become friends again. It even occurred to me that you might enjoy meeting the daughter of my future wife. Cécile is a delightful, intelligent girl of eighteen — a literature student, an excellent pianist, just the kind of person who would interest you.

No thanks, Walker says, standing up from the table. I don't need you to play matchmaker for me. You already did that once, remember?

Well, if you ever change your mind, give me a call. I'd be happy to introduce her to you.

At that point, just as Walker is turning to go, Born reaches into the breast pocket of his cream-colored blazer and withdraws a business card with his address and telephone number on it. Here, he says, handing the card to Walker. All my coordinates. Just in case.

For a brief moment, Walker is tempted to tear up the card and throw the pieces onto the ground — the same way he tore up the check in New York last spring — but then he decides against it, not wanting to disgrace himself with such a cheap and petty insult. He slips the card into his pocket and says good-bye. Born nods but says nothing. As Walker leaves, the sun shoots across the sky and explodes into a hundred thousand splinters of molten light. The Eiffel Tower falls down. Every building in Paris bursts into flame. End of Act I. Curtain.

★ ★ ★

He has put himself in an untenable position. As long as he was ignorant of Born's whereabouts, he could live with the uncertainty of a potential encounter, all the while deluding himself into believing that luck would be with him and the dreaded moment would never come, or come late, so late that his time in Paris would not be destroyed by fears of another encounter, other encounters. Now that it has happened, and happened early, much earlier than he would have thought possible, he finds it unbearable to have Born's address in his pocket and not be able to go to the police to demand that he be arrested.

189

Nothing would make him happier than to see the murderer of Cedric Williams brought to justice. Even if they let him off, he would have to suffer through the expense and humiliation of a trial, and even if the case never went to court, he would have to endure the unpleasantness of being grilled by the police, the rigors of a drawn-out investigation. But short of abducting Born and hauling him back to New York, what can Walker do? He ponders the situation for the rest of the day and deep into the night, and then an idea occurs to him, a diabolical idea, an idea so cruel and underhanded that he is stunned by the mere fact that he is capable of imagining such a thing. It won't put Born in prison, alas, but it will make his life extremely uncomfortable, and if Walker can pull off his plan successfully, it will deprive Hélène Juin's future husband of the one object he covets most in the world. Walker is both thrilled and disgusted with himself. He has never been a vengeful person, has never actively sought to hurt anyone, but Born is in a different category, Born is a killer, Born deserves to be punished, and for the first time in his life Walker is out for blood.

The plan calls for a practiced liar, a social acrobat skilled in the fine art of duplicity, and since Walker is neither one of those things, he knows that he is the worst man for the job he has given himself. Right from the start, he will be forced to act against his own nature, again and again he will slip and fall as he struggles to gain a secure footing on the battleground he has mapped out in his mind, and yet in spite of his misgivings, he marches off to the Café Conti the next morning to drop another *jeton* into the pay telephone and put his scheme into operation. He is dumbfounded by his boldness, his resolve. When Born answers on the third ring, the surprise in the man's voice is palpable.

Adam Walker, he says, doing his best to mask his astonishment. The last person on earth I was expecting to hear from.

Forgive the intrusion, Walker says. I just wanted you to know that I've done some serious thinking since we talked yesterday.

Interesting. And where have your thoughts led you?

I've decided I want to bury the hatchet.

Doubly interesting. Yesterday, you accuse me of murder, and today you're willing to forgive and forget. Why the sudden turnaround?

Because you convinced me you were telling the truth.

Am I to take this as a sincere apology — or are you angling for some new favor from me? You wouldn't be thinking of trying to resurrect your dead magazine, for example?

Of course not. That's all in the past.

It was a hurtful thing you did, Walker. Tearing up the check into little pieces and sending it back to me without a word. I was deeply insulted.

If I offended you in any way, I'm truly sorry. I was more or less in shock after what happened. I didn't know what I was doing.

And you know what you're doing now?

I think so.

You think so. And tell me young man, what exactly do you want?

Nothing. I called because you asked me to call. In case I changed my mind.

You want to get together, then. Is that it? You're telling me you'd like to resume our friendship.

That was the idea. You mentioned meeting your fiancée and her daughter. I thought that would be a nice way to begin.

Nice. Such an insipid word. You Americans have a real gift for banalities, don't you?

No doubt. We're also good at apologizing when we feel we're in the wrong. If you don't want to see me, just say so. I'll understand.

Forgive me, Walker. I was being nasty again. I'm afraid it comes with the territory.

We all have our moments.

Indeed. And now you want to break bread with Hélène and Cécile. As per my invitation of yesterday. Consider it done. I'll leave word at your hotel as soon as I've made the arrangements.

★ ★ ★

The dinner is set for the following night at Vagenende, a turn-of-the-century brasserie on the Boulevard Saint-Germain. Walker arrives promptly at eight, the first member of the party to show up, and as he is led to Monsieur Born's table, he is too nervous and distracted to pay much attention to his surroundings: the dark, oak-paneled walls, the brass fixtures, the stiff white table-cloths and napkins, the hushed conversations in other parts of the room, the sound of silver utensils clanking against china. Thirty-four hours after his demented, groveling conversation with Born, this is what his lies have earned him: unending fear, unmitigated self-contempt, and the priceless opportunity to meet Born's future wife and stepdaughter. Everything hinges on what happens with Hélène and Cécile Juin. If he can manage to form a connection with them, with either one of them, a relation independent of any connection with Born, then sooner or later it will become possible for him to reveal the truth about Riverside Drive, and if Walker can persuade them to accept his story about the killing of Cedric Williams, then there is a chance, a better than even chance, that the wedding will be called off and Born will be forsaken by his bride-to-be. That is all Walker has set out to accomplish: to break up the marriage before it becomes a legal fact. Not such an onerous punishment for the crime of murder, perhaps, but, given the available options, harsh enough. Born rejected. Born humiliated. Born crumpled up in misery. Hateful as Walker finds it to be pandering to him with false apologies and insincere avowals of friendship, he understands that he has no other choice. If Hélène and Cécile prove to be intractable, then he will abandon the effort and quietly declare defeat. But only if, and only when, and until that moment comes, he is determined to go on playing cards with the devil.

His initial findings are inconclusive. By temperament or circumstance, both mother and

193

daughter come across as modest and reserved, not easily approachable or given to lighthearted talk, and since Born dominates the early going with introductions, explanations, and various other comments, little is said by either one of them. When Walker gives a brief account of his first days in Paris, Hélène compliments him on his French; at another point, Cécile blandly inquires if he enjoys living in a hotel. The mother is tall, blond, and well dressed, by no means a beauty (her face is too long, Walker thinks, a bit on the horsey side), but like many middle-class Frenchwomen of a certain age, she carries herself with considerable poise and assurance — a question of style, perhaps, or else the product of some arcane Gallic wisdom concerning the nature of femininity. The daughter, who has just turned eighteen, is a student at the Lycée Fénelon on the rue de l'Éperon, which is less than a five-minute walk from the Hôtel du Sud. She is a smaller, less-imposing creature than her mother, with short brown hair, thin wrists and narrow shoulders, and alert, darting eyes. Walker notices that those eyes have a tendency to squint, and it occurs to him (correctly, as it turns out) that Cécile normally wears glasses and has decided to live without them for the duration of the dinner. No, not a pretty girl, almost mousy in fact, but nevertheless an interesting face to look at: tiny chin, long nose, round cheeks, an expressive mouth. Every now and then, that mouth tugs downward with a clandestine sort of amusement, not quite blossoming into a smile, but for all that showing a sharply developed sense of humor, someone awake to the comic possibilities of any given moment. There is no question that she is extremely intelligent (for the past four minutes Born has been bragging to Walker about her outstanding grades in literature and philosophy, her passion for the piano, her mastery of ancient Greek), but much as Cécile has working in her favor, Walker sadly acknowledges that he is not attracted to her, at least not in the way he would have hoped. She is not his type, he says to himself, falling back on that vague, overused term, which stands in for the infinite complexities of physical desire. But what is his type? he wonders. His own sister? The sex-hungry Margot, who is ten years older than he is? Whatever it is he wants, it is not Cécile Juin. He looks at her and sees a child, a work in progress, a not yet fully formed person, and at this point in her life she is too withdrawn and self-conscious to give off any of the erotic signals that would inspire a man to run after her. That isn't to say he won't do his best to cultivate a friendship with her, but there will be no kissing or touching, no romantic entanglements, no attempt to lure her into bed.

He despises himself for thinking such thoughts, for looking upon the innocent Cécile as if she were nothing more than a sex object, a potential victim of his seductive powers (assuming he has any), but at the same time he knows that he is fighting a war, an underground guerrilla war, and this dinner is the first battle of that war, and if he could win the battle by

195

seducing his adversary's future stepdaughter, he would not hesitate to do it. But the young Cécile is not a candidate for seduction, and therefore he will have to devise more subtle tactics to advance his purpose, shifting from an all-out assault on the daughter to a two-pronged offensive against mother and daughter both — in an attempt to ingratiate himself with them and eventually lure them over to his side. All this must be accomplished under Born's watchful gaze, the intolerable, suffocating presence of a man he can barely bring himself to look at. The wily, skeptical Born is no doubt deeply suspicious of the two-faced Walker, and who knows if he hasn't merely pretended to accept the latter's pretend apology in order to find out what mischief the boy is up to? There is an edge to Born's voice buried under the pleasant chatter and false bonhomie, an anxious, straining tone that seems to suggest he is on his guard. It will not be wise to see him again, Walker tells himself, which makes it all the more imperative to establish his separate peace with the Juins tonight, before the dinner comes to an end.

The women are on the other side of the table. He is opposite Cécile, and Born is sitting to his left, face to face with Hélène. Walker studies Hélène's eyes as she looks at her betrothed, and he becomes just as baffled as Margot was when he detects no spark emanating from them. Other feelings lurk in those eyes, perhaps — wistfulness, kindness, sadness — but love is not among them, much less happiness or a single trace of joy. But how can there be happiness for a woman

196

in Hélène's position, for someone who has spent the past six or seven years living in a state of grief and suspended animation as her half-dead husband languishes in a hospital? He imagines the comatose Juin stretched out in bed, his body hooked up to countless machines and a tangle of respiration tubes, the only patient in a large, deserted ward, living but not living, dying but not dying, and suddenly he remembers the film he saw with Gwyn two months ago, *Ordet*, the film by Carl Dreyer, sitting next to his sister in the balcony of the New Yorker theater, and the dead farmer's wife laid out in her coffin, and his tears when she sat up and came to life again, but no, he says to himself, that was just a story, a make-believe story in a make-believe world, and this is not that world, and there will be no miraculous resurrections for Juin, Hélène's husband will never sit up and come back to life. From Juin's bed in the hospital Walker's mind jumps to another bed, and before he can put a stop to it, he is revisiting the repugnant scene Margot described to him a few days ago: Margot in bed with the two men, Born and the other one, what was his name, François, Margot in bed with Born and François, the three of them naked, fucking, and now he sees Born watching François push his hardened cock into Margot, and there is Born, naked in his chunky, odious flesh, swept up in the throes of arousal, jerking off as he watches his girlfriend do it with another man . . .

Walker smiles at Cécile in an attempt to dissolve the image, and as she smiles back at him

197

— a bit puzzled, but apparently pleased by the attention — he wonders if this kind of debauchery doesn't explain why Born is so keen on marrying Hélène. He is struggling to turn his back on himself, to resist his sordid, malevolent urges, and she represents respectability to him, a wall against his own madness. Walker notes how decorously he behaves with Hélène, addressing her by the formal *vous* instead of the more intimate, familiar *tu*. It is the language of counts and countesses, the language of marriage in the highest reaches of the upper class, and it creates a distance from both self and world that serves as a form of protection. It is not love that Born is looking for but safety. The libidinous Margot brought out the worst in him. Will the calm and repressed Hélène turn him into a new man? Dream on, Walker says to himself. A person of your intelligence should know better than to think that.

By the time they place their orders, Walker has been told that Hélène works as a speech pathologist at a clinic in the fourteenth arrondissement. She has been in the profession since the early fifties — in other words, long before her husband's accident — and although she now depends on this job to generate the income needed to support her small household, Walker quickly understands that she is a dedicated practitioner, that her career gives her immense satisfaction and is probably the single most important element of her life. Find yourself drowning in a sea of trouble, and hard work can become the raft that ends up keeping you afloat.

Walker reads it in her eyes, is impressed by how noticeably they have brightened now that Born has mentioned the subject, and suddenly there is a possible opening, a chance to engage her in pertinent dialogue. The truth is that Walker is genuinely interested in what she does. He has read Jakobson and Merleau-Ponty on aphasia and language acquisition, has given serious thought to these matters because of his engagement with words, and therefore he does not feel like a fraud or a conniver when he starts pelting her with questions. At first, Hélène is taken aback by his enthusiasm, but once she realizes that he is in earnest, she begins to talk about articulation disorders in children, her methods of treating the lisping, garble-mouthed, stuttering youngsters who come to her clinic, but no, she doesn't only work with children, there are the adults as well, the old people, the victims of stroke and various brain injuries, the aphasics, the ones who have lost the power of speech or can't remember words or jumble words to such an extent that *pen* becomes *paper* and *tree* becomes *house*. There are several different forms of aphasia, Walker learns, depending on which part of the brain is affected — Broca's aphasia, Wernicke's aphasia, conduction aphasia, transcortical sensory aphasia, anomic aphasia, and so on — and isn't it intriguing, Hélène says, smiling for the first time since she entered the restaurant, truly smiling at last, isn't it intriguing that thought cannot exist without language, and since language is a function of the brain, we would have to say that language — the ability to experience the world through symbols — is in some sense a physical property of human beings, which proves that the old mind-body duality is so much nonsense, doesn't it? Adieu, Descartes. The mind and the body are one.

He is discovering that the best way to get to know them is to leave himself out of it, to ask questions rather than give answers, to make them talk about themselves. But Walker is not adept at this kind of interpersonal manipulation, and he falls into an uncomfortable silence when Born barges in with some pointedly negative comments about the Israeli army's refusal to withdraw from Sinai and the West Bank. Walker senses that he is trying to goad him into an argument, but the fact is that he agrees with Born's stance on this issue, and rather than let him know that, he says nothing, waiting for the harangue to run its course by looking at Cécile's mouth, which is again tugging downward in response to some secret inner mirth. He could be wrong, but it appears that she finds the intensity of Born's opinions rather funny. A couple of minutes later, the rant is interrupted when the appetizers are set before them. Seizing his opportunity, Walker breaks the sudden silence by asking Cécile about her study of ancient Greek. Greek wasn't offered at the high school he went to, he says, and he envies her for having the chance to learn it. He has only two years of college left, and by now it's probably too late for him to start.

Not really, she says. Once you learn the alphabet, it's not as hard as it looks.

200

They talk about Greek literature for a while, and before long Cécile is telling him about her summer project — a crazy, overly ambitious plan that has led to three months of constant frustration and regret. God knows what possessed her to try in the first place, she says, but she got it into her head to take on a book-length poem by the most difficult writer imaginable and translate it into French. When Walker asks who the writer is, she shrugs and says that he hasn't heard of him, that no one has heard of him, and indeed, when she mentions the poet's name, Lycophron, who lived around 300 B.C., Walker admits that she is right. The poem is about Cassandra, she goes on, the daughter of Priam, the last king of Troy — poor Cassandra, who had the misfortune to be loved by Apollo. He offered her the gift of prophecy, but only if she agreed to sacrifice her virginity to him in exchange. At first she said yes, then she said no, and the jilted Apollo took his revenge on her by poisoning his gift, making sure that none of Cassandra's prophecies would ever be believed. Lycophron's poem is set during the Trojan War, and Cassandra is in prison, already mad, about to be murdered with Agamemnon, spewing forth endless ravings and visions of the future in a language so complex, so crammed with metaphors and allusions, that it is almost unintelligible. It is a poem of shrieks and howls, Cécile tells him, a great poem in her opinion, a wild and utterly modern poem, but so daunting and elusive, so far beyond her powers of comprehension, that after hours and hours of work she has managed to translate only a hundred and fifty lines. If she keeps it up, she says, mouth tugging downward once again, it will take her only ten or twelve years to finish.

In spite of her self-deprecating manner, Walker can't help admiring the girl's courage for tackling such a formidable poem, a poem he himself would now like to read, and consequently he asks her if any translations exist in English. She doesn't know, she says, but she would be happy to find out for him. Walker thanks her and then adds (out of simple curiosity, with no ulterior motive) that he would like to read her version of the opening lines in French. But Cécile demurs. It couldn't possibly interest you, she says. It's pure rubbish. At which point Hélène pats her daughter's hand and tells her not to be so hard on herself. Born then pipes in and addresses Cécile as well: Adam is a translator, too, you know. A poet first, but also a translator of poems. From Provençal, no less. He once gave me a work by my would-be namesake, Bertran de Born. An impressive fellow, old Bertran. He tended to lose his head at times, but a good poet, and Adam did an excellent translation.

Oh? Cécile says, looking at Walker. I wasn't aware of that.

I don't know about excellent, he says, but I have done a little translating.

Well, she replies, in that case . . .

And just like that, with no forewarning, with no devious maneuvers on his part, Walker finds himself arranging to get together with Cécile tomorrow afternoon at four o'clock to have a look at her manuscript. A small victory, perhaps, but quite suddenly he has accomplished everything he set out to do this evening. There will be further contact with the Juins, and Born will be nowhere in sight.

★ ★ ★

The following morning, he is sitting at his wobbly desk with a pen in his hand, looking over a recent poem and becoming more and more disenchanted with it, wondering if he should forge on with his efforts, put the manuscript aside for later reflection, or simply chuck it into the wastebasket. He lifts his head for a peek out the windows: gray and overcast, a mountain of clouds bulking up to the west, yet another shift in the ever-shifting Paris sky. He finds the gloom indoors rather pleasant — a soothing gloom, as it were, a companionable gloom, a gloom one could converse with for hours. He puts down his pen, scratches his head, exhales. Unbidden, a forgotten verse from Ecclesiastes comes roaring into his consciousness. *And I gave my heart to know wisdom, and to know madness and folly* . . . As he jots down the words in the right-hand margin of his poem, he wonders if this isn't the truest thing he has written about himself in months. The words might not be his own, but he feels that they belong to him.

Ten-thirty, eleven o'clock. The yellowish glow of the electric bulb radiating from the wine-bottle lamp on the desk. The dripping faucet, the peeling wallpaper, the scratching of his pen. He hears the sound of footsteps on the stairs. Someone is approaching, slowly mounting the circular staircase toward his floor, the top floor, and at first he assumes it is Maurice, the semi-inebriated hotel manager, coming to deliver a telegram or the morning mail, affable Maurice Petillon, man of a thousand stories about nothing at all, but no, it can't be Maurice, for now Walker detects the clicking sound of high heels, and therefore it must be a woman, and if it's a woman, who else can it be but Margot? Walker is glad, inordinately glad, positively stupid with happiness at the prospect of seeing her again. He jumps out of his chair and rushes to open the door before she has time to knock.

She is holding a small, wax-coated patisserie bag filled with freshly baked croissants. Under normal circumstances, a person who shows up bearing gifts is a person in a happy frame of mind, but Margot looks peeved and out of sorts today, and she barely manages a smile as she plants a frosty, perfunctory kiss on Walker's mouth. When Walker puts his arms around her, she wriggles out of his grasp and strides into the room, tossing the bag onto the desk and then sitting down on the unmade bed. Walker closes the door behind him, advances as far as the desk, and stops.

What's wrong? he says.

There's nothing wrong with me, Margot replies. I want to know what's wrong with you.

With me? Why should anything be wrong with me? What are you talking about?

Last night, I happened to be walking with a

204

friend down the Boulevard Saint-Germain. It was about eight-thirty or nine o'clock. We passed that restaurant, you know the one I'm talking about, the old brasserie, Vagenende, and for no particular reason, giant idiot that I am, or maybe because I used to go there with my parents when I was a little girl, I looked through the window. And who do you think I saw?

Ah, Walker says, feeling as if he has just been slapped across the face. You don't have to tell me. I already know the answer.

What are you up to, Adam? What kind of warped game are you involved in now?

Walker lowers himself onto the chair behind the desk. There is no air left in his lungs; his head is about to detach itself from his body. He looks away from Margot, whose eyes never leave him, and begins fiddling with the bag of croissants.

Well? she says. Aren't you going to talk?

I want to, he says at last. I want to tell you everything.

Then why don't you?

Because I don't know if I can trust you. You can't breathe a word about this to anyone, do you understand? You have to promise me that.

Who do you think I am?

I don't know. Someone who disappointed me. Someone I like very much. Someone I want to be friends with.

But you don't think I can keep a secret.

Can you?

No one ever asked me before. How can I know unless I try?

Well, at least that's honest.

You decide. I'm not going to force you to talk when you don't want to talk. But if you don't talk, Adam, I'm going to stand up and leave this room, and you'll never see me again.

That's blackmail.

No it's not. It's the simple truth, that's all.

Walker lets out a prolonged sigh of defeat, then stands up from the chair and begins pacing back and forth in front of Margot, who watches him in silence from the bed. Ten minutes go by, and in those minutes he tells her the story of the past several days: the accidental meeting with Born, which he now suspects was not an accident, Born's spurious denials about the murder of Cedric Williams, the invitation to meet Hélène and Cécile, the business card he almost tore up, hatching the plan to block Born's marriage to Hélène, the contrite telephone call to set the plan in motion, the dinner at Vagenende, his upcoming date with Cécile at four o'clock this afternoon. When Margot has heard him out, she pats the bed with her left hand and asks Walker to sit down beside her. Walker sits, and the moment his body touches the mattress, Margot grabs hold of his two shoulders with her two hands, turns him toward her, brings her face to within inches of his, and says in a low voice filled with determination: Give it up, Adam. You don't have a chance. He'll slice you into little pieces.

It's too late, Walker says. I've already started now, and I'm not going to stop until I've seen it through to the end.

You talk about trust. What makes you think you can trust Hélène Juin? You've only just met her.

I know. It's going to take a while before I'm sure. But my first impression of her is a good one. She strikes me as a solid, honest person, and I don't think she really cares that much about Born. She's grateful to him, he's been kind to her, but she's not in love with him.

The minute you tell her about what happened in New York, she'll turn around and go straight to Rudolf. I promise you.

Maybe. But even if she does, what can happen to me?

All kinds of things.

Born might try to punch me in the face, but he's not going to come after me with his knife.

I'm not talking about the knife. Rudolf has connections, a hundred powerful connections, and before you start to mess with him, you should know who you're dealing with. He's not just anyone.

Connections?

With the police, with the military, with the government. I can't prove anything, but I've always felt he's something more than just a university professor.

Such as?

I don't know. Secret intelligence, espionage, dirty work of some kind or another.

And why on earth do you suspect that?

Telephone calls in the middle of the night . . . mysterious, unexplained absences . . . the people he knows. Cabinet ministers, army generals.

How many young professors go out to dinner with top government officials? Rudolf is on the inside, and that makes him a dangerous person for you to know. Especially here in Paris.

It sounds rather flimsy to me.

Do you remember the dinner at our apartment in New York last spring?

Vividly. How could I forget it?

He was on the phone when I let you into the apartment. Then he came out — furious, breathing fire, hysterical. *How many years have I given them?* What did he mean by that? Principles! Battles! The ship is going down! There was a problem in Paris, and I can tell you now that it had nothing to do with academic business or his father's estate. It was connected to the government, to his secret life in whatever agency he works for. That's why he got so worked up when you started talking about the CIA. Don't you remember? He told you all those things about your family, and you were shocked, you couldn't believe how much information he'd managed to dig up about you. You said he must be an agent of some kind. You were right, Adam. You sniffed out something about him, and he started laughing at you, he tried to turn it into a joke. That's when I knew I was right.

Maybe. But it's still just a guess.

Then why wouldn't he tell me what the problem was? He didn't even bother to make up an excuse. It doesn't concern you, he said, don't ask so many questions. So off he flies to Paris, and when he comes back, he's engaged to Hélène Juin and I'm thrown out the door.

They go on talking for another fifteen or twenty minutes, and the more vehement Margot becomes about her suspicions concerning undercover operations, government conspiracies, and the psychological pressures of leading a double life, the less Walker seems to care. Margot is puzzled by his indifference. She calls it curious, unhealthy, irrational, but Walker explains that Born's activities are of no interest to him. The only thing that counts is the murder of Cedric Williams, and even if Born turned out to be the head of the entire French intelligence system, it wouldn't matter to him. There is just one moment when his attention seems fully engaged, and that follows a tossed-off comment from Margot about Born's past — something to do with spending his childhood in a large house outside Paris, which was where she first met him when she was three years old. What about Guatemala? Walker asks, remembering that Born said to him that he had grown up in Guatemala.

He was pulling your leg, Margot replies. Rudolf has never been anywhere near the place.

I thought as much. But why Guatemala?

Why not Guatemala? He enjoys making up stories about himself. Fooling people, telling little lies — they're grand entertainment for Rudolf.

Although little of concrete value emerges from this conversation (too many assumptions, not enough facts), it nevertheless seems to mark a turning point in his relations with Margot. She is worried about him, worried for him, and the anxiety and concern he sees in her eyes is both comforting (the issue of trust is no longer in doubt) and somewhat troubling. She is drawing closer to him, her affection has become more manifest, more sincere, and yet there is something maternal about that anxiety, a sense of wisdom frowning down on the errors of youth, and for the first time in the months he has known her, he can feel the difference in their ages, the gap of ten years that stands between them. He hopes this will not become a problem. He needs Margot now. She is his only ally in Paris, and being with her is the only medicine that can prevent him from brooding about Gwyn, from longing for Gwyn. No, he is not unhappy that she spotted him in the restaurant last night with Born and the Juins. Nor is he unhappy that he has just bared his soul to her. Her reaction has proved that he means something to her, that he represents more than just another body to climb into bed with, but he knows that he mustn't abuse her friendship, for Margot is not entirely there, and she has only just so much of herself to give. Ask for too much, and she is liable to resent it, perhaps even abscond.

Leaving the untouched croissants on the desk, they go out into the dank, sunless weather to look for a place to eat. Margot holds his hand as they walk along in silence, and ten minutes later they are sitting across from each other at a corner table in the Restaurant des Beaux-Arts. Margot buys him a copious three-course lunch (refusing to let him pay, insisting that he order dessert and a second cup of coffee), and then they move on to the rue de l'Université. The Jouffroy apartment is on the fifth floor of a six-story building, and as they squeeze into the cramped birdcage of an elevator to begin their ascent, Walker puts his arms around Margot and covers her face with a barrage of short, intense kisses. Margot bursts out laughing, and she is still laughing as she extracts a key from her purse and unlocks the door of the apartment. It turns out to be a sumptuous place, far more lavish than anything Walker could have imagined, an immense palace of comfort expressing wealth on a scale he has not encountered before. Margot once told him that her father worked in banking, but she neglected to add that he was the president of the bank, and now that she is giving Walker a brief tour of the rooms, with their thick Persian rugs and gilt-edged mirrors, with their crystal chandeliers and antique furnishings, he feels he is gaining new insight into the disaffected, elusive Margot. She is a person at odds with the environment she was born into, at odds with it but not in outright rebellion (for here she is, temporarily back with her parents as she searches for a place of her own), yet what a disappointment it must be to them that she is still unmarried at thirty, nor can her halfhearted attempts to become a painter sit terribly well in this dominion of bourgeois respectability. Ambiguous Margot, with her love of cooking and her love of sex, still struggling to find a place for herself, still not entirely free.

Or so Walker muses as he follows her into the kitchen, but a minute later he learns that the

211

portrait is somewhat more complex than the one he has been fashioning in his mind. Margot does not live in the apartment with her parents. She has a room upstairs, a tiny maid's room that her grandmother bought for her as a twenty-first-birthday present, and the only reason she entered the apartment this afternoon was to look for a pack of cigarettes (which she now finds in a drawer next to the sink). The tour was a little bonus, she adds, so Walker would have an idea of how and where she grew up. When he asks her why she prefers camping out in a minute *chambre de bonne* to sleeping in comfort down here, Margot smiles and says: Figure it out for yourself.

It is a spartan room, less than a third the size of his room at the hotel. Space for a small desk and chair, a small sink, and a small bed with storage drawers under the mattress. Pristine in its cleanliness, no adornments anywhere — as if they have stepped into the cell of a novitiate nun. Just one book in sight, lying on the floor beside the bed: a collection of poems by Paul Éluard, *Capitale de la douleur*. A few sketchbooks piled up on the desk along with a drinking glass filled with pencils and pens; some canvases on the floor, leaning against the wall with their backs facing out. Walker would love to turn them around, would love to open the sketchbooks, but Margot doesn't offer to show them to him, and he doesn't dare touch anything without her permission. He is awed by the simplicity of the room, awed by this unearthly glimpse into Margot's inner world. How many people has she

212

allowed to come in here? he wonders.

He would like to think he is the first.

★ ★ ★

They spend two hours together in Margot's narrow bed, and when Walker finally leaves, he is running late for his appointment with Cécile Juin. It is entirely his fault, but the truth is that he forgot all about the meeting. From the moment he started kissing Margot, the four o'clock rendezvous vanished from his mind, and if not for Margot herself, who glanced over at the alarm clock and said to him: *Aren't you supposed to be somewhere in fifteen minutes?*, he would still be lying next to her — rather than bounding from the bed, jumping into his clothes, and scrambling to get out of there.

He is mystified by this gesture of help. Just hours earlier, she was adamantly opposed to his plan, and now she seems to be acting as his accomplice. Has she rethought her position, he asks himself, or is she subtly mocking him in some way, testing him to find out if he is actually stupid enough to walk into the trap she feels he has set for himself? He suspects the latter interpretation is the correct one, but even so, he thanks her for reminding him of the date, and then, just as he is about to open the door and leave the tiny room, he rashly tells Margot that he loves her.

No you don't, she says, shaking her head and smiling. But I'm glad you think you do. You're a crazy boy, Adam, and every time I see you,

you're crazier than you were the last time. Before long, you'll be just as crazy as I am.

★ ★ ★

He walks into La Palette at twenty-five past four, almost half an hour late. He would not be surprised if Cécile has already left, storming out in a huff and vowing to rain down a thousand curses on him if he should ever cross her path again. But no, she is still there, sitting calmly at a table in the back room, reading a book, a half-finished bottle of Orangina in front of her, wearing glasses this time, and a fetching little dark blue hat that resembles a beret. Embarrassed, out of breath from running, his clothes disheveled, his body no doubt reeking of sex, and with the word *crazy* still resounding in his head, Walker approaches the table, already stammering a multitude of apologies as Cécile glances up at him and smiles — a wholly undeserved smile of forgiveness.

Still, even as he sits down in the chair across from her, Walker goes on apologizing, inventing some far-fetched excuse about standing in line at the post office for more than an hour to make a long-distance call to New York, but Cécile shrugs it off, telling him not to worry, there's no problem, he doesn't have to explain anything. Then, holding up her left wrist, she taps her watch with her right index finger and says: We have a rule in Paris. Whenever people arrange to get together, the first one to arrive gives the other person an extra half hour to show up — no questions asked. It's four twenty-five now. By my reckoning, that makes you five minutes early.

Well, Walker says, impressed by the daffiness of this logic, then I'm rattling on for nothing, aren't I?

That's what I've been trying to tell you.

Walker orders a coffee, his sixth or seventh of the day, and then, with a characteristic downward tug of her mouth, Cécile points to the book she was reading when he came in — a small green hardcover volume with no dust jacket, apparently quite old, a frayed and battered object that looks like something rescued from a trash bin.

I found it, she says, unable to control her mouth anymore as it breaks into a full-fledged smile. Lycophron in English. The Loeb Classical Library, published by Harvard University Press. Nineteen twenty-one. With a translation by — (she opens the book to the title page) — A. W. Mair, professor of Greek, Edinburgh University.

That was fast, Walker says. How in the world did you manage to find it?

Sorry. I can't tell you.

Oh? And why not?

It's a secret. Maybe I'll tell you when you give it back to me, but not before then.

You mean I can borrow it?

Of course. You can keep it for as long as you like.

And what about the translation? Have you looked at it?

My English isn't very good, but it strikes me

as stuffy and pedantic, rather old-school, I'm afraid. Worse yet, it's a literal prose translation, so all the poetry is missing. But at least it gives you a sense of the thing — and why it's given me so much trouble.

Cécile opens the book to the second page of the poem and points to line thirty-one, where Cassandra's monologue begins. She says to Walker: Why not read some of it out loud to me? Then you can judge for yourself.

Walker takes the book from her and immediately plunges in: Alas! hapless nurse of mine burnt even aforetime by the warlike pineships of the lion that was begotten in three evenings, whom of old Triton's hound of jagged teeth devoured with his jaws. But he, a living carver of the monster's liver, seething in steam of cauldron on a flameless hearth, shed to ground the bristles of his head; he the slayer of his children, the destroyer of my father-land; who smote his second mother invulnerable with grievous shaft upon the breast; who, too, in the midst of the racecourse seized in his arms the body of his wrestler sire beside the steep hill of Cronus, where is the horse-affrighting tomb of earth-born Ischenus; who also slew the fierce hound that watched the narrow straits of the Ausonian sea, fishing over her cave, the bull-slaying lioness whom her father restored again to life, burning her flesh with brands; she who feared not Leptynis, the goddess of the underworld . . .

Walker puts down the book and smiles. This is insane, he says. I'm absolutely lost.

216

Yes, it's a terrible translation, Cécile says. Even I can hear that.

It's not just the translation. I have no idea what's going on.

That's because Lycophron is so indirect. *Lycophron the obscure*. There's a reason why they called him that.

Still . . .

You have to know the references. The nurse is a woman named Ilios, for example, and the lion is Heracles. Laomedon promised to pay Poseidon and Apollo for building the walls of Troy, but after he reneged, a sea monster appeared — Triton's hound — to devour his daughter, Hesione. Heracles climbed into the monster's belly and cut it to bits. Laomedon said he would reward Heracles for killing the monster by giving him the horses of Tros, but again he broke his word, and the angry Heracles punished him by burning down the city of Troy. That's the background of the first few lines. If you don't know the references, you're bound to be lost.

It's like trying to translate *Finnegans Wake* into Mandarin.

I know. That's why I'm so sick of it. Summer vacation ends next week, but my summer project is already kaput.

You're giving up?

When I came home from dinner last night, I read over my translation again and dumped it in the garbage. It was dreadful, positively dreadful.

You shouldn't have done that. I was looking forward to reading it.

Too embarrassing.

But you promised. That's why we're sitting here now — because you were going to show me your translation.

That was the original idea, but then I changed the plan.

Changed it to what?

To giving you this book. At least I've accomplished something today.

I don't think I want it anymore. The book belongs to you. You should hold on to it, as a keepsake from your summer of struggle.

But I don't want it either. Just looking at it makes me ill.

What should we do with it, then?

I don't know. Give it to someone else.

We're in France, remember? What French person in his right mind would be interested in a bad English translation of an impenetrable Greek poem?

Good point. Why don't we just throw it away?

Too harsh. Books should be treated with respect, even the ones that make us ill.

Then we'll leave it behind. Right here on this bench. An anonymous gift to an unknown stranger.

Perfect. And once we pay the bill and walk out of this café, we'll never talk about Lycophron again.

★ ★ ★

So begins Walker's friendship with Cécile Juin. In many ways, he finds her a thoroughly impossible creature. She fidgets and trembles, she bites her nails, she doesn't smoke or drink, she is a militant vegetarian, she puts too many demands on herself (e.g., the destroyed translation), and at times she is shockingly immature (e.g., the silly business about not telling him where she found the book, her girlish fixation on *secrets*). On the other hand, she is without question one of the most brilliant people he has ever met. Her mind is a wondrous instrument, and she can think circles around him on any topic imaginable, dazzling him with her knowledge of literature and art, music and history, politics and science. Nor is she simply a memory machine, one of those prototypical top students with a capacity for ingesting vast amounts of unfiltered information. She is sensitive and acute, her opinions are unfailingly original, and, shy and nervous as she is, she stubbornly holds her ground in any argument. For six straight days, Walker meets her for lunch at the student cafeteria on the rue Mazet. They spend the afternoons together wandering in and out of bookstores, going to movies, visiting art galleries, sitting on benches along the Seine. He is relieved that he is not physically attracted to her, that he can confine his thoughts about sex to Margot (who spends one night with him in his hotel during this period) and to the absent Gwyn, who is never far from him. In a word, despite Cécile's maddening idiosyncrasies, he enjoys the company of her mind more than enough to forgo any thoughts about her body, and he gladly keeps his hands to himself.

Proceeding cautiously, he does not ask her any direct questions about Born. He wants to know what she thinks of him, wants to know how she feels about her mother's impending marriage to this *old family friend*, but there is ample time in front of him, the divorce will not go through until the spring, and he prefers to wait until their friendship has firmly taken root before delving into such private matters. Nevertheless, her silence is instructive, he believes, for if she were especially fond of Born, or if she were enthusiastic about the marriage, she would inevitably talk about those things every now and then, but Cécile says nothing, and therefore he concludes that she has misgivings about her mother's decision. Perhaps she looks on it as a betrayal of her father, he thinks, but that is far too delicate a subject for him to bring up with her, and until Cécile mentions it herself, he will continue to pretend he knows nothing about the man in the hospital, the all but dead father who will never wake again.

On the fifth day of their daily rambles, Cécile tells him that her mother would like to know if he is free to come to their apartment for dinner the following night, the last night before the new term at the lycée begins. Walker's first impulse is to decline the invitation, since he fears Born will be included in the company, but it turns out that Born is in London on family business (family business?) and that it will just be the three of them, Hélène, Cécile, and himself. Of course, he says, he will be happy to go to such a small dinner. Large gatherings make him uncomfortable, but a quiet evening with mother and daughter Juin sounds terrific. When he says the word *terrific* (*formidable*), Cécile's face lights up with an expression of blazing, untempered joy. In that instant, Walker suddenly understands that the invitation has not come from Hélène but from Cécile, that she has put her mother up to asking him to their apartment and in all likelihood has been badgering her about it for days. Until now, Cécile has been rather guarded in his presence, holding back from any spontaneous outbursts of emotion, and this look of joy spreading across her face is a deeply worrying sign. The last thing he wants is for her to start developing a crush on him.

They live on the rue de Verneuil in the seventh arrondissement, a street that runs parallel to the rue de l'Université, but unlike the palatial residence of Margot's family, the Juins' apartment is small and simply furnished, no doubt a reflection of Hélène's reduced financial circumstances following her husband's accident. But the place is extremely well cared for, Walker notices, everything is where it should be, immaculate, tidy, trim, from the spotless glass coffee table to the waxed and gleaming parquet floors, as if this will for order is an attempt to keep the chaos and unpredictability of the world at arm's length. Who can blame Hélène for such fanatical diligence? Walker thinks. She is trying to hold herself together. She is trying to hold both herself and Cécile together, and with the heavy burden she has to bear, who knows if this isn't why she is planning to divorce her husband and marry Born: to get out from under, to be able to breathe again?

With Born missing from the equation, Walker finds Hélène to be somewhat softer and more congenial than the woman he met at the restaurant several days ago. She is still reserved, still enveloped in an air of rectitude and propriety, but when she greets him at the door and shakes his hand, he is startled by how warmly she looks into his eyes, as if she is genuinely glad that he has turned up. Maybe he was wrong about Cécile having to twist her arm to get him invited to the house. When all is said and done, maybe it was Hélène who proposed the idea herself: What about this odd American boy you've been palling around with, Cécile? Why don't you ask him to dinner so I can learn something more about him?

Again, Cécile has chosen to dispense with her glasses for the evening, but contrary to what happened at the dinner in the restaurant, she is not squinting. Walker assumes that she has started wearing contact lenses, but he refrains from asking her about it on the off chance that such a question will embarrass her. She seems more quiet than usual, he thinks, more poised and in control of herself, but he can't tell if it's because she is making a conscious effort to act in a certain way or because she feels more inhibited with him in front of her mother. Course by course, the food is brought to the table: pâté with cornichons to start with, a pot-au-feu, an endive salad, three different cheeses, and crème caramel for dessert. Walker compliments Hélène on each dish, and while he honestly enjoys every morsel that enters his mouth, he knows that her cooking is not in the same league as Margot's. Innumerable matters of no importance are discussed. School and work, the weather, the differences between the subway systems in Paris and New York. The conversation brightens considerably when he and Cécile begin to talk about music, and when the meal is over he finally persuades her (after how many truculent refusals?) to play something for him, something for him and her mother. There is a small upright piano in the room — which serves as a combination living room-dining room — and as Cécile stands up from the table and begins walking toward the instrument, she asks: Anything in particular? Bach, he says, without hesitation. A two-part invention by Bach.

She plays well, she hits all the notes of the piece with dogged precision, her dynamics are steady, and if her phrasing is a bit mechanical, if she doesn't quite attain the fluency of a seasoned professional, who can fault her for being anything other than what she is? She is not a professional. She is an eighteen-year-old high school student who plays the piano for her own pleasure, and she renders the Bach efficiently, dexterously, and with much feeling. Walker remembers his own fumbling attempts to learn the piano when he was a boy and how disappointed he was to discover that he had no aptitude for it whatsoever. He therefore applauds Cécile's performance with great enthusiasm, praising her efforts and telling her how good he thinks she is. Not really good, she says, with that annoying modesty of hers. So-so. But even as she

223

denigrates herself, Walker can see her mouth tugging downward, see her struggling to suppress a smile, and he understands how much his compliments have meant to her.

A moment later, she excuses herself and marches off down the hall (no doubt to visit the bathroom), and for the first time all evening, Walker is alone with her mother. Since Hélène knows it will not be long before Cécile returns, she gets right to the point, not wanting to waste a second.

Be careful with her, Mr. Walker, she says. She's a complex, fragile person, and she has no experience with men.

I like Cécile very much, he says, but not in the way you seem to be suggesting. I enjoy being with her, that's all. As a friend.

Yes, I'm sure you like her. But you don't love her, and the problem is that she's fallen in love with you.

Has she told you that?

She doesn't have to tell me. All I have to do is look.

She can't be in love with me. I've only known her for a week.

A year, a week, what difference does it make? These things happen, and I don't want her to get hurt. Please be careful. I beg of you.

★ ★ ★

Dread has become fact. Innocence has turned into guilt, and hope is a word that rhymes with despair. In every part of Paris, people are jumping out of windows. The metro is flooded with human excrement. The dead are crawling from their graves. End of Act II. Curtain.

Act III. As Walker leaves the Juin apartment and staggers out into the chilly September night, there is no doubt in his mind that Hélène has told him the truth. He already suspected it himself, and now that these suspicions have been confirmed, he understands that he will have to come up with a new strategy. To begin with, there will be no more daily jaunts with Cécile. Fond as he has become of her, he must be careful (yes, Hélène was right), he must be very careful not to do anything that will hurt her. But what does careful mean? Cutting off relations with her strikes him as unnecessarily cruel, and yet if he goes on seeing her, would she not then interpret his continued interest in her as a sign of encouragement? There is no simple solution to this dilemma. For the fact is that he must see her, perhaps not as often as before, perhaps not for so many hours at a stretch, but he must see her because she is the person he has decided to unburden himself to, the one who is going to be told about the killing of Cedric Williams. Cécile will believe the story. If he goes to her mother instead, there is a good chance that Hélène will not. But if Cécile believes the story, then his chances with Hélène will improve, since it is more than likely that she will believe what her daughter tells her.

He calls Margot the next morning, hoping to distract himself from this muddle of uncertainties by spending some time with her — depending on her mood, of course, and

225

depending on whether she is free.

That's funny, Margot says. I was just about to pick up the phone and call your hotel.

I'm glad, Walker replies. That means we were thinking about each other at the same moment. Mental telepathy is the best indication of a strong bond between people.

You say the strangest things . . .

Do you want to tell me why you were going to call, or should I tell you why I called?

You first.

Very simple. I'm dying to see you.

I would love to get together, but I can't. That's why I wanted to talk to you.

Is something wrong?

No, not at all. I'm going away for a week and I wanted to let you know.

Away?

Yes, to London.

London?

Why do you keep repeating what I say?

I'm sorry. But someone else is in London, too.

Along with about ten million other people. Are you thinking of anyone in particular?

I thought maybe you knew.

What are you talking about?

Born. He went to London three days ago.

And why should I care about that?

You're not going to see him, are you?

Don't be ridiculous.

Because if you are going to see him, I don't think I could take it.

What's gotten into you? Of course I'm not going to see him.

Then why are you going?

Don't do this, Adam. You have no right to ask that question.

I thought I did.

I don't have to account for myself to anyone — least of all to you.

Sorry. I'm acting like an idiot, aren't I? The question is withdrawn.

If you must know, I'm going to see my sister. She's married to an Englishman and lives in Hampstead. Her little boy is turning three, and I'm invited to the birthday party. Also — just to complete the picture — my mother is traveling with me.

Can I see you before you go?

We're leaving for the airport in an hour.

Too bad. I'm going to miss you. Really, really miss you.

It's only eight days. Get a grip on yourself, little man. I'll be back before you know it.

★ ★ ★

After this dispiriting talk with Margot, he returns to his room at the hotel and mopes around for a few hours, unable to summon the energy to begin working at his desk, unable to concentrate on the book he is trying to read (Georges Perec's *Les Choses: Une Histoire des années soixante*), and before long he is thinking about Cécile again, remembering that today is her first day of school and that not far from where he is sitting she is in a classroom at the Lycée Fénelon, listening to one of her teachers expound on

Molière's prosody as she fiddles with her bag of newly sharpened pencils. He will avoid her for the time being, he says to himself, and when his own classes begin in eight days (the exact day of Margot's return), he will have a legitimate excuse for seeing her less often, and as the time they spend together diminishes, perhaps her infatuation with him will diminish as well.

For the next three days, he steadfastly adheres to this regimen of silence. He sees no one, talks to no one, and bit by bit he begins to feel somewhat stronger in his loneliness, as if the stringencies he has forced upon himself have ennobled him in some way, reacquainting him with the person he once imagined himself to be. He writes two short poems that might actually have something to them (*never nothing but the dream of nothing/never anything but the dream of all*), spends an entire afternoon setting down his thoughts about the resurrection scene in Dreyer's film, and composes a long, lushly rhapsodic letter to Gwyn about the vagaries of the Paris sky as seen through the windows of his room: *To live here is to become a connoisseur of clouds, a meteorologist of whims.* Then, early on the fourth day, just after he has woken up, as he is taking his first sips of the bitter instant coffee he prepares each morning with water boiled on the electric hot plate beside his bed, there is a knock on the door.

Still blurred, still dopey from the warmth of the bed, the tousled, undressed Walker slips into a pair of pants and heads for the door, tiptoeing gingerly on his bare feet, not wanting to pick up any splinters from the crumbling planks. Again he assumes it is Maurice, and again his assumption is wrong, but thinking that it must be Maurice, he doesn't bother to ask who is there.

Cécile is standing in front of him. She is tense, she is biting her lower lip, and she is trembling, as if small electric currents were passing through her body, as if she were about to rise up into the air and levitate.

Walker says: Aren't you supposed to be in school?

Don't worry about school, she answers, stepping across the threshold before he can invite her in. This is more important than school.

All right, it's more important than school. In what way?

You haven't called me since the night of the dinner. What's happened to you?

Nothing. I've been busy, that's all. And I figured you were busy, too. You just started your classes this week, and you must be drowning in homework. I wanted to give you a few days to settle in.

That's not it. That's not it at all. My mother talked to you, that's what happened. My stupid mother talked to you and scared you off. Well, just for your information, my mother doesn't know anything about me. I can take care of myself just fine, thank you.

Slow down, Cécile, Walker says, raising his right arm and thrusting it toward her with an open palm — the pose of a cop directing traffic. I woke up about three minutes ago, he continues, and I'm still trying to shake the cobwebs out of my head. Coffee. That's what I was doing. I was drinking coffee. You wouldn't want some, would you?

I don't like coffee. You know that.

Tea?

No thank you.

All right. No coffee, no tea. But please sit down. You're making me nervous.

He gestures to the chair behind the desk, then approaches the desk to pull out the chair for her, and as Cécile walks toward it, he retrieves his bowl of coffee and carries it over to the bed. He sits down on the sagging, U-shaped mattress at the same instant she sits down on the creaking chair. For some reason, he finds the effect comical. He takes a sip of the no longer hot coffee and smiles at her, hoping their simultaneous touchdown was as funny to her as it was to him, but nothing is funny to Cécile just now, and she does not smile back.

Your mother, he says. Yes, she talked to me. It happened when you left the room after playing the piano, and the conversation lasted for all of fifteen or twenty seconds. She talked and I listened, but she didn't scare me off.

No?

Of course not.

Are you sure?

Positively.

Then why have you disappeared?

I haven't disappeared. I was planning to call you on Saturday or Sunday.

For real?

Yes, for real. Stop it now. No more questions, all right? No more doubts. I'm your friend, and I want to stay your friend.

It's just —

Enough. I want to stay your friend, Cécile, but I can't do that unless you begin to trust me.

Trust you? What are you talking about? Of course I trust you.

Not really. We've spent a lot of time together lately, and in that time we've talked about all sorts of things — books and philosophers, art and music, films, politics, even shoes and hats — but you've never once opened up to me about yourself. You don't have to hide. I know what trouble is. I know what happens to families when things go wrong. The other day, when I told you about what happened to my brother, Andy, I thought that might get you talking, but you never said a word. I know about your father's accident, Cécile, I know about the hell you and your mother have been living in, I know about the divorce, I know about your mother's marriage plans. Why don't you ever mention these things to me? That's what friends are for. To share each other's pains, to help each other out.

It's too hard, she says, lowering her eyes and looking at her hands as she speaks. That's why I'm so happy when I'm with you. Because I don't have to think about those things, because I can forget how rotten and terrible the world is . . .

★ ★ ★

231

She is still talking, but he is no longer listening to her, no longer paying close attention because a sudden thought has taken hold of him, and he is wondering if this might not be the moment to tell her the story, the story of Born and Cedric Williams, the killing of Cedric Williams, the right moment because of the reassurances he has just given her, his declarations of friendship, which might make her receptive enough to listen to him in a state of relative calm, to absorb the brutal account of what Born did to that boy without causing irreparable damage to her, this *fragile person*, as her mother put it, this trembling, nail-biting person, the vulnerable Cécile who nevertheless spent the summer translating a poem of such excessive violence, such nightmarish horror, that he himself was shocked by Cassandra's howling monologue about ripping apart she-dog monsters and burning down cities and slaughtering one's own children, and yet all that is in the realm of myth, imaginary violence from long ago, whereas Born is a real person, a living, breathing person whom she has known all her life, the man who intends to marry her mother, and whether she is for or against that marriage, what will it do to her when she learns what this man is capable of, when he tells her about the murderous attack he witnessed with his own eyes, and even as he thinks that now is the time to talk to her about that night in New York last spring, he hesitates, he cannot bring himself to do it, he mustn't do it, he will not do it, and come what may he will not enlist Cécile as an intermediary to carry the news to her mother, he will go directly to Hélène himself, that is the proper solution, the only decent solution, and even if he fails to win her over, he must not and will not involve Cécile in this ugly business.

Is everything all right, Adam?

The spell is finally broken. Walker looks up, nods his head, and gives her a brief, apologetic smile. I'm sorry, he says. I was thinking about something.

Something important?

No, not at all. I was remembering the dream I had last night. You know how it is when you wake up. Your body springs into action, but your mind is still in bed.

You're not angry with me for coming here, are you?

Not in the least. I'm glad you came.

You do like me a little bit, don't you?

What kind of question is that?

Do you think I'm ugly or repulsive?

Don't be absurd.

I know I'm not pretty, but I'm not too disgusting to look at, am I?

You have a lovely face, Cécile. A delicate face with beautiful, intelligent eyes.

Then why don't you ever touch me or try to kiss me?

What?

You heard what I said.

Why? I don't know. Because I haven't wanted to take advantage of you, I suppose.

You think I'm a virgin, don't you?

To tell you the truth, I haven't thought about

it one way or the other.

Well, I'm not. Just so you know. I'm not a virgin anymore, and I never will be again.

Congratulations.

It happened last month in Brittany. The boy's name was Jean-Marc, and we did it three times. He's a good person, Jean-Marc, but I'm not in love with him. Do you understand what I'm saying?

I think so.

And?

You have to give me time.

What does that mean?

It means that I'm deeply in love with someone in New York. She broke up with me just before I left for Paris, and I'm still suffering, still trying to regain my balance. I'm not ready for anything new right now.

I understand.

Good. That makes things a lot simpler.

Not simpler — more complicated. But that won't change anything in the end.

Oh?

Once you get to know me better, you'll see that I have one very special quality, something that sets me apart from everyone else.

And what quality is that?

Patience, Adam. I'm the most patient person in the world.

★ ★ ★

It has to be a Saturday, he decides. Hélène is off from work, Cécile has a half day of school, and

234

therefore Saturday is the only day of the week when he can go to the Juin apartment with the certainty that he will be alone with Hélène. And he wants to act now, to talk to her while Born is still in London, since that is the only way he can eliminate the risk of having Born walk in on them in the middle of their conversation. He calls Hélène at the clinic. He says he has something important to discuss with her about Cécile. No, nothing catastrophic, he replies, in fact quite the opposite, but he needs to talk to her, and it would be best for all concerned if they can meet at a time when Cécile will not be present. It is Hélène herself who suggests that he come to the apartment on Saturday morning. Cécile will be at the lycée then, and if he shows up at around nine o'clock, they will be able to finish their talk before Cécile comes home. What does he prefer? she asks. Coffee or tea? Croissants, brioches, or tartines beurrées? Coffee and tartines, he says. Yogurt? Yes, yogurt would be very nice. It's settled, then. He will come for breakfast on Saturday morning. Hélène's voice on the phone is so accommodating, so full of kindness and playful complicity that Walker has no choice but to revise his opinion of her after they hang up. She is awkward with strangers, perhaps, but once she gets to know someone a little bit, she relaxes her guard and begins to show her true colors. Those colors have become more and more attractive to him. Hélène clearly likes him, and the fact of the matter is, he likes her too. All the more motivation to remove Born from the premises as quickly as possible. If it can

235

be done. If he has the wherewithal to make her believe him.

The rue de Verneuil, Saturday morning. For the first half hour, Walker concentrates on Cécile, doing what he can to put Hélène's mind at rest about her daughter's feelings for him and prove that the situation is not as dire as she thought it was. He tells her about his conversation with Cécile on Thursday (neglecting to mention that it took place in the morning, when she was supposed to have been at school) and says that everything is out in the open now. Cécile knows that he is unavailable to her, that he has just been through a shattering breakup with someone in New York and is in no condition to begin a romance with her or anyone else.

Is that true, Hélène asks, or were you just making it up to protect her?

I wasn't making it up, Walker says.

Poor boy. You must be having a hard time of it.

I am. But that doesn't mean I don't deserve to.

Ignoring this cryptic remark, Hélène pushes on: And what did she say when you told her about your . . . situation?

She said she understood.

That's all? She didn't make a scene?

No scene. She was very calm.

I'm surprised. That isn't like her.

I know she's high-strung, Madame Juin, I know she isn't terribly stable, but she's also a remarkable person, and my feeling is that she's a lot stronger than you think she is.

236

That's a matter of opinion, of course, but let's hope you're right.

Also, and this will interest you, you were wrong when you told me she has no experience with men.

Well, well. And where did she acquire this experience?

I've already said enough. If you want to know, you'll have to ask Cécile herself. I'm not a spy, after all.

How tactless of me. You're absolutely right. Forgive me for asking the question.

My only point is that Cécile is growing up, and maybe it's time to let her go. You don't have to worry about her so much anymore.

It's impossible not to worry about that girl. That's my job, Adam. I worry about Cécile. I've been worrying about her all her life.

★ ★ ★

[After the word *life*, there is a break in Walker's manuscript, and the conversation abruptly comes to an end. Until this point, the notes have been continuous, an uninterrupted march of densely packed, single-spaced paragraphs, but now there is a blank that covers approximately a quarter of a page, and when the text resumes below this white rectangle, the tone of the writing is different. There isn't much left to tell (we are on page 28 by now, which means there are just three pages to go), but Walker abandons the meticulous, step-by-step approach he has taken so far and rapidly summarizes the final events of the narrative. I can only assume that he was in the middle of the conversation with Hélène when he stopped writing for the day, and when he woke up the next morning (if he slept at all), his condition had taken a turn for the worse. These were the last days of his life, remember, and he must have felt too ravaged, too depleted, too frail to go on as before. Even earlier, over the course of the first twenty-eight pages, I had noticed a slow but ineluctable dwindling of strength, a loss of attention to detail, but now he is too incapacitated to put in anything but the bedrock essentials. He begins *Fall* with a fairly elaborate description of the Hôtel du Sud, he mentions what Born is wearing during their first encounter at the café, but little by little his descriptions begin to have less to do with the physical world than with inner states. He stops talking about clothes (Margot, Cécile, Hélène — not one word about how they are dressed), and only when it seems crucial to his purpose does he bother to depict his surroundings (a few sentences about the atmosphere in Vagenende, a few sentences about the Juin apartment), but mostly the story consists of thought and dialogue, what people are thinking and what people are saying. By the last three pages, the collapse is nearly total. Walker is vanishing from the world, he can feel the life ebbing out of his body, and yet he forges on as best he can, sitting down at his computer one last time to bring the story to an end.]

★ ★ ★

H. and W. at the kitchen table. Coffee, bread and butter, a pot of yogurt. There is little left to talk about concerning C. Before it is too late, he must push H. in a new direction, get her to start talking about her husband, about Born. Must confirm that facts are correct before diving in. Born mentioned the marriage to him last spring, M. has echoed this with added information about the divorce, C. has not contradicted this, but H. has yet to broach the subject with him. How to proceed? He begins by mentioning *Rudolf*, describes their meeting in New York back in April, never hints they are anything to each other but warm friends, then tells about Born's return from Paris in May and how excited he was when he announced that he was *marrying her*. Is it true? H. nods. Yes, it's true. Then she says it is the most wrenching decision she has ever made. In a flood, she begins to talk about her husband, to tell him about the car accident in the Pyrenees, the hairpin turn and the crash down the side of the mountain, the hospital, the anguish of the past six and a half years, the devastation wrought on C. — a flood of words, and then a flood of tears. W. barely has the heart to go on. The tears abate. She is embarrassed, apologetic. How strange that she should be confiding in him, she says, a young boy from New York scarcely older than her daughter, a person she scarcely knows. But Rudolf thinks the world of you, and you've been so kind to C. — maybe that's the reason.

He is ready to abandon the whole business. Keep your mouth shut, he says to himself, leave

239

the poor woman alone. But he can't. His anger is simply too great, and so he jumps off the cliff and begins talking about Cedric Williams and Riverside Drive — regretting it, hating himself with every word he speaks, but unable to stop. H. listens in stunned silence. His words are a sharpened axe, and he is chopping off her head, he is killing her.

There is no question that she believes him. He can see from the way she looks at him that she knows he is telling the truth. But it makes no difference. He is demolishing her life, and she has no alternative but to defend herself. How dare you make these hideous accusations — with no proof, with nothing to support what you're saying?

I was there, he says. The proof is in my eyes, in what I saw.

But she will not accept this. Rudolf is a distinguished professor, an intellectual, a man from one of the finest families, etc. He is her friend, he has rescued her from years of misery, he is like no other man in the world.

Hard face. No more tears, no more self-pity. Furious in her self-righteousness.

W. stands up to go. There is nothing more to say to her. Only this, which he delivers just before he walks out of the apartment: I thought it was my duty to tell you. Step back from it for a moment, and you'll understand that I have no possible reason to lie to you. I want you and Cécile to be happy — that's all — and I think you're about to make a terrible mistake. If you don't believe me, then do yourself a favor and ask Rudolf why he carries around a switchblade in his pocket.

★ ★ ★

Sunday morning. A knock on the door. The bleary-eyed, unshaven Maurice, still recovering from his Saturday night binge. A telephone call for you, *jeune homme.*

W. walks downstairs to the reception desk and picks up the phone. Born's voice says to him: I hear you've been saying bad things about me, Walker. I thought we had an understanding, and now you turn around and stab me in the back. Just like a Jew. Just like the stinking Jew you are, with your bogus Anglo-Saxon name and your filthy little mouth. There are laws against this kind of thing, you know. Slander, defamation of character, spreading lies about people. Why don't you go home? Pack up and leave Paris. Quit the program and get out of here. If you stay around, you'll regret it, Walker, I promise you. Your ass will be so cooked, you won't be able to sit down again for the rest of your life.

★ ★ ★

Monday afternoon. He parks himself in front of the Lycée Fénelon, waiting for Cécile to emerge from the building. When she finally comes out, encircled by a throng of other students, she looks him in the eye and turns her head away. She begins walking toward the rue Saint-André des Arts. W. runs to catch up with her. He grabs her

241

by the elbow, but she shrugs him off. He grabs her again, forcing her to stop. What's wrong? he says. Why won't you talk to me?

How could you? she answers, barking at him in a loud, strident voice. Saying all those *monstrous things* to my mother. You're sick, Adam. You're no good. Your tongue should be ripped out of your mouth.

He tries to calm her down, to make her listen to him.

I never want to see you again.

He makes one last effort to reason with her.

She begins to cry. Then she spits in his face and walks off.

★ ★ ★

Monday night. The voluminous, gum-chewing whore on the rue Saint-Denis. It is his first experience with a prostitute. The room smells of insecticide, sweat, and traces of vomit.

★ ★ ★

Tuesday. He spends the entire day walking through Paris. He sees a priest playing cricket with a gang of schoolboys in the Luxembourg Gardens. He gives ten francs to a clochard on the rue Monge. The late-September sky darkens around him, turning from metallic blue to the deepest shade of indigo. He has run out of ideas.

★ ★ ★

Tuesday night. At 3 A.M., a loud noise just outside his room. He is fast asleep, exhausted from his marathon trek through the city. Someone is knocking. No, not someone, several someones. An army of fists is pounding on his door.

Two policemen in uniform, young French gendarmes with guns in their holsters and sticks in their hands. An older man in a business suit. Befuddled Maurice lurking at the door. They ask if his name is Adam Walker — *Valk-air*. They ask for his papers, meaning his American passport, and when he gives it to one of the gendarmes, it is not returned to him. Then the older man instructs the other gendarme to search the armoire. The bottom drawer is opened, and out comes a large brick wrapped in aluminum foil. The younger man gives it to the older man, who begins peeling back the foil. Hashish, he says. A good two and a half kilos, maybe three.

The exquisite irony of Born's retaliation. The boy who never took drugs is charged with possession of drugs.

They take him away. In the backseat of the car, W. tells the older man that he is innocent, that someone planted the drugs in his room while he was out walking. The man tells him to shut up.

They lead him into a building, put him in a room, and lock the door. He has no idea where he is. All he knows is that he is sitting in a small, empty room somewhere in Paris and that handcuffs have been placed around his wrists. Has he been arrested? He isn't sure. No one said

243

a word to him, but he finds it odd that he hasn't been photographed and fingerprinted, that he is sitting in this small, empty room and not in the lockup cell of some prison.

He sits there for close to seven hours. At ten-thirty, he is taken from the building and driven to the Palais de Justice. The handcuffs are removed from his wrists. He goes into an office and talks to a man who claims to be the *juge d'instruction*. It could be that the man is who he says he is, but W. suspects not. He is growing more and more convinced that he is in a farce directed by Rudolf Born, and *all the men and women are merely players*.

The examining magistrate, assuming he is the examining magistrate, tells W. that he is a lucky young man. Possession of such a large quantity of illicit drugs is a serious crime in France, punishable by X many years in prison. Fortunately for W., a man with considerable influence in government circles has interceded on his behalf, arguing for clemency in light of the accused's heretofore unblemished record. The Ministry of Justice is therefore prepared to strike a bargain with W. They will drop the charges if he agrees to deportation. He will never be allowed to enter France again, but he will be a free man in his own country.

The *juge d'instruction* opens the top drawer of his desk and takes out W.'s passport (which he holds up in his right hand) and an airline ticket (which he holds up in his left). This is a one-time offer, he says. Take it or leave it.

W. will take it.

244

Good, the man says. A wise decision. The plane leaves this afternoon at three. That will give you just enough time to return to your hotel and pack. An officer will accompany you, of course, but once the plane takes off and leaves French soil, the affair will be closed. We earnestly hope that this is the last we'll ever see of you. Have a pleasant journey, Mr. Walker.

★ ★ ★

And so ends W.'s brief sojourn in the land of Gaul — expelled, humiliated, banned for life.

★ ★ ★

He will never go back there, and he will never see any of them again.

★ ★ ★

Good-bye, Margot. Good-bye, Cécile. Good-bye, Hélène.

★ ★ ★

Forty years later, they are no more substantial than ghosts.

★ ★ ★

They are all ghosts now, and W. will soon be walking among them.

IV

Riding back on the plane from San Francisco to New York, I searched my memory for the exact moment when I had first spotted Walker in the fall of 1967. I hadn't known that he had gone off to study in Paris for the year, but a few days into the semester, when we held our first editorial meeting of the *Columbia Review* (Adam and I were both on the board), I noticed that he wasn't there. What happened to Walker? I asked someone, and that was when I learned he was in Europe, enrolled in the Junior Year Abroad Program. Not long after that (a week? ten days?), he suddenly appeared again. I was taking Edward Tayler's seminar on sixteenth- and seventeenth-century poetry (Wyatt, Surrey, Raleigh, Greville, Herbert, Donne), the same Edward Tayler who had taught Milton back in the spring. Walker and I had been in that class together, and we were both of the opinion that Tayler was hands down the best professor in the English Department. Since the seminar was primarily for graduate students, I felt lucky to have been admitted as a third-year undergraduate, and I worked my head off for the sly, ironical, tight-lipped, ever-brilliant Tayler, wanting to earn the respect of this demanding, much-admired person. The seminar met twice a week for an hour and a half, and at the third or fourth session, with no explanation from anyone, there was Walker again, unexpectedly among us, the thirteenth member of a class officially limited to twelve.

We talked in the hall afterward, but Adam seemed distracted, unwilling to say much about his precipitous return to New York (I now know why). He mentioned that the program in Paris had been a disappointment to him, that the courses he was allowed to take had not been interesting enough (all grammar, no literature), and rather than waste a year in the sub-basement of the French educational bureaucracy, he had opted to come back. Quitting the program on such short notice had caused some upheavals, but Columbia had acted with unusual kindness, he felt, and even though classes had already begun when he bolted from Paris, a long talk with one of the deans had settled the matter, and he had been reinstated as a full-time student in good standing — which meant that he didn't have to worry about the draft, at least not for another four semesters. The only problem was that he had no permanent place to live. He had shared his old apartment with his sister in July and August, but after he left for what he had thought would be a full year, she had found another roommate, and now he was out in the cold. For the time being, he was crashing with different friends in the neighborhood while he hunted for a new apartment of his own. In fact, he said, glancing down at his watch, he had an appointment in twenty minutes to look at a small studio that had just opened up on 109th Street, and he had to be off. See you later, he said, and then he began running toward the stairs.

I knew that Adam had a sister, but this was the first I'd heard about her being in New York — a resident of Morningside Heights, no less, and doing graduate work in English at Columbia. Two weeks later, I caught my first sight of her on campus. She was walking past Rodin's statue of the thinker on her way into Philosophy Hall, and because of the strong, almost eerie resemblance to her brother, I felt certain that the young woman flitting past me was Walker's sister. I have already mentioned how beautiful she was, but saying that doesn't do justice to the overwhelming impact she had on me. Gwyn was ablaze with beauty, an incandescent being, a storm in the heart of every man who laid eyes on her, and seeing her for the first time ranks as one of the most astonishing moments of my life. I wanted her — from the first second I wanted her — and, with the passionate obstinacy of a daydreaming fool, I went after her.

Nothing ever happened. I got to know her a little bit, we met for coffee a couple of times, I asked her out to the movies (she turned me down), I invited her to a concert (she turned me down), and then, accidentally, we both wound up at a large Chinese dinner one night and discussed the poems of Emily Dickinson for half an hour. A short time after that, I persuaded her to go for a walk with me in Riverside Park, tried to kiss her, and was pushed away. Don't, Jim, she said. I'm involved with someone else. I can't do this.

That was the end of it. Several swings of the

bat, failure to make contact on any pitch, and the game was over. The world fell apart, the world put itself together again, and I muddled on. To my great good fortune, I have been with the same woman for close to thirty years now. I can't imagine my life without her, and yet every time Gwyn enters my thoughts, I confess that I still feel a little pang. She was the impossible one, the unattainable one, the one who was never there — a specter from the Land of If.

An invisible America lay silent in the darkness beneath me. As I sat on the jet from San Francisco to New York, revisiting the bad old days of 1967, I realized that I would have to write her a condolence letter first thing the next morning.

★ ★ ★

It turned out that Gwyn had already been in touch. When I walked through the door of my house in Brooklyn, my wife gave me a warm, fervent hug (I had called from San Francisco, she knew Adam was dead), and then she told me that earlier in the day a message had been left for me on the answering machine by someone named Gwyn Tedesco.

Is that the Gwyn I think it is? she asked.

I called her at ten o'clock the next morning. I had wanted to write a letter, to express my feelings on paper, to give her something more than the empty platitudes we sputter forth at such times, but her message had sounded urgent, there was an important matter she needed to discuss with me, and so I called her back and never wrote the letter.

Her voice was the same, remarkably the same as the one that had mesmerized me forty years ago. A lilting gravity, crystal enunciation, the barest residue of the mid-Atlantic accent of her childhood. The voice was the same, but Gwyn herself was no longer the same, and as the conversation continued, I began projecting various pictures of her in my head, wondering how well or badly her beautiful face had fared over the course of time. She was sixty-one years old now, and it suddenly occurred to me that I had no desire to see her again. It could only lead to disappointment, and I didn't want my hazy memories of the past to be blown apart by the hard facts of the present.

We exchanged the customary platitudes, rambling on for several minutes about Adam and his death, about how difficult it was for her to accept what had happened, about the rough blows life deals us. Then we caught up on the past for a little while, talking about our marriages, our children, and our work — a comfortable back-and-forth, very friendly on both sides, so much so that I even found the nerve to ask her if she remembered the day in Riverside Park when I tried to kiss her. Of course she remembered, she said, laughing for the first time, but how was she to know that scrawny Jim the college boy would grow up to become James Freeman? I never grew up, I said. And I'm still just Jim. Not so scrawny anymore, but still just Jim.

Yes, it was all quite amiable, and even though we had vanished from each other's lives decades earlier, Gwyn talked as if little or no time had elapsed, as if those decades amounted to nothing more than a month or two. The familiarity of her tone lulled me into a kind of drowsy openness, and because my defenses were down, when she finally got to the business at hand, that is, when she finally explained why she had called me, I made a terrible blunder. I told her the truth when I should have lied.

Adam sent me an e-mail, she said, a long e-mail written a few days before he . . . just a few days before the end. It was a beautiful letter, a farewell letter I now realize, and in one of the paragraphs toward the bottom he mentioned that he was writing something, a book of some kind, and if I wanted to read it, I should contact you. But only after he was dead. He was very insistent about that. Only after he was dead. He also warned me that I might find the manuscript extremely upsetting. He apologized for that in advance, asking me to forgive him if the book hurt me in any way, and then he said no, I shouldn't bother to read it, I should forget the whole thing. It was terribly confusing. In the very next sentence, he changed his mind again and told me to go ahead if I wanted to, that I had a right to see it, and if I did want to see it, I should contact you, since you had the only copy. I didn't understand that part. If he wrote the book on a computer, wouldn't he have saved it on his hard drive?

He told Rebecca to delete it, I said. It's gone

254

from the computer now, and the only copy is the one he printed out and sent to me.

So the book really exists.

Sort of. He meant to write it in three chapters. The first two are in fairly good shape, but he didn't manage to finish the third. Just some notes for it, a hastily written outline.

Did he want you to help him get it published?

He never talked about publishing, not directly in any case. All he wanted was for me to read the manuscript, and then it would be up to me to decide what to do with it.

Have you decided?

No. To tell you the truth, I haven't even thought about it. Until you mentioned publishing just now, the idea had never crossed my mind.

I think I should have a look at it, don't you?

I'm not sure. It's your call, Gwyn. If you want to see it, I'll make a copy and FedEx it to you today.

Will I be upset?

Probably.

Probably?

Not by all of it, but one or two things might upset you, yes.

One or two things. Oh dear.

Don't worry. As of this moment, I'm putting the decision in your hands. Not a word of Adam's book will ever be published without your approval.

Send it, Jim. Send it today. I'm a big girl now, and I know how to swallow my medicine.

★ ★ ★

How simple it would have been to cover my tracks and deny the existence of the book, or tell her that I had lost it somewhere, or claim that Adam had promised to send it to me but never did. The subject had caught me by surprise, and I couldn't think fast enough to start spinning out a fake story. Even worse, I had told Gwyn there were three chapters. Only the second one had the potential to wound her (along with a couple of remarks in the third, which I easily could have crossed out), and if I had said that Adam had written only two chapters, *Spring* and *Fall*, she would have been spared from having to go back to the apartment on West 107th Street and relive the events of that summer. But she was expecting three chapters now, and if I sent her only two, she would call right back and ask for the missing pages. So I photocopied everything I had — *Spring, Summer,* and the notes for *Fall* — and shipped them off to her address in Boston that afternoon. It was a rotten thing to do to her, but by then I no longer had a choice. She wanted to read her brother's book, and the only copy in the world belonged to me.

She called two days later. I don't know what I was expecting from her, but I had taken it for granted somehow that intense emotions would be involved — angry tears, threats, shame that her secret had been exposed — but Gwyn was unnaturally subdued, more numb than insulted, I think, as if the book had clobbered her into a state of puzzled disbelief.

I don't understand, she said. Most of it is so accurate, so exactly right, and then there are all those things he made up. It doesn't make any sense.

What things? I asked, knowing full well what she was referring to.

I loved my brother, Jim. When I was young, he was closer to me than anyone else. But I never slept with him. There was no grand experiment when we were kids. There was no incestuous affair in the summer of 1967. Yes, we lived together in that apartment for two months, but we had separate bedrooms, and there was never any sex. What Adam wrote was pure make-believe.

It's probably not my place to ask, but why would he do such a thing? Especially if the other parts of the story are true.

I don't know that they're true. At least I can't verify that they're true. But all those other things tally with what Adam told me back then, forty years ago. I never met Born or Margot or Cécile or Hélène. I wasn't with Adam in New York that spring. I wasn't with him in Paris that fall. But he did talk to me about those people, and everything he said about them in 1967 matches up with what he says about them in the book.

All the odder, then, that he should make up those things about you.

I know you don't believe me. I know you think I'm trying to protect myself, that I don't want to admit those things could have happened between us. But it wasn't like that, I promise. I've been thinking about it for the past twenty-four hours, and the only answer I've come up with is that those pages are a dying man's fantasy, a dream

257

of what he wished had happened but never did.

Wished?

Yes, wished. I'm not denying those feelings were in the air, but I had no interest in acting on them. Adam was too attached to me, Jim. It was an unhealthy attachment, and after we'd been living together for a while that summer, he started telling me that I'd spoiled him for other women, that I was the only woman he could ever love, and that if we weren't brother and sister, he would marry me in a second. Sort of joking, of course, but I didn't like it. To be perfectly honest, I was relieved when he went to Paris.

Interesting.

And then, as we both know, less than a month later he was back — booted out in disgrace, as he put it to me at the time. But I had another roommate by then, and Adam had to look for a new apartment of his own. We were still friends, still the best of friends, but I started to put a little distance between us, to back away from him for his own good. You saw a fair amount of him during your last two years of college, but how often did you see him with me?

I'm trying to remember . . . Not a lot. No more than a couple of times.

I rest my case.

So what happens to his book now? Do we put it in a drawer and forget about it?

Not necessarily. In its present form, the book is unpublishable. Not only is it untrue — at least partly untrue — but if those untrue pages ever found their way into the world, they would create misery and disaster for untold numbers of people. I'm a married woman, Jim. I have two daughters and three grandchildren, dozens of relatives, hundreds of friends, a stepniece I'm very fond of, and it would be a crime to publish the book as it stands now. Agreed?

Yes, yes. You won't get an argument from me.

On the other hand, I was deeply moved by the book. It brought my brother back to me in ways I hadn't expected, in ways that utterly surprised me, and if we can transform it into something publishable, I would give the project my blessing.

I'm a little lost. How do you make an unpublishable book publishable?

That's where you come into it. If you're not interested in helping, we'll drop the matter now and never talk about it again. But if you do want to help, then this is what I propose. You take the notes for the third part and put them into decent shape. That shouldn't be too hard for you. I could never do it myself, but you're the writer, you'll know how to handle it. Then, most important, you go through the manuscript and change all the names. Remember that old TV show from the fifties? *The names have been changed to protect the innocent.* You change the names of the people and the places, you add or subtract any material you see fit, and then you publish the book under your own name.

But then it wouldn't be Adam's book anymore. It feels dishonest somehow. Like stealing . . . like some weird form of plagiarism.

Not if you frame it correctly. If you give credit to Adam for the passages he wrote — to the real

Adam under the false name you'll invent for him
— then you won't be stealing from him, you'll be
honoring him.

But no one will know it's Adam.

Does it matter? You and I will know, and as far
as I'm concerned, we're the only ones who
count.

You're forgetting my wife.

You trust her, don't you?

Of course I trust her.

Then the three of us will know.

I'm not sure, Gwyn. I need to think about it.
Give me a little time, okay?

Take all the time you need. There's no rush.

★ ★ ★

Her story was convincingly told, more than
plausible, I felt, and for her sake I wanted to
believe it. But I couldn't, at least not entirely, at
least not with a strong doubt that the text of
Summer was a story of lived experience and not
some salacious dream of a sick and dying man.
To satisfy my curiosity, I took a day off from the
novel I was writing and went up to the Columbia
campus, where I learned from an administrator
at the School of International Affairs that Rudolf
Born had been employed as a visiting professor
during the 1966–67 academic year, and then,
after a session in the microfilm room of Butler
Library, the same Castle of Yawns where Walker
had worked over the summer, that the corpse of
eighteen-year-old Cedric Williams had been
discovered one May morning in Riverside Park

with more than a dozen knife wounds in his chest and upper body. These *other things*, as Gwyn had called them, had been accurately reported in Walker's manuscript, and if these other things were true, why would he have gone to the trouble of fabricating something that wasn't true, damning himself with a highly detailed, self-incriminating account of incestuous love? It's possible that Gwyn's version of those two summer months was correct, but it's also possible that she lied to me. And if she lied, who can blame her for not wanting the facts to be dragged out into the open? Anyone would lie in her situation, everyone would lie, lying would be the only alternative. As I rode back to Brooklyn on the subway, I decided that it didn't matter to me. It mattered to her, but not to me.

Several months went by, and in that time I scarcely thought about Gwyn's proposal. I was hard at work on my book, entering the last stages of a novel that had already consumed several years of my life, and Walker and his sister began to recede, to melt away, turning into two dim figures on the far horizon of consciousness. Whenever Adam's book happened to make an appearance in my mind, I was fairly certain that I didn't want to get involved with it, that the episode was finished. Then, two things happened that led me to reverse my thinking. I came to the end of my own book, which meant that I was free to turn my attention to other things, and I stumbled upon some new information connected to Walker's story, a coda, as it were, a last little chapter that gave the project new meaning for me — and with that meaning an impetus to begin.

I have already described how I revamped Walker's notes for *Fall*. As for the names, they have been invented according to Gwyn's instructions, and the reader can therefore be assured that Adam Walker is not Adam Walker. Gwyn Walker Tedesco is not Gwyn Walker Tedesco. Margot Jouffroy is not Margot Jouffroy. Hélène and Cécile Juin are not Hélène and Cécile Juin. Cedric Williams is not Cedric Williams. Sandra Williams is not Sandra Williams, and her daughter, Rebecca, is not Rebecca. Not even Born is Born. His real name was close to that of another Provençal poet, and I took the liberty to substitute the translation of that other poet by not-Walker with a translation of my own, which means that the remarks about Dante's *Inferno* on the first page of this book were not in not-Walker's original manuscript. Last of all, I don't suppose it is necessary for me to add that my name is not Jim.

Westfield, New Jersey, is not Westfield, New Jersey. Echo Lake is not Echo Lake. Oakland, California, is not Oakland, California. Boston is not Boston, and although not-Gwyn works in publishing, she is not the director of a university press. New York is not New York, Columbia University is not Columbia University, but Paris is Paris. Paris alone is real. I managed to keep it in because the Hôtel du Sud vanished long ago, and all recorded evidence of not-Walker's stay there in 1967 has long since vanished as well.

★ ★ ★

I finished my novel late last summer (2007). Soon after that, my wife and I began organizing a trip to Paris (her sister's daughter was marrying a Frenchman in October), and the talk about Paris got me thinking about Walker again. I wondered if I could track down some of the players from the unsuccessful revenge drama he mounted there forty years ago, and if I could, whether any of them would be willing to talk to me. Born was of particular interest, but I would have been glad to sit down with any of the others I managed to find — Margot, Hélène, or Cécile. I had no luck with the first three, but when I googled Cécile Juin on the Internet, abundant amounts of information came flying up onto the screen. After my encounter with the eighteen-year-old girl in Walker's manuscript, I wasn't surprised to learn that she had grown up to be a literary scholar. She had taught at universities in Lyon and Paris, and for the past ten years she had been attached to the CNRS (the National Center for Scientific Research) as part of a small team investigating the manuscripts of eighteenth- and nineteenth-century French writers. Her specialty was Balzac, about whom she had published two books, but numerous other papers and articles were mentioned as well, a whole catalogue of work spanning three decades. Good for her, I thought. And good for me, too, since I was now in a position to write to her.

We exchanged two short letters. In mine, I introduced myself as a friend of Walker's, told

263

her the news of Adam's recent death, and asked if it would be possible for us to get together during my upcoming visit to Paris. It was short and to the point, with no questions about her mother's marriage to Born, nothing about Walker's notes for *Fall*, simply a request to meet her in October. She wrote back promptly. In my translation from the French, her letter read as follows:

I am devastated to learn of Adam's death. I knew him briefly when I was a young girl in Paris many years ago, but I have never forgotten him. He was the first love of my life, and then I did him an ugly turn, a thing so cruel and unforgivable that it has been weighing on my conscience ever since. I sent him a letter of apology after he returned to New York, but the letter came back to me, marked *Addressee Unknown*.

Yes, I will be happy to see you when you come to Paris next month. Please be warned, however. I am a silly old woman, and my emotions tend to run away from me. If we talk about Adam (which I assume we will), there's a good chance that I will break down and start crying. You mustn't take it personally.

Fifty-eight wasn't old, of course, and I doubted there was anything about Cécile Juin that could be described as silly. The woman's sense of humor was apparently intact, then, and successful as she was in her narrow world of

264

academic research, she must have understood how peculiar a life she had chosen for herself: sequestered in the small rooms of libraries and underground vaults, poring over the manuscripts of the dead, a career spent in a soundless domain of dust. In a P.S. to her letter, she revealed how sardonically she looked upon her work. She recognized my name, she said, and if I was the James Freeman she thought I was, she wondered if I would be willing to participate in a survey she and her staff were conducting on the composition methods of contemporary writers. Computer or typewriter, pencil or pen, notebook or loose sheets of paper, how many drafts to finish a book. Yes, I know, she added, very dull stuff. But that's our job at the CNRS: to make the world as dull as possible.

There was self-mockery in her letter, but there was also anguish, and I was somewhat startled by how vividly she remembered Walker. She had known him for only a couple of weeks in the distant days of her girlhood, and yet their friendship must have opened up something in her that altered her perception of herself, that thrust her for the first time into a direct confrontation with the depths of her own heart. *I have never forgotten him. He was the first love of my life.* I hadn't been prepared for such a forthright confession. Walker's notes had dealt with the problem of her growing crush on him, but her feelings turned out to have been even more intense than he had imagined. And then she spat in his face. At the time, she must have felt her anger was justified. He had slandered

Born, he had upset her mother, and Cécile had felt betrayed. But then, not long after that, she had written him a letter of apology. Did that mean she had rethought her position? Had something happened to make her believe Walker's accusations were true? It was the first question I was intending to ask her.

My wife and I booked a room at the Hôtel d'Aubusson on the rue Dauphine. We had stayed there before, had stayed in several Paris hotels over the years, but I wanted to go back to the rue Dauphine this time because it happened to be smack in the middle of the neighborhood where Walker had lived in 1967. The Hôtel du Sud might have been gone, but many of the other places he had frequented were not. Vagenende was still there. La Palette and the Café Conti were still open for business, and even the cafeteria on the rue Mazet was still dishing out inedible food to hungry students. So much had changed in the past forty years, and the once down-at-the-heels neighborhood had evolved into one of the most fashionable areas of Paris, but most of the landmarks from Walker's story had survived. After checking into the hotel on the first morning, my wife and I went outside and wandered through the streets for a couple of hours. Every time I pointed out one of those places to her, she would squeeze my hand and emit a small, sarcastic grunt. You're incorrigible, she finally said. Not at all, I replied. Just soaking up the atmosphere . . . preparing myself for tomorrow.

Cécile Juin showed up at four o'clock the

following afternoon, striding into the hotel bar with a small leather briefcase tucked under her left arm. Judging from Walker's descriptions of her in the notes for *Fall*, her body had expanded dramatically since 1967. The thin, narrow-shouldered girl of eighteen was now a round, plumpish woman of fifty-eight with short brown hair (dyed, some gray roots visible when she shook my hand and sat down across from me), a slightly wrinkled face, a slightly sagging chin, and the same alert and darting eyes Walker had noticed when they first met. Her manner was a bit skittish, perhaps, but she was no longer the trembling, nail-biting bundle of nerves who had caused her mother so much worry in the past. She was a woman in full possession of herself, a woman who had traveled great distances in the years since Walker had known her. A few seconds after she sat down, I was a little surprised to see her pull out a pack of cigarettes, and then, as the minutes rolled on, doubly surprised to learn that she was a heavy smoker, with a deep, rumbling cough and the rough-edged contralto voice of a tobacco veteran. When the barman arrived at our table and asked us what we wanted, she ordered a whiskey. Neat. I told him to make it two.

I had prepared myself for a prissy, school-marmish eccentric. Cécile might have had her eccentricities, but the woman I met that day was down-to-earth, funny, enjoyable to be with. She was simply but elegantly dressed (a sign of confidence, I felt, a sign of self-respect), and although she wasn't someone who bothered with lipstick or nail polish, she looked thoroughly feminine in her gray woolen suit — with silver bracelets around each wrist and a bright, multicolored scarf wrapped around her neck. During the course of our long, two-hour conversation, I found out that she had spent fifteen years in psycho-analysis (from age twenty to thirty-five), had been married and divorced, had married again to a man twenty years older than she was (he died in 1999), and that she had no children. On this last point she commented: A few regrets, yes, but the truth is I probably would have been a terrible mother. No aptitude, you understand.

For the first twenty or thirty minutes, we mostly talked about Adam. Cécile wanted to know everything I could tell her about what had happened in his life from the moment she lost touch with him. I explained that I had lost touch with him as well, and since we hadn't resumed contact until just before his death, my only source of information was the letter he had written to me last spring. One by one, I took her through the salient points Walker had mentioned — falling down the stairs and breaking his leg on the night of his graduation from college, the luck of drawing a high number in the draft lottery, his move to London and the years of writing and translating, the publication of his first and only book, the decision to abandon poetry and study law, his work as a community activist in northern California, his marriage to Sandra Williams, the difficulties of being an interracial couple in America, his stepdaughter, Rebecca, and her two children — and then I added that if she wanted to learn more, she should probably arrange to meet with his sister, who would no doubt be glad to fill her in on the smallest details. As promised, Cécile broke down and cried. It touched me that she understood herself well enough to have been able to predict those tears, but even though she knew they were coming, there was nothing forced or willed about them. They were genuine, spontaneous tears, and although I had been expecting them myself, I genuinely felt sorry for her.

She said: He lived around here, you know. Just thirty seconds away, on the rue Mazarine. I walked past the building on my way to see you just now — the first time I've been on that street in years. Odd, isn't it? Odd that the hotel should be gone, that terrible, broken-down place where Adam lived. It's so alive in my memory, how can it possibly be gone? I was there only once, one time for an hour or two, but I can't forget it, it's still burning inside me. I went there because I was angry at him. One day early in the morning. I cut school and walked over to the hotel. I climbed the rickety stairs, I knocked on his door. I wanted to strangle him because I was so angry, because I loved him so much. I was an idiot girl, you understand, an impossible, unlikable girl, a gawky imbecile girl with glasses on my nose and a sick, quivering heart, and I had the temerity to fall in love with a boy like Adam, perfect Adam, why in God's name did he even talk to me? He let me in. He calmed me down. He was kind to me, so kind to me, my life was in his hands, and he was kind to me. I should have known then what a good person he was. I never should have doubted a word he said. Adam. I dreamed of kissing him. That was all I ever wanted — to be kissed by Adam, to give myself to Adam — but time ran out on me, and we never kissed, we never touched, and before I knew it he was gone.

That was when Cécile broke down and started to cry. It took two or three minutes before she was able to talk again, and when the conversation continued, the first thing she said opened the door onto the next phase of our encounter. I'm sorry, she mumbled. I'm blathering on like a madwoman. You have no idea what I'm talking about.

But I do, I said. I know exactly what you're talking about.

You can't possibly know.

Believe me, I do. You were angry at Adam because he hadn't called you for several days. The night before you went back to school, he had dinner with you and your mother at your apartment on the rue de Verneuil. After dessert, you played the piano for him — a two-part invention by Bach — and then, because you left the room for a while, your mother had a chance to speak to Adam one-on-one, and what she said to him, in your words, *scared him off.*

Did he tell you this?

No, he didn't tell me. But he wrote about it, and I've read the pages he wrote.

He sent you a letter?

It was a short book, actually. Or an attempt to write a book. He spent the last months of his life working on a memoir about nineteen sixty-seven.

It was an important year for him.

Yes, a very important year. I think I'm beginning to understand.

If not for Adam's manuscript, I never would have heard of you.

And now you want to find out what happened, is that it?

I can see why Adam thought you were so intelligent. You catch on fast, don't you?

Cécile smiled and lit another cigarette. I seem to be at a disadvantage, she said.

In what way?

You know a lot more about me than I know about you.

Only the eighteen-year-old you. Everything else is a blank. I looked for Born, I looked for Margot Jouffroy, I looked for your mother, but you were the only one I could find.

That's because all the others are dead.

Oh. How awful. I'm so sorry . . . especially about your mother.

She died six years ago. In October — exactly six years ago tomorrow. About a month after the attacks on New York and Washington. She'd had heart trouble for some time, and one day her heart simply gave out on her. She was seventy-six. I wanted her to live to a hundred, but as you know, what we want and what we get are rarely the same thing.

And Margot?

I barely knew her. I was told she killed herself. A long time ago now — all the way back in the seventies.

And Born?

271

Last year. I think. But I'm not absolutely sure. There's a slim chance he's still alive somewhere.

Did he and your mother stay married until her death?

Married? They were never married.

Never married? But I thought —

They talked about it for a while, but it never happened.

Was Adam responsible for stopping it?

Partly, I suppose, but not entirely. When he talked to my mother and made those wild accusations about Rudolf, she didn't believe him. Nor did I, for that matter.

You were so incensed, you spat in his face, didn't you?

Yes, I spat in his face. It was the single worst thing I've done in my life, and I still can't forgive myself for it.

You wrote to Adam to apologize. Does that mean you changed your mind about his story?

No, not then. I wrote because I was ashamed of what I did, and I wanted him to know how bad I felt about it. I tried to talk to him in person, but when I finally found the courage to call his hotel, he wasn't there anymore. They told me he'd gone back to America. I couldn't understand it. Why would he leave so suddenly? The only explanation I could think of was that he was so upset by what I'd done to him that he couldn't bear the thought of staying in Paris. How's that for a selfish reading of events? When I asked Rudolf to talk to the head of the Columbia program and find out what had happened, he reported that Adam had left because he wasn't satisfied with the courses he was taking. That seemed utterly feeble to me, and I didn't buy it for a second. I was convinced he'd left because of me.

You know better now, don't you?

Yes, I know better. But it took years before I learned the truth.

Years. Which means that Adam's story had no effect on your mother's decision.

I wouldn't say that. After Adam left, Rudolf couldn't stop talking about him. He had been accused of murder, after all, and he was outraged, quite bonkers really, and he fumed and railed against Adam for weeks. He should be put in jail for twenty years, he said. He should be strung up and hanged from the nearest lamppost. He should be carted off to Devil's Island. It was all so excessive, so over the top, that my mother began to feel a little annoyed with him. She had known Rudolf for a long time, many years, almost as long as she'd known my father, and for the most part he had been extremely gentle with her — considerate, thoughtful, gracious. There were a few hot-headed moments, of course, especially when he started talking about politics, but that was politics, not personal business. Now he was on a rampage, and I think she was beginning to have some doubts about him. Was she honestly prepared to spend the rest of her life with a man who had such a violent temper? After a month or two, Rudolf began to calm down, and by Christmastime the fits and crazy outbursts had stopped. The winter was tranquil, I recall,

273

but then it was spring, May sixty-eight, and the whole country exploded. For me, it was one of the greatest periods of my life. I marched, I demonstrated, I helped shut down my school, and suddenly I had turned into an activist, a bright-eyed revolutionary agitating to bring down the government. My mother was sympathetic to the students, but right-wing Rudolf had nothing but contempt for them. He and I got into some dreadful arguments that spring, fierce shouting matches about law and justice, Marx and Mao, anarchy and rebellion, and for the first time politics was no longer just politics, it was personal business. My mother was caught in the middle, and it made her more and more unhappy, more and more silent and withdrawn. The divorce from my father was supposed to become final at the beginning of June. In France, divorcing couples have to talk to a judge one last time before he can sign the papers. They're asked to reconsider, to rethink their decision and make sure they want to go ahead with it. My father was in the hospital — I imagine you know all about that — and my mother went to see the judge on her own. When he asked her if she had any second thoughts about her decision, she said yes, she had changed her mind and didn't want a divorce. She was protecting herself against Rudolf, you understand. She didn't want to marry him anymore, and by staying married to my father, she *couldn't* marry him anymore.

How did Born react?

With tremendous kindness. He said that he

274

understood why she couldn't go through with it, that he admired her for her steadfastness and courage, that he thought she was an extraordinary and noble woman. Not what you would expect, but there you have it. He behaved beautifully.

How much longer did your father go on living?

A year and a half. He died in January nineteen seventy.

Did Born come back and propose again?

No. He left Paris after sixty-eight and started teaching in London. We saw him at my father's funeral, and a couple of weeks after that he wrote my mother a long, heartfelt letter about the past, but that was the end of it. The subject of marriage never came up again.

And what about your mother? Did she find someone else?

She had some male friends over the years, but she never remarried.

And Born moved to London. Did you ever see him again?

Once, about eight months after my mother died.

And?

I'm sorry. I don't think I can talk about it.

Why not?

Because if I tried to tell you what happened, I couldn't begin to convey what a strange and disturbing experience it was for me.

You're pulling my leg, right?

Just a little bit. To use your terms, I can't *tell* you anything, but you can *read* about it if you want to.

Ah, I see. And where is this mysterious text of yours?

In my apartment. I've been keeping a diary since I was twelve years old, and I wrote a number of pages about what happened during my visit to Rudolf's house. An on-the-spot, eyewitness account, if you will. I think it might interest you. If you like, I can photocopy the pages and bring them here tomorrow. If you're not in, I'll drop them off at the desk.

Thank you. That's very generous of you. I can't wait to read them.

And now, Cécile said, grinning broadly as she reached into her leather bag and pulled out a large red notebook, shall we get on with the survey for the CNRS?

★ ★ ★

The next afternoon, when my wife and I returned to the hotel after a long lunch with her sister, the package was waiting for me. In addition to the photocopied pages from her diary, Cécile included a short cover letter. She thanked me for the whiskeys, for tolerating her *grotesque and unpardonable* tears, and for giving up so much of my time to talk to her about Adam. Then she apologized for her illegible handwriting and offered to help me if I had any trouble deciphering it. I found it perfectly legible. Every word was clear, not one letter or punctuation mark confused me. The diary was written in French, of course, and what follows is my translation of that French into English, which

276

I am including with the author's full permission.

I have nothing more to say. Cécile Juin is the last person from Walker's story who is still alive, and because she is the last, it seems fitting that she should have the last word.

CÉCILE JUIN'S DIARY

4/27. A letter today from Rudolf Born. Six months after the fact, he has only just now learned of Mother's death. How long has it been since I last saw him, last heard from him? Twenty years, I think, perhaps twenty-five.

He sounds distraught, shattered by the news. Why would it mean so much to him now, after all these years of silence? He writes eloquently about the strength of her character, her dignified bearing and inner warmth, her attunement to the minds of others. He never stopped loving her, he says, and now that she has left this world, he feels that a part of him has left it with her.

He is retired. 71, unmarried, in good health. For the past six years, he has been living in a place called Quillia, a small island between Trinidad and the Grenadines at the juncture of the Atlantic and the Caribbean, just north of the equator. I have never heard of it. I must remember to look it up.

In the last sentence of the letter, he asks for news of me.

4/29. I have written back to R.B. Much more openly than I intended to, but once I started to talk about myself, I found it difficult to stop. When the letter reaches him, he will know about my work, about my marriage to Stéphane, about Stéphane's death three years ago, and how lonely and burnt out I feel most of the time. I wonder if I haven't gone a bit too far.

What are my feelings toward this man? Complicated ones, ambiguous ones, combining compassion and indifference, friendship and wariness, admiration and bemusement. R.B. has many excellent qualities. High intelligence, good manners, a ready laugh, generosity. After Father's accident, he stepped in and became our moral support, the rock on which we stood for many years. He was saintly with Mother, a chivalrous companion, helpful and doting, always there in time of trouble. As for me, who was not even twelve when our world caved in, how many times did he lift me out of the doldrums with his encouragement and praise, his pride in my meager accomplishments, his indulgent attitude toward my adolescent sufferings? So many positive attributes, so much to feel grateful for, and yet I continue to resist him. Does it have something to do with our bitter clashes in May '68, those frantic weeks in May when we were at perpetual war with each other, causing a rift between us that was never fully repaired? Perhaps. But I like to think of myself as a person who doesn't bear grudges, who is capable of forgiving others — and deep down I believe he was forgiven long ago. Forgiven because I laugh when I think about that time now and feel no anger. Instead, what I feel is doubt, and that was something which began to take hold in me several months earlier — back in the fall, when I fell in love with Adam Walker. Dear Adam, who came to Mother with those horrible accusations about R.B. Impossible to believe him, but now that so many years have passed, now that one has pondered and dissected and endlessly reexamined Adam's motive for saying such things, it becomes difficult to know what to think. Surely there was bad blood between Adam and R.B., surely Adam felt it would be in Mother's best interest to call off the marriage, and so he made up a story to frighten her into changing her mind. A terrifying story, too terrifying to be true, and therefore a miscalculation on his part, but Adam was essentially a good person, and if he thought there was something tainted about R.B.'s past, then perhaps there was. Hence my doubt, which has been festering in me for years. But I can't condemn a man on the strength of doubt alone. There must be proof, and since there is no proof, I must take R.B. at his word.

5/11. A response from R.B. He writes that he is living in seclusion in a large stone house overlooking the ocean. The house is called Moon Hill, and conditions there are quite primitive. The windows are broad apertures cut out of the rock with no glass covering them. The air blows in, the rain blows in, the insects and birds blow in, and there is little distinction between indoors and outdoors. He has a private generator for producing electricity, but the machine breaks

279

down often, and half the time they light the rooms with kerosene lamps. There are four people in the household: a handyman-caretaker named Samuel, an old cook, Nancy, and a young cleaning woman, Melinda. There is a telephone and a radio, but no television, no mail delivery, and no running water. Samuel goes to the post office in town to pick up his letters (twelve miles away), and water is stored in wooden tanks above the sinks and toilets. Shower water comes out of a disposable plastic bag that hangs from a hook above your head. The landscape is both lush and barren. Profuse vegetation everywhere (palm trees, rubber plants, a hundred varieties of wildflowers), but the volcanic earth is strewn with rocks and boulders. Land crabs plod through his garden (he describes them as small armored tanks, prehistoric creatures who look as if they belong on the moon), and because of the frequent infestations of mosquitoes, not to mention the constant threat of tarantulas, everyone sleeps in beds covered with protective white netting. He spends his days reading (for the past two months he has been diligently plowing through Montaigne again) and taking notes for a memoir he hopes to begin in the near future. Every evening, he settles into his hammock by the window in the living room and videotapes the sunset. He calls it the most astonishing spectacle on earth.

My letter has overwhelmed him with nostalgia, he says, and he regrets now that he allowed himself to disappear from my life. We were once so close, such good friends, but after he and my mother parted ways, he didn't feel he had the right to remain in touch. Now that the ice has been broken again, he has every intention of keeping up a correspondence with me — assuming that is something I would want as well.

He is saddened to learn of my husband's death, saddened to learn of the difficulties I have been having of late. But you're still young, he adds, still in your early fifties, with much to look forward to, and you mustn't give up hope.

These are trite and conventional remarks, perhaps, but I sense that he means well, and who am I to scorn well-meant gestures of earnest sympathy? The truth is that I am touched.

Then, a sudden inspiration. Why not pay him a visit? The holidays are approaching, he says, and perhaps a little jaunt to the West Indies would do me some good. There are several spare bedrooms in his house, and putting me up would pose no problem. How happy it would make him to see me again, to spend some time together after so many years. He writes down his telephone number in case I'm interested.

Am I interested? It is difficult to say.

5/12. Information about Quillia is scant. I have already combed the Internet, which has yielded a couple of short, superficial histories and various bits of tourist data. With the latter entries, the writing is atrocious, banal to the point of absurdity: *the resplendent sun . . . the glorious beaches . . . the bluest blue water this side of heaven.*

I am sitting in the library now, but it turns out

that there are no books devoted exclusively to Quillia — only a smattering of references buried in the larger volumes about the region. During pre-Columbian times, the inhabitants were the Ciboney Indians, who subsequently left and were supplanted by the Arawaks, who in their turn were followed by the Caribs. When colonization began in the 16th century, the Dutch, the French, and the English all took an interest in the place. There were skirmishes with the Indians, skirmishes among the Europeans, and when black slaves started arriving from Africa, much slaughter ensued. By the 18th century, the island was declared a neutral zone, exploited equally by the French and the English, but after the Seven Years' War and the Treaty of Paris, the French decamped and Quillia fell under the control of the British Empire. In 1979, the island became independent.

It is five miles across. Subsistence farming, fishing, boat-building, and an annual hunt for a single whale. The population is three and a half thousand — mostly of African descent, but also Carib, English, Irish, Scottish, Asian, and Portuguese. One book reports that a large contingent of Scottish sailors was stranded on Quillia in the 18th century. With no possibility of returning home, they settled there and mingled with the blacks. Two centuries later, the result of this interbreeding is a curious mixed race of redheaded Africans, blue-eyed Africans, and albino Africans. As the author notes: *The island is a laboratory of human possibilities. It explodes our rigid, preconceived ideas about race — and perhaps even destroys the concept of race itself.*

A nice phrase, that. *A laboratory of human possibilities.*

5/14. A hard day. This afternoon, I realized that it has been exactly four months since my last period. Does this mean it's finally happened? I keep hoping for the old, familiar cramps, the bloat and irritation, the blood flowing out of me. It isn't a question of no longer being able to bear children. I never particularly wanted them. Alexandre more or less talked me into it, but we split up before anything ever happened. With Stéphane, children were out of the question.

No, it isn't about children anymore. I'm too old for that now, even if I wanted to become pregnant. It's more about losing my place as a woman, of being expelled from the ranks of femininity. For forty years, I was proud to bleed. I bore up under *the curse* with the happy knowledge that I was sharing an experience with every other woman on the planet. Now I have been cut adrift, neutered. It feels like the beginning of the end. A post-menopausal woman today, an old crone tomorrow, and then the grave. I'm too worn out even to cry.

Perhaps I should go to Quillia, after all, in spite of my reservations. I need to shake things up for myself, to breathe new air.

5/17. I have just spoken to R.B. Odd to hear that voice again after all this time, but he sounded vigorous, in top form. When I told him I'd decided to accept his invitation, he began shouting into the phone. Splendid! Splendid! What excellent news!

One month from now (in R.B.'s words), we will be drinking Samuel's rum punches, taking turns filming the sunset, and having the time of our lives.

I will book the tickets tomorrow. Five days in late June. Subtract the two days of travel, and that leaves three full days on Quillia. If I'm having the time of my life, I can always extend the visit. If I find it unbearable, I don't suppose three days will be too much to bear.

6/23. After a long flight across the Atlantic, I am sitting in a transit lounge at the Barbados airport, waiting for the small, one-propeller plane that will take me to Quillia two and a half hours from now (if it leaves on time).

Insufferable heat, everywhere a dense circle of heat closing around my body, the heat of the tropics, a heat that melts the thoughts in your head.

In the main terminal, a dozen soldiers patrolling the floor with machine guns. An air of menace and mistrust, hostility in every glance. What is going on? A dozen black soldiers with machine guns in their hands, and the crowds of grim, sweating travelers with their overstuffed bags and cranky children.

In the transit lounge, nearly everyone is white. Long-haired American surfers, Australians drinking beer and talking in loud voices, Europeans of various unknown nationalities, a couple of Asian faces. Boredom. Fans circling overhead. Piped-in music that is not music. A place that is not a place.

★ ★ ★

Nine hours later. The one-propeller plane was the smallest flying machine I have ever been in. I sat up front with the pilot, the other two passengers sat directly behind us, and the instant we took off, I understood that we were at the mercy of every puff of wind that might blow our way, that even the smallest disturbance in the surrounding air could throw us off course. We lurched and wobbled and dipped, my stomach was in my mouth, and yet I enjoyed myself, enjoyed the feathery weightlessness of the ride, the sense of being in such close contact with that unstable air.

Seen from above, the island is no more than a small dot, a gray-green speck of cooled lava jutting out of the ocean. But the water around it is blue — yes, the bluest blue water this side of heaven.

It would be an exaggeration to call the Quillia airport an airport. It is a landing strip, a ribbon of tarmac unspooled at the base of a tall, hulking mountain, and it can accommodate nothing bigger than planes the size of toys. We retrieved our bags in the terminal — a tiny cinder-block hut — and then went through the ordeal of customs and passport control. Not even in post-9/11 Europe have I been subjected to such a thorough examination of my belongings. My suitcase was opened, and every article of clothing was lifted out and inspected, every book was shaken by the spine, every shoe was turned upside down, peered into, searched — slowly and methodically, as if this were a procedure that could not, under any circumstances, be conducted in haste. The man in charge of passport control was dressed in a snappy, neatly pressed uniform, a symbol of authority and officialdom, and he too took his sweet time before letting me go. He asked the purpose of my visit, and in my mediocre, heavily accented English, I told him that I'd come to spend a few days with a friend. Which friend? Rudolf Born, I said. The name seemed to ring a bell with him, and then he asked (inappropriately, I believe) how long I had known Mr. Born. All my life, I said. All your life? My answer seemed to have thrown him. Yes, all my life, I repeated. He was a close friend of my parents'. Ah, your parents, he said, nodding in contemplation, apparently satisfied by my answer. I thought we had come to the end of our business, but then he opened my passport, and for the next three minutes he scrutinized it with the zealous, patient eye of a forensics expert, carefully studying each page, pausing over each marking, as if my past travels were the key to solving the mystery of my life. At last, he took out a form printed on a narrow slip of paper, positioned it at right angles with the edge of his desk, and filled in the blanks with a small, meticulous hand. After stapling the form into my passport, he inked his rubber stamp, pressed the rubber onto a spot beside the form, and delicately added the name of Quillia to the roster

286

of countries I have been allowed to enter. French bureaucrats are notorious for their maniacal exactitude and cold efficiency. Next to this man, they are all amateurs.

I stepped out into the broiling four o'clock heat, expecting to find R.B. waiting for me, but he wasn't there. My escort to the house was Samuel, the handyman-caretaker, a strong, well-built, exceedingly handsome young man of around thirty — with exceedingly black skin, which would suggest he is not descended from that band of Scottish sailors marooned here in the 18th century. After my encounter with the remote and taciturn men at the airport terminal, I found it a relief to be smiled at again.

It didn't take long to understand why the job of accompanying me to Moon Hill had been given to Samuel. We rode in a car for the first ten minutes, which led me to assume we would drive all the way to the house, but then Samuel stopped the car, and the rest of the journey — that is to say, the bulk of the journey, the more than one-hour journey still in front of us — was made on foot. It was an arduous trek, an excruciating climb up a steep, root-entangled path that sapped my strength and left me gasping for breath after five minutes. I am a person who sits in libraries, a fifty-three-year-old woman who smokes too many cigarettes and weighs twenty pounds more than she should, and my body is not cut out for exertions of this sort. I was thoroughly humiliated by my ineptitude, by the sweat that poured out of me and drenched my clothes, by the swarms of mosquitoes dancing around my head, by my frequent calls to stop and rest, by the slippery soles of my sandals, which made me fall, not once, not twice, but again and again. But even worse, far worse than my petty physical woes, there was the shame of watching Samuel in front of me, the shame of seeing Samuel *carry my suitcase on his head*, my too heavy suitcase, loaded down with the weight of too many unnecessary books, and how not to see in that image of a black man carrying a white woman's possessions *on his head* the horrors of the colonial past, the atrocities of the Congo and French Africa, the centuries of affliction —

I mustn't go on like this. I'm working myself into a lather, and if I mean to get through these days with my mind intact, I must maintain my composure. The reality is that Samuel wasn't the least bit distressed about what he was doing. He has been up and down this mountain thousands of times, he carries provisions on his head as a matter of course, and for someone born on an island as poor as this one, working in the house of a man like R.B. is considered a good job. Whenever I asked him to stop, he did so without complaint. No trouble, ma'am. Just take it nice and easy. We'll get there when we get there.

R.B. was napping in his room when we reached the top of the mountain. Incomprehensible as that might have been, it gave me a chance to settle into my own room (high, high up, overlooking the ocean) and pull myself together. I showered, put on a fresh set of clothes, and did my hair. Minor improvements, perhaps, but at least I didn't have to live through the embarrassment of being seen in such a sorry state. The walk up the mountain had nearly destroyed me.

In spite of my efforts, I could see the disappointment in his eyes when I entered the living room an hour later — the first look after so many years, and the sad acknowledgment that the young girl of long ago had turned into a frowsy, none-too-attractive, post-menopausal woman in late middle age.

Unfortunately — no, I think I mean fortunately — the disappointment was mutual. In the past, I had found him to be a seductive figure, good-looking in a rough sort of way, something close to an ideal embodiment of male confidence and power. R.B. was never a thin man, but in the years since I last saw him, he has put on considerable amounts of weight, a truckload of excess poundage, and as he stood up to greet me (dressed in shorts, with no shirt, no shoes or socks), I was astonished to see how large his stomach had grown. It is a great medicine ball of a stomach now, and with most of the hair gone from his head, his skull reminded me of a volleyball. A ridiculous image, I know, but the mind is always churning forth its quirky nonsense, and that was what I saw when he stood up and approached me: a man composed of two spheres, a medicine ball and a volleyball. He is much bigger, then, but not whalelike, not blubbery or drooping with flab — just large. The skin around his stomach is quite taut, actually, and except for the fleshy creases around his knees and neck, he looks fit for a man his age.

An instant after I saw it, the crestfallen look vanished from his eyes. With all the aplomb of a practiced diplomat, R.B. broke into a smile, opened his arms, and hugged me. It's a miracle, he said.

That hug proved to be the high point of the evening. We drank the rum punches Samuel prepared for us (very good), I watched R.B. film the sunset (I found it inane), and then we sat down to dinner (heavy food, beef drowned in a thick sauce, inappropriate fare for this climate — better suited to Alsace in midwinter). The old cook, Nancy, is not old at all — forty, forty-five at most — and I wonder if she doesn't have two jobs in this household: cook by day, R.B.'s bed partner at night. Melinda is in her early twenties, and therefore is probably too young to fill the latter role. She is a beautiful girl, by the way, as beautiful as Samuel is handsome, a tall, lanky thing with an exquisite gliding walk, and from the little looks they give each other, I would guess that she and Samuel are an item. Nancy and Melinda served us the food, Samuel cleared the table and washed the dishes, and as the meal wore on I found myself growing increasingly uncomfortable. I don't like being waited on by servants. It offends me somehow, especially in a situation like this one, with three people working for just two others, three black people working for two white people. Again: unpleasant echoes of the colonial past. How to get rid of this feeling of shame? Nancy, Melinda, and Samuel went about their tasks with stolid equanimity, and though I received a number of courteous smiles, they seemed guarded and aloof, indifferent. What must they think of us? They probably laugh at us behind our backs — with good reason.

The servants got me down, yes, but not as much as R.B. himself did. After his warm welcome, I felt as if he no longer knew what to do with me. He kept saying that I must be tired, that the trip must have worn me out, that jet lag is a modern invention designed to ruin the human body. I won't deny that I was exhausted and jet-lagged, that my muscles ached from my battle with the mountain, but I wanted to stay up and talk, to *reminisce about old times* as he put it in one of his letters, and he seemed reluctant to go there with me. Our conversation over dinner was brutally dull. He told me about his discovery of Quillia and how he had managed to buy this house, discussed some of the particulars of local life, and then lectured me on the flora and fauna of the island. Mystifying.

I am in bed now, encased in a dome of white mosquito netting. My body is smeared with an odious product called OFF, a mosquito repellent that smells of toxic, life-threatening chemicals, and the green anti-mosquito coils on either side of the bed are slowly burning down, emitting curious little trails of smoke.

I wonder what I am doing here.

★ ★ ★

6/26. Nothing for two days. It has been impossible to write, impossible to find a moment's peace, but now that I have left Moon Hill and am on my way back to Paris, I can pick up the story and push on to the bitter end. Bitter is precisely the word I want to use here. I feel bitter about what happened, and I know I will be tasting that bitterness for a long time to come.

It started the next morning, the morning after my arrival at the house, the 24th. Sitting over breakfast in the dining room, R.B. calmly put down his cup of coffee, looked me in the eye, and asked me to marry him. It was so far-fetched, so utterly unexpected, I burst out laughing.

— You can't be serious, I said.

— Why not? he answered. I'm all alone here. You have no one in Paris, and if you came to Quillia and lived with me, I would make you the happiest woman in the world. We're perfect for each other, Cécile.

— You're too old for me, old friend.

— You've already been married to a man older than I am.

— That's just it. Stéphane is dead, isn't he? I have no desire to become a widow again.

— Ah, but I'm not Stéphane, am I? I'm strong. I'm in perfect health. I have years and years ahead of me.

— Please, Rudolf. It's out of the question.

— You're forgetting how much we adored each other.

— I liked you. I always liked you, but I never adored you.

— Years ago, I wanted to marry your mother. But that was only an excuse. I wanted to live with her so I could be near you.

— That's ridiculous. I was a child back then — an awkward, undeveloped child. You weren't interested in me.

— It was all working so well. It was about to happen, it would have happened, the three of us wanted it to happen, and then that American boy came to Paris and ruined everything.

— It wasn't because of him. You know that. My mother didn't believe his story, and neither did I.

— You were right not to believe him. He was a liar, a twisted, angry boy who turned against me and tried to wreck my life. Yes, I've made terrible mistakes over the years, but killing that kid in New York wasn't one of them. I never put a hand on him. Your boyfriend made it all up.

— My boyfriend? That's a good one. Adam Walker had better things to do than fall for someone like me.

— And to think ... I was the one who introduced him to you. I thought I was doing you a favor. What a miserable joke.

— You did do me a favor. And then I turned around and insulted him. I called him a crazy person. I said his tongue should be torn out of his mouth.

— You never told me that. Good work, Cécile. I'm proud of you for showing such spirit. The boy got what he deserved.

— Deserved? What does that mean?

— I'm alluding to his hasty departure from France. You know why he left, don't you?

— He left because of me. Because I spat in his face.

— No, no, nothing as simple as that.

— What are you talking about?

— He was deported. The police caught him with three kilos of drugs — marijuana, hashish, cocaine, I can't remember the substance now. They were tipped off by the manager of that putrid hotel he lived in. The cops searched his room, and that was the end of Adam Walker. He had two choices: stand trial in France or leave the country.

— Adam with drugs? It isn't possible. He was against drugs, he hated them.

— Not according to the police.

— And how do you know that?

— The examining magistrate was a friend of mine. He told me about the case.

— How convenient. And why would he bother to talk to you about a thing like that?

— Because he knew I was acquainted with Walker.

— You were involved in it, weren't you?

— Of course not. Don't be silly.

— You were. Admit it, Rudolf. You were the one who got Adam kicked out of the country.

— You're wrong, my darling. I can't say that I was sorry to see him go, but I wasn't responsible.

— It's so far in the past. Why tell lies about it now?

— I swear on your mother's grave, Cécile. I had nothing to do with it.

I didn't know what to think. Perhaps he was telling the truth, perhaps he wasn't, but the moment he started talking about my mother's grave, I realized that I didn't want to be in the room with him anymore. I was too upset, too close to tears, too distracted to go on talking. First his insane proposal of marriage, and then the ghastly news about Adam, and suddenly I couldn't sit at that table a second longer. I stood up from my chair, told him I wasn't feeling well, and quickly retreated to my room.

Half an hour later, R.B. knocked and asked if he could come in. I hesitated for a few moments, wondering if I had the strength to confront him again. Before I could decide, there was another knock, louder and more insistent than the first one, and then he opened the door himself.

— I'm sorry, he said, as his large, half-naked body lumbered toward a chair in the far corner of the room. I didn't mean to unnerve you. I'm afraid I took the wrong approach.

— Approach? Approach to what?

As R.B. lowered himself into the chair, I sat down on a small wooden bench just below the window. We were no more than three feet apart. I wished he hadn't walked in on me so soon after my abrupt exit from the dining room, but he looked sufficiently contrite for me to think that further conversation might be possible.

— Approach to what? I repeated.

— To certain . . . how shall I put it? . . . to certain future . . . to certain possible domestic arrangements in the future.

— I'm sorry to disappoint you, Rudolf, but I'm not interested in marriage. Not with you or anyone else.

— Yes, I know. That's your position today, but tomorrow you might have a different view of the matter.

— I doubt it.

— It was a mistake not to share my thoughts with you. I've been living with this idea ever since I received your letter last month, and after turning it around in my mind for so long, it felt real to me, as if all I had to do was say the word and it would happen. I've probably been alone too much these past six years. I sometimes confuse my thoughts about the world with the world itself. I'm sorry if I offended you.

— I wasn't offended. Surprised would be the appropriate word, I think.

— Given your position — the position you hold now, in any case — I would like to suggest an experiment. An experiment in the form of a business proposal. Do you remember the book I told you about in one of my letters?

— You mentioned that you were taking notes for a memoir you wanted to write.

— Exactly. I'm nearly ready to begin, and I want you to help me with it. I want us to write the book together.

— You're forgetting that I already have a job in Paris. A job that means quite a lot to me.

— Whatever salary they give you at the CNRS, I'll double it.

— It isn't a question of money.

— I'm not asking you to quit your job. All you have to do is apply for a leave of absence. The book should take us about a year to write, and if you don't want to stay with me here after we're finished, go back to Paris. In the meantime, you'll be earning twice what you earn now — with free room and board, by the way — and in the process you might discover that you want to marry me. An experiment in the form of a business proposal. Do you see what I'm talking about?

— Yes, I see. But why would I be interested in working on someone else's book? I have my own work to do.

— Once you know what the book is about, you'll be interested.

— It's a book about your life.

— Yes, but do you know anything about my life, Cécile?

— You're a retired professor of government and international affairs.

— Among other things, yes. But I didn't only teach government, I worked for it as well.

— The French government?

— Of course. I'm French, aren't I?

— And what kind of work did you do?

— Secret work.

— Secret work . . . Are you talking about espionage?

— Skullduggery in all its many forms, my dear.

— Well, well. I had no idea.

— It goes all the way back to Algeria for me. I started young, and I went on working for them straight through to the end of the Cold War.

— In other words, you have some gripping stories to tell.

— More than gripping. Stories to curdle your blood.

— Are you allowed to publish these stories? I thought there were laws that prevented government workers from exposing state secrets.

— If we run into any difficulties, we'll redo the manuscript and publish it as a novel — under your name.

— My name?

— Yes, your name. I'll keep myself out of it, and you can have all the glory.

★   ★   ★

I no longer believed a word he was saying. By the time R.B. left the room, I was convinced he was mad, that he had lost his mind and gone stark raving mad. He'd spent too many years on Quillia, and the tropical sun had cooked the wires in his brain and pushed him over the edge of sanity. Espionage. Marriage. Memoirs that transformed themselves into novels. He was like a child, a desperate child who made up things as he went along, saying whatever popped into his head and then spinning it out into a fiction that would serve his purpose at any given moment — in this case, the bizarre, wholly preposterous idea that he wanted to marry me. He didn't want to marry me. He couldn't want to marry me. But if he did, and if he thought he could, then it only proved that he was no longer in his right mind.

I pretended to play along with him, acting as if I took his *experiment in the form of a business proposal* seriously. Was I too afraid to challenge him, or was I simply trying to avoid an unpleasant scene? A little of both, I think. I didn't want to say anything that would provoke his anger, but at the same time I found the conversation unbearably tedious, and I wanted to get rid of him as quickly as I could. So you'll think it over? he asked. Yes, I said, I promise to think it over. But you'll have to tell me more about the book before I make my decision. Of course, he answered, that goes without saying. I have some chores to do with Samuel now, but we can talk about it over lunch. Then he patted me on the cheek and said: I'm so glad you've come. The world has never looked more beautiful to me.

I didn't go to lunch. I said that I wasn't feeling well, which was partly true and partly not true. I could have gone if I had pushed myself, if I had actively wanted to go, but I wasn't in the mood to push myself, and I didn't want to go. I needed a break from R.B., and the fact was that the trip had taken its toll on me. I felt exhausted, jet-lagged, spent. Without bothering to take off my clothes, I lay down on the bed and napped for three solid hours. I woke up in a sweat, perspiration gushing from every pore of my body, my mouth dry, my head pounding. Stripping off my clothes, I went into the bathroom, hung one of the water-filled plastic bags on the shower hook, opened the nozzle, and let the water rush down onto my head. A lukewarm shower in the midday heat. The bathroom was out in the open, a small, niche-like space carved into the stone and perched on top of the cliff, with nothing below me but the immense, glittering ocean. *The world has never looked more beautiful.* Yes, I said to myself, this is beyond doubt a beautiful place, but it is a harsh beauty, an inhospitable beauty, and I am already looking forward to leaving it.

I thought about writing in my diary, but I was too agitated to sit still. Then it occurred to me that I should suspend all writing for the duration of my visit. What if R.B. sneaked into my room and found the diary, I wondered, what if he saw the things I was saying about him? All hell would break loose. I might even be in danger.

I tried to read, but reading was beyond my powers of concentration just then. All the useless books I had packed for my holiday in the sun. Novels by Bernhard and Vila-Matas, poems by Dupin and du Bouchet, essays by Sacks and Diderot — all worthy books, but useless to me now that I had reached my destination.

I sat in the chair by the window. I paced around the room. I sat down in the chair again.

And what if R.B. hadn't gone mad? I asked myself. What if he was playing with me, proposing marriage in order to tease me and make fun of me, having a good laugh at my expense? That too was possible. Anything was possible.

He drank heavily at dinner that night. A couple of tall rum punches before we sat down at the table, then ample doses of wine throughout

300

the meal. At first, it seemed to have no effect on him. He solicitously asked if I was feeling better, and I said yes, the nap had done me a world of good, and after that we talked about small, inconsequential things, with no mention of marriage, no mention of Adam Walker, no mention of books about undercover intelligence work that can be turned into novels. Although we were speaking French, I wondered if he preferred not to talk about these matters in front of the servants. I also wondered if he wasn't going senile, in the early stages of Alzheimer's or dementia, and had simply forgotten the things we had talked about earlier in the day. Perhaps thoughts flitted through his head like butterflies or mosquitoes — ephemeral notions that came and went so fast that he couldn't keep track of them anymore.

About ten or fifteen minutes into the meal, however, he began talking about politics. Not in any personal way, not with any stories about his own experiences, but abstractly, theoretically, sounding very much like the professor he had been for most of his adult life. He began with the Berlin Wall. Everyone in the West was so happy when the wall came down, he said, everyone thought a new era of peace and brotherly love had dawned on earth, but in fact it was the most alarming event of recent times. Distasteful as it might have been, the Cold War had held the world together for forty-four years, and now that the simple, black-and-white binary world of us versus them was gone, we had entered a period of instability and chaos similar to the years prior to World War I. Mutual Assured Destruction, MAD. It was a frightening concept, yes, but when one half of humanity is in a position to blow up the other half, and when the other half is in a position to blow up the first half, neither side will pull the trigger. Permanent stalemate. The most elegant answer to military aggression in the history of mankind.

I didn't interrupt. R.B. was talking rationally for once, even if his argument was rather crude. What about Algeria and Indochina, I wanted to ask him, what about Korea and Vietnam, what about U.S. interference in Latin America, the assassinations of Lumumba and Allende, the Soviets rolling their tanks into Budapest and Prague, the long war in Afghanistan? There was little point in asking these questions. I had sat through enough lectures of this sort as a girl to know that tangling with R.B. wasn't worth the trouble. Let him rant, I said to myself, let him spout forth his simplistic opinions, and before long he'll talk himself out and the evening will be over. This was the R.B. of old, and for the first time since I'd set foot in his house, I felt I was on familiar ground.

But he didn't talk himself out, and the evening dragged on much longer than I thought it would. He was only warming up with those comments about the Cold War, clearing his throat, as it were, and for the next two hours he subjected me to the most blistering harangue I had ever heard from him. Arab terrorism, September 11th, the encroaching war in Iraq, the price of oil, global warming, food shortages, mass starvation, a world depression, dirty bombs, anthrax attacks, the annihilation of Israel — what didn't he talk about, what dire, death-rattling prophecy did he not conjure up and spew in my face? Some of the things he said were so mean and ugly, so vicious in their hatred of anyone who was not a European with white skin, of anyone who was not, finally, Rudolf Born himself, that a moment came when I couldn't bear to listen to him anymore. Stop it, I said. I don't want to hear another word. I'm going to bed.

As I stood up from my chair and left the room, he was still talking, still preaching to me in his drunken, rasping voice, not even aware that I was no longer sitting at the table. The polar ice caps are melting, he said. Fifteen years from now, twenty years from now, the floods will come. Drowned cities, obliterated continents, the end of everything. You'll still be alive, Cécile. You'll get to see it happen, and then you'll drown. You'll drown with all the others, all the billions of others, and that will be the end. How I envy you, Cécile. You'll be there to see the end of everything.

★ ★ ★

He didn't show up for breakfast the next morning (yesterday). When I asked Nancy if he was all right, she made a small sound in the back of her throat, something akin to a muted, inward laugh, and said that Mr. Born was still in dreamland. I wondered how long he had gone on drinking after I left the dining room.

Four hours later, he emerged for lunch, apparently in good cheer, his eyes bright and focused, ready for action. For the first time since I'd been there, he had taken the trouble to put on a shirt.

— Excuse my intemperate remarks last night, he began. I didn't mean half the things I said — less than half of them, actually, almost nothing.

— Why would you say something you didn't mean? I asked, somewhat thrown by this odd retraction. It wasn't like him to examine his own behavior, to back down from anything he said or did — intemperate or not.

— I was testing out certain ideas, trying to get myself into the proper frame of mind for the work ahead.

— And what work is that?

— The book. The book we're going to make together. After our discussion yesterday morning. I'm convinced you're right, Cécile. The true story can never be published. There are too many secrets, too many bits of dirty business to expose, too many deaths to account for. The French would arrest me if I tried to talk about them.

— Are you saying you want to give up the project?

— No, not at all. But in order to tell the truth, we'll have to fictionalize it.

— That's what you said yesterday.

— I know. It popped into my head while we were talking, but now that I've had time to think it over, I believe it's the only solution.

— A novel, then.

— Yes, a novel. And now that I'm thinking novel, I understand that limitless possibilities have suddenly opened up to us. We can tell the truth, yes, but we'll also have the freedom to make things up.

— Why would you want to do that?

— To make the story more interesting. We'll be basing the action on my life, of course, but the character who plays me in the book will have to be given a different name. We can't call him Rudolf Born, can we? He'll have to be someone else — Mr. X, for example. Once I become Mr. X, I won't be myself anymore, and once I'm not myself, we can add as many new details as we like.

— Such as?

— Such as . . . maybe Mr. X isn't the person he appears to be. We present him as a man who leads a double life. The world knows him as a dull professor, a man who teaches government and international affairs at some dull institute or university, but in fact he's also a special undercover agent, fighting the good fight against the Soviet Communists.

— We already know that. That's the premise of the book.

— Yes, yes — but wait. What if his double life isn't a double life but a triple life?

— I don't follow.

— He seems to be working for the French, but he's actually working for the Russians. Mr. X is a mole.

— It's beginning to sound like a thriller —

— Thriller. Don't you just love that word? *Thriller.*

— But why would Mr. X betray his country?

— Any number of reasons. After years of work in the field, he becomes disillusioned with the West and converts to the Communist cause. Or else he's a cynic who doesn't believe in anything, and the Russians are paying him good money, more money than the French are paying him, which means that he's earning more than twice as much as he would if he worked for just one side.

— He doesn't seem to be a very sympathetic character.

— He doesn't have to be sympathetic. Just interesting and complex. Think back to May sixty-eight, Cécile. Do you remember all those terrible arguments we had?

— I'll never forget them.

— What if Mr. X, the double agent in league with the enemy, is in perfect accord with the young Cécile Juin character? What if he's delighted to see France erupt in anarchy, bursting with joy over the disintegration of France and the imminent fall of the government? But he has to protect his cover, and to do that he espouses views directly opposed to the ones he believes in. It adds a nice little twist, don't you think?

— Not bad.

— I've thought of another scene. It might be difficult to pull off, but if we stick with the idea of turning Mr. X into a mole, it would be crucial

— one of the darkest, most lacerating moments in the book. Mr. X has a French colleague, Mr. Y. They've been close friends for many years, they've lived through some harrowing adventures together, but now Mr. Y suspects that Mr. X is working for the Soviets. He confronts Mr. X and tells him that if he doesn't quit the service immediately, he will have him arrested. These are the early sixties, remember. Capital punishment was still in force, and arrest means the guillotine for Mr. X. What can he do? He has no choice but to kill Mr. Y. Not with a bullet, of course. Not with a blow to the head or a knife in the belly, but by more subtle means that will allow him to escape detection. It's summer. Mr. Y and his family are vacationing in the mountains somewhere in the south of France. Mr. X goes down there, sneaks onto the property in the middle of the night, and disconnects the brakes of Mr. Y's car. The next morning, on his way into town to buy bread at the local bakery, Mr. Y loses control of the car and crashes down the side of a mountain. Mission accomplished.

— What are you saying, Rudolf?

— Nothing. I'm telling you a story, that's all. I'm describing how Mr. X kills Mr. Y.

— You're talking about my father, aren't you?

— Of course not. Why would you think that?

— You're telling me how you tried to kill my father.

— Nonsense. Your father was never in the service. You know that. He worked for the Ministry of Culture.

— So you say. Who knows what he really did?

— Stop it, Cécile. We're just having a little fun.

— It's not funny. It's not the least bit funny. You're making me sick to my stomach.

— My dear girl. Calm down. You're acting like a simpleton.

— I'm walking out of here, Rudolf. I can't stand to be with you for another minute.

— Right now, in the middle of lunch? Just like that?

— Yes, just like that.

— And I thought —

— I don't care what you thought.

— All right, go if you want to. I won't try to stop you. I've done nothing but shower you with kindness and affection since you came here, and now you turn on me like this. You're a ridiculous, hysterical woman, Cécile. I'm sorry I invited you to my house.

— I'm sorry I came.

★ ★ ★

I was already standing by then, already making my way across the room, already in tears. Just before I reached the hall, I turned around for a last look at the man my mother almost married, the man who had asked me to be his wife, and there he was, sitting with his back to me, hunched over his plate, shoveling food into his mouth. Total indifference. I hadn't even left the house, and already I had been expunged from his mind.

I went into my bedroom to gather up my things. There would be no Samuel to accompany me this time, and since I wouldn't be able to get down the mountain with the suitcase in my hand, the bag would have to stay. I transferred some clean underwear into my purse, kicked off my sandals and put on a pair of sneakers, then checked to make sure that my passport and money were where they should have been. The thought of leaving my clothes and books behind caused a small twinge of regret, but the feeling evaporated after a couple of seconds. My plan was to walk to the town of Saint Margaret and buy a ticket for the next available flight to Barbados. It was twelve miles from the house. I could do that. As long as I was on flat ground, I could walk forever.

Climbing down the mountain was less of a challenge than climbing up had been. I broke into a sweat, of course, I was bedeviled by the same aerial attacks of gnats and mosquitoes, but I didn't fall this time, not even once. I moved at a moderate pace, neither too plodding nor too rushed, pausing every now and then to examine wildflowers by the side of the road — bright, beautiful things whose names were unknown to me. Burning red. Burning yellow. Burning blue.

As I approached the bottom of the mountain, I began to hear something, a sound or collection of sounds that I was unable to identify. At first, I thought it resembled the chirping of crickets or cicadas, the persistent metallic cries of insects in the afternoon heat. But it was too hot for insects to be calling to one another just then, and as I drew closer, I understood that the sounds were too loud, that the rhythms of the sounds were too complex, too pulsing and intricate to be coming from any living thing. A barrier of trees blocked my view. I kept on walking, but the barrier didn't end until I reached the very bottom. Once I got there, I stopped, turned to my right, and finally saw where the sounds were coming from, finally saw what my ears had been telling me.

A barren field stretched out before me, a barren, dusty field cluttered with gray stones of various shapes and sizes, and scattered among the stones in that field were fifty or sixty men and women, each holding a hammer in one hand and a chisel in the other, pounding on the stones until they broke in two, then pounding on the smaller stones until they broke in two, and then pounding on the smallest stones until they were reduced to gravel. Fifty or sixty black men and women crouching in that field with hammers and chisels in their hands, pounding on the stones as the sun pounded on their bodies, with no shade anywhere and sweat glistening on every face. I stood there watching them for a long time. I watched and listened and wondered if I had ever seen anything like it. This was the kind of work one usually associated with prisoners, with people in chains, but these people weren't in chains. They were working, they were making money, they were keeping themselves alive. The music of the stones was ornate and impossible, a music of fifty or sixty clinking hammers, each one moving at its own speed, each one locked in its own cadence, and together they formed a fractious, stately harmony, a sound that worked itself into my body and stayed there long after I had left, and even now, sitting on the plane as it flies across the ocean, I can still hear the clinking of those hammers in my head. That sound will always be with me. For the rest of my life, no matter where I am, no matter what I am doing, it will always be with me.

We do hope that you have enjoyed reading
this large print book.

Did you know that all of our titles
are available for purchase?

We publish a wide range of high quality
large print books including:
Romances, Mysteries, Classics
General Fiction
Non Fiction and Westerns

Special interest titles available in
large print are:
The Little Oxford Dictionary
Music Book
Song Book
Hymn Book
Service Book

Also available from us courtesy of
Oxford University Press:
Young Readers' Dictionary
(large print edition)
Young Readers' Thesaurus
(large print edition)

For further information or a free
brochure, please contact us at:
Ulverscroft Large Print Books Ltd.,
The Green, Bradgate Road, Anstey,
Leicester, LE7 7FU, England.
Tel: (00 44) 0116 236 4325
Fax: (00 44) 0116 234 0205

Other titles published by
The House of Ulverscroft:

LOSING CHARLOTTE

Heather Clay

Born and raised at Four Corners, a thoroughbred horse farm in Kentucky, Knox Bolling has grown up within the comforting rhythms of family life and the cycle of growth that transforms the foals into yearlings. Deep ties bind her to her safe, if predictable life, but Knox knows that the world offers more — excitements that her tempestuous older sister, Charlotte, has within her grasp when she marries and moves away to Manhattan's West village. Then disaster strikes. Nothing could have prepared Knox for the loss of her sister. But the powerful bond remains, as her loyalty to Charlotte is profoundly and fatefully tested. Whilst she starts to come to terms with her elusive sister's life, Knox learns deeply moving lessons for her own . . .

CRAZY HEART

Thomas Cobb

At the age of fifty-seven, Bad Blake is on his last legs. His weight, his ticker, his liver, even his pick-up truck are all giving him trouble. A renowned songwriter and 'picker' who hasn't recorded in five years, Bad now travels the countryside on gigs that take him mostly to motels and bowling alleys. Enter Ms. Right. Can Bad stop living the life of a country-western song and tie a rope around his crazy heart?